Carrie Snyder is a Canadian writer. Her 2012 short story collection *The Juliet Stories* was a finalist for the Governor General's Award for English fiction, and a *Globe and Mail* Top 100 book. *Girl Runner*, her debut novel, has been shortlisted for the Rogers Writers' Trust Fiction Prize. Carrie lives in Waterloo, Ontario with her family, and blogs as *Obscure CanLit Mama*.

Visit her website at carriesnyder.com

GIRL RUNNER

A former Olympic athlete, Aganetha Smart was famous in the 1920s; but now at age 104, she lives in a nursing home, alone and forgotten by history. When her quiet life is disturbed by the unexpected arrival of two young strangers, she begins to reflect on her childhood in rural Ontario and her struggles to make an independent life for herself in the city. Without revealing who they are or what they may want from her, the visitors take her on an outing to the family farm where she was raised. Here, the devastation of WWI and the Spanish flu epidemic, the optimism of the 1920s and the sacrifices of the 1930s come vividly back to mind as Aganetha wrestles with the confusion and displacement of the present.

CARRIE SNYDER

♦

GIRL RUNNER

Complete and Unabridged

CHARNWOOD
Leicester

First published in Great Britain in 2015 by
Two Roads
an imprint of
John Murray Press
London

First Charnwood Edition
published 2017
by arrangement with
John Murray Press
An Hachette UK company
London

A catalogue record for this book is available
from the British Library.

ISBN 978–1–4448–3253–2

Published by
F. A. Thorpe (Publishing)
Anstey, Leicestershire

Set by Words & Graphics Ltd.
Anstey, Leicestershire
Printed and bound in Great Britain by
T. J. International Ltd., Padstow, Cornwall

This book is printed on acid-free paper

To Kevin, who helped me find
my inner athlete
And to our kids, Angus, Annabella,
Flora, and Calvin,
who've always
known how to play

CONTENTS

Prologue

Love Song

This is not the love song of Aganetha Smart.

No, and don't talk to me of being weary and claiming one's well-earned rest.

All my life I've been going somewhere, aimed toward a fixed point on the horizon that seems never to draw nearer. In the beginning, I chased it with abandon, with confidence, and somewhat later with frustration, and then with grief, and later yet with the clarity of an escape artist. It is far too late to stop, even if I run in my mind only, out of habit.

You do what you do until you're done. You are who you are until you're not.

My name is Aganetha Smart, and I am 104 years old.

Do not imagine this is an advantage.

I have outlived everyone I've ever loved, and everyone who ever loved me. Nor have I aged well. Just look at me.

I am surrounded by strangers. By day, I am propped in a wheeled chair in a room that smells of chicken fat and diapers. By night, I am lifted into a rigid bed and tamped down with a blanket that stinks of bleach. This pattern has held for much longer than I care to estimate. I am a bit deaf — though not so deaf as they think — and not-quite blind, so I'll admit that my descriptive capacity may be lacking. It is entirely possible that I am living in a cathedral of light and sleeping in a vast canopied bed, and cannot appreciate it. But I suspect otherwise: my sense of smell is perfectly intact.

As for speech, the words do not exit my mouth entirely at my command. It is only at great cost that I make myself clear. So much easier to loop lazily, mumbling a string of disconnected yet familiar phrases, the ones that wait poised at the front of the tongue in case of emergency, or occasion for social nicety: 'Well, now, I don't know, but why . . .'

It's a barrier, I won't pretend.

I'm in a state that appears simple. Pared down. Reduced. Boiled clean away.

What astonishes me is how little remains. What proof? A rattling shoe box of scorched medals and no one to claim them. My name at rest in a column in a forgotten record book. Daily blasts of words, produced on deadline, inked onto newsprint, out-of-date by dinnertime.

My achievement is to have lived long enough to see my life vanish. Who will write my obituary? This is not something I fret overly about, mind you. But there it is.

It is too late to change tactics, to go wide around trouble, to save my best burst of speed for the final stretch. There's no starting this race over again. And still I run. I run and I run, without rest, as if even now there is time and purpose and I will gain, at last — before my spool of silence unwinds — what I've yet to know.

2

1

Visitors

'Coming, Aggie?' Fannie squeezes my fingers.

We walk the dusty lane, her hand around mine. Fannie is not like anyone else. She moves like water in a muddy creek. We stop to gather wildflowers, ripping their tough stems free, the delicate flowers expiring in our hands. Tall grasses vibrate with heat. We cut a path through the raspberry brambles and along the edge of the front field, planted with corn, the corn taller than my head, taller than Fannie's too.

Fannie's hair is falling out of her bun. Wisps halo her. I look up into her face, like the face of the moon, looking down into mine.

We are going to the graveyard. We are always going to the graveyard.

'Here we are,' Fannie says in a comfortable way. I climb the mossy split rails. Dark and grooved, the wood is cool and damp against my knees. Fannie enters at the gate. 'Hello, everyone,' she says. 'Hello, boys. Good morning, Mother.'

I leap from the fence and drop the dying wildflowers. My job is to clear away the crabapples that fall from the overhanging trees. Fannie hitches her skirt, swings it out of the way, and kneels on a grave to pick it clean of weeds. That is her job.

I throw handfuls of crabapples, making noises like guns firing, like grenades exploding, like I imagine war to sound. Our brother Robbie is at war — my half-brother, Fannie's full.

Fannie pats the grass to call me closer. I chew open a crabapple, spit it out.

'Born too early,' Fannie begins. I know her stories by heart. 'Born too early,' she repeats, waiting for me, sitting now on her bottom, arms gathering her legs into her bosom. 'Their skin was thinner than crepe, blue as baby birds.'

She's got me. I kneel and brush the grass over the twins, buried together in a tiny square coffin. I can almost see its outlines under the ground, of thin dark wood pressed on all sides by the weight of the earth.

'Were they boys or girls?' I ask. Fannie is waiting for me to ask.

'Boys, of course.'

I already know, but her answer still gives me a shiver. This is a graveyard of dead children, all boys, my half-brothers. I am relieved to have been born a girl.

The twins: the first and second babies born to our father Robert Smart and his first wife, who was Fannie's mother — not mine — and whose name I know was Tilda. The twins lived for a few minutes each, not even an hour, let alone a day.

Next born came Robbie, who is alive and well and fighting in the mud fields of France. His letters home are scant on details, but for the mud. He writes that his feet are always wet, and that the boys suffer from foot rot. Some of their toes turn black.

4

I would like to know more about this. I am thinking about it now.

'Do their toes fall off?' I ask Fannie.

'Whose toes?'

'The boys in the war, in the mud.'

'Robbie doesn't say.'

'Can you write to him and ask?' (I don't yet know how to write.)

'I think we have nicer things to say in our letters, don't we? Robbie doesn't want to think about his toes falling off.'

'Maybe they've already fallen off.'

'He would tell us.'

But I wonder: would he? I look forward to inspecting his feet, surreptitiously, when he's home again, whenever that may be. The newspaper says our boys will be home by Christmas, but Christmas is a long way off.

After Robbie was born, along came Fannie, and then Edith, a string of good luck.

Fannie is older than Edith, but Edith is no longer at home with us. Last fall, she married a man named Carson Miller, and they live across the cornfield, on the next farm over. I like to close my eyes and see Edith standing under the arbour built by our father for the wedding — I think she looks beautiful and I don't understand why my mother grieved over the bareness of the arbour. In my mind, Edith stands alone holding fresh-cut late-blooming flowers, her newly sewn dress tight at the wrists and close at the neck, a raven blue hue.

Fannie moves to the next grave, pulling me along with her. I poke at the initials in the flat stone, scraping away flecks of moss with my fingernails.

Here is another boy. After Edith was born, the string of good luck came to an end.

'Fever,' says Fannie, her fingers plucking at minuscule weeds. 'Only six months old.'

But six months isn't *only*, and I know it.

Edith's baby is already six months. I get to haul around his squirming protesting self as often as I please. I might go whenever I want, so long as I tell Mother — she likes to send along a basket of something: fresh salt buns, or a ball of butter, or beans and tomatoes from our garden. At home, I am the youngest and I like the novelty of being in charge of 'Little Robbie,' named so as to tell him apart from Robbie, my brother, and Robert, my father.

I feel torn, on visiting Edith's. There is something unfinished about the house and yard, and it feels different from home. Strange.

Edith's vegetable garden is half the size of ours, and weedy. The flowers grow scanty in their beds, as if they've given up trying. The house is cramped and smells of damp and dirty laundry and soup.

Edith greets my surprise arrivals with an irritated 'Oh, Aggie,' flushed and hurrying, her hairline damp with sweat. She never sits down, and she never offers me a cookie. (Maybe she doesn't bake any?) She hands off the baby and rushes to other business — not baking cookies — muttering to herself.

Little Robbie and I go a long time without seeing her — it is like she's disappeared — until

6

he is howling and I am hot and cannot soothe him and my arms ache and I feel like howling too. This is when Edith pops into the scene: 'There you are!' Annoyed, as if she's been looking and looking everywhere for us.

So I might go as often as I like, but I don't go very often.

Fannie is shifting her weight slowly from the baby who died of fever to the next grave, the grave that grieves her most of all, the one we've both been moving toward: little James.

'It was haying time,' says Fannie, drawing out each word slow and plain. 'Maybe he was hot and wanted cooling down. Maybe he was lost. He was only two years old — how did he find his way across the back field to the pond? Drowned before we even knew he was missing, that's how fast it happened. That's how fast it can.'

Neighbour boys fishing at the pond discovered James floating facedown in the water, and they pulled him out and ran screaming to the farmhouse, carrying him between them.

When they set him down in the yard, little James was not yet stiff, the life fresh out of him.

'I was seven years old,' says Fannie. 'Older than you. The neighbour boys — they're in the war now, but they were just boys then — Jerry and Jack — I can hear them hollering. They laid him on the patch of grass by the summer kitchen door. Everyone came running, my mother falling down over him, trying to lift him, telling him to breathe, please, breathe. And then I knew he must be dead. So I ran and hid in the barn, in the mow, under the straw. The shock of it. It

7

broke my mother's heart.'

For a moment I forget that when Fannie says 'my mother,' she means the first mother, not mine, and it jolts me to think, even for a breath, even mistakenly, that my own mother's heart might be broken by anything.

None of my mother's babies are dead; none of the graves are hers to mourn. I believe this is because my mother gave birth only to girls, three of us: Olive, then Cora, and me, Aganetha, last of all.

I have decided that my mother is nothing like the first mother. The first mother — *Tilda*, I mouth her name — is fuzzy around the edges, shrouded in black netting from all her years of mourning. The stories about Tilda are not really about her. She is in the background, weeping for her dead babies, and then, suddenly, she's buried too.

'Puerperal fever,' says Fannie, but that is not what I hear, and so I imagine the first mother purple from scalp to toenail when she died.

All of this happened almost at once: little James drowned, our brother George came early — 'So tiny we kept him in a drawer' — and the first mother died.

I imagine Fannie hiding under the straw past dusk, refusing to come out, like a kitten in a nest. Who pulls her out? Fannie doesn't say.

The neighbour men came to finish the haying. Father sat in silence at the table and ate whatever the neighbour women laid before him. Fannie and Edith, aged seven and six, spooned milk into the tiny new baby's mouth — my half-brother

George. Everyone watched Father eat and eat and eat, like he had a hole in his stomach through which the food was falling, and they wondered whether he would ever speak again. (He must have; he married my mother before the next spring.)

Nothing so sad has ever happened to me.

'It was James drowning that killed my mother,' says Fannie. 'I don't think it was George at all. George wasn't to blame.'

I know what she's going to say next, and I wait for it.

'I was supposed to be watching him, Aggie. Watching him was my job. What was I doing instead?'

We are nearly done. In another moment, I'll go back to gathering and throwing crabapples. There is just one more thing Fannie needs to say as we kneel here beside each other.

Thin yellow hair lifts from my scalp. I can't see my own face, looking up at my sister's, and don't know that it is wildly freckled, and in my silence looks long and carven. Fannie is both smiling and serious.

'I'll never stop watching you, Aggie. I promise.'

There.

It is the clearest air. The quietest sky. The hummingest bugs. The sun shines.

★ ★ ★

'Friends here to see you, Mrs. Smart!'

The nurse has woken me. I've been lying in a

9

shallow drift of sleep, not an unpleasant place to linger, and it is with irritation that I'm wrenched back into this room, surfacing into a pattern that has the sensation of being chronic.

'Wakey, wakey, Mrs. Smart!'

My mouth is dry, lips peeling off each other as I open them to say again the obvious: *I never married!*

I keep telling them, but they do insist on *Missus*, as if I've cause to be shamed by my spinster state. Do they practice their chirping in the mirror, these nurses? This one is arranging my sweater like I am her plaything, a dried-apple-head doll she's crafted herself and would like to show off to someone who's come to play.

I hear myself looping, 'Goodness, why now . . .'

'Mrs. Smart, we have a lovely surprise for you this morning! Friends come to see you! Isn't that something!'

She's got me there — I would have to agree. I would have to call that *something*. Who would come to see me? I don't know anyone, anymore. Everyone's dead.

I am trying to explain that I am very thirsty. I've got her by the wrist, but she's stronger. She evades me and goes around behind to unlock the brake — I hear its click releasing — and she begins pushing the chair out of the corner where they've arranged it beside the window that is never opened and that steams opaque with moisture on chilly days. The radiator mumbles. I don't mind the spot. I'll know I'm a goner when they park me in front of the blithering television.

'I'm thirsty,' I croak.

No, she doesn't hear. She bends with hushed excitement and breathes into my hair, what's left of it, tufted like the threads of root on an old red radish.

'It's a young man and a young woman come to visit, Mrs. Smart. They'd like to take you for a stroll. And what a lovely day for it. We'll bundle you up with blankets and tuck you right in. I've forgotten their names. But here they are. Smile, Mrs. Smart. Say hello to your friends.'

I refuse to do as I'm told, on principle.

The scent of scrubbed skin rushes toward me. I feel a hand alight awkwardly on mine, as if it's afraid of elderly bones and tendons and veins, as if its owner might break me. Hair swings loose and shiny, a flash of red, between our faces. The girl is saying a name, and it isn't mine, though it might be hers. It means nothing to me. No bells. No symphony of recognition.

'Louder, dear, she's nearly deaf. Aren't you, Mrs. Smart?' Voice raised. 'But we know she can hear us. Can't you, Mrs. Smart? She's not completely lost in there.'

'Hello, again,' the girl says, to me, and then to the nurse, 'it's been awhile. She might not remember us.'

I don't reply.

'And you know Mrs. Smart from . . . ?' The nurse's question trails off.

I could tell her, because I'm quite sure — this girl doesn't know me from a stranger off the street. She couldn't possibly, young as she is.

11

Everyone known to me is dead, buried, departed, gone, x-ed from my life, ties severed, bridges burnt, lost, misplaced.

'It's a long story,' I hear the girl say. She adds that she's a distant relative, but her laugh is nervous, a kid's laugh. The girl is lying, I decide, trying to parse a rumbling under my breastbone that might just be excitement. I've been sitting in this chair for years, day in, day out, as the light outside the window fades and lengthens and fades again, and the seasons trail, and the sky grows dark with snowflakes and flat with summer's glare. Every change here is incremental. Which makes this girl's arrival monumental.

She is speaking — not to the nurse, but to me.

'Coming?' she asks, as if in my wheeled chair I have some choice, some agency. She touches my hand again, her fingers sliding under mine, around mine, so lightly I only just register the pressure of her hold on me.

I say to her, You remind me of someone. Come closer, I'll whisper it.

Fannie.

Fannie is still so young. She's stayed the same and I have not. But when she visits, her face always turned away from mine, hidden behind her hair, behind a shadow, I feel the girl in me, the years dissolving. I feel the comfort of her, my big sister, offering her hand.

Coming, Aggie?

She has been dead nearly a century, but she walks effortlessly across the undulations of my mind, hair loose, hips broad, apron bleached white.

'Coming?' The girl's touch brushes the skin on my wrist, like an offer, waiting for me.

I slip my hand into hers.

2

Sisters and Brothers

We're on the move, from stuffy room to antiseptic hall.

A confiding tone from the nurse: 'Do you know, you're the first visitors she's had since I started working here. It's nice of you to come!' I register this tone often, spoken over my head. *She pulled the bowl of soup down on her lap. She soiled the sheets. We found her wandering the hall, she could have fallen and broken something. Who knew she could still walk!*

Keep on talking. Just so long as I'm going somewhere, squeaking on rubber wheels away from the nagging television, the muffled room, the whistles and cackles, belches and groans. For a moment the chair is caught on the lip of the threshold, but a professional shove with the wrists has us over and out.

I hear from my throat a chortle of excitement that comes out quite strangled. Quiet, old woman, I think. They've forgotten you're here.

We stall in the hall, lit by fluorescent tubes and smelling of disinfectant. The nurse won't let me go just yet. She's worried about that chortle.

She's saying, 'If you sign your name here, and today's date, and the time.'

I could do with that information. What if I've had a birthday and I'm already 105? What if it's

14

past breakfast and no one's spooned me my tea? What is the girl's name? That might come in handy. I might be able to use that.

''Kaley,'' says the nurse, reading it off the page. 'That's an unusual name.'

'Not really,' the girl says.

'I guess nothing's unusual these days, ha-ha!' The nurse wants a person to like her, which, I could tell her, generally guarantees a person won't.

'Kaley,' says the girl. 'It's Celtic,' and we're back to the name.

Kaley. I hum the word inside my head. Kaley, like the leafy vegetable, bitter until the first frost and then virtually indestructible. Kaley, and the other one — there's a second visitor, a boy — says he's called Max. It's the first he's opened his mouth. The nurse doesn't ask Max to sign the form. She doesn't ask me either.

We begin an elaborate exit ritual, not of my choosing. The tucking of the flannel blanket. The fixing of the belt around my midsection to prevent me from slipping out of the wheeled chair. More patting, more fixing, more fussing, more lifting and shifting of the sweater and of my hands. The nurse pulls a woollen hat down over my ears, bound to be unflattering. It already itches.

The girl says, 'Are we ready?'

She adjusts the woollen hat, an unnecessary action that is nevertheless reassuring. Excellent. I feel the nurse relaxing. The woman will let us go, soon. She will let us go, together.

As the girl leans into my line of sight, her face

sharpens suddenly from dull blur to distinct blur. I would guess her hair to be coloured and not a natural shade of red. No one in my family had red hair, although Edith married a boy with red hair. Carson, that was his name. But their son came out dark, like most of us — all but me. Their daughter was fair, as I suspect this girl is, but I am getting confused. She's too young to be Edith's, much too young, if I am as old as I think I am.

'When should we expect Mrs. Smart back?' the nurse asks.

The girl looks to the quiet one, the one called Max, as if asking a question, and she says, 'I don't know. An hour, maybe two?'

'Perfect! A little stroll, a little sunshine, a cup of tea, maybe? She loves her cups of tea, don't you, Mrs. Smart?' She is very gullible, this one, busy with her bossing, her certainty about a person's likes and dislikes.

But I've heard it in the girl's voice: the catch, the sweet spot in which to hide the lie. I hardly dare believe it. They've no intention of bringing me back.

★　★　★

Lies, let me count the ways.

There is the lie of omission, the lie of avoidance, the lie outright, the boast, the tiny indulgence or fudging, the sly miscalculation, the rounding up or down, there is flattery, and the little white lie, and there is the bold sweep, the lie of epic proportions with a million smaller lies to

16

underpin it, there are the muddling lies that confuse or confound, the lie of distraction, the lie that knows it will be caught out, the cold-blooded lie and the quick-witted lie and the lie made in terror and haste, the lie that must lie and lie again to cover its tracks, and, of course, there is the lie that fools even the liar, who knows not what he or she propagates.

That last one is the most dangerous of all, for it can trick almost everyone. It can come to look like the truth.

And so I think of another lie. The lie of my own choosing, that lives with me yet, and without me. The lie that protects. That shelters. That builds its fragile hiding place of love.

★   ★   ★

Fannie is shooing me away.

'But where are you going?' I say. 'Can't I come too? Why not?'

She walks down the lane in no kind of hurry even as she brushes me away. Calm.

'Is it Robbie? Are you sad? Are you mad?' I pursue her through the raspberry canes. This summer our front field is planted with wheat, and it waves and bends, thick and green.

Fannie doesn't stop at the graveyard. She goes on by. Edith's husband, Carson, has planted their field in corn, again, and that is where Fannie seems headed.

'Why won't you say anything? Why can't I come?'

She is well beyond the split rail fence when she

17

turns: 'Aggie, I'm going on now. You must not follow me.'

'But why?' My face crumples. I blink wildly against tears. Fannie is the only person in the whole world who never refuses me, never pushes me away, never fails to enjoy the whirl I cannot help but make.

She calls me to her, and I run, thinking she has changed her mind. She hugs me warmly against her soft front. I am gaining on her in height, the top of my head past her chin. I am eight years old and growing, and she is twenty-one, long since done. She holds me at arm's length and gazes into my eyes, and I see, as if through a window freshly cleaned with vinegar and brown paper, that she is hiding something.

Fannie is hiding something — Fannie, who shares with me everything she knows, clear as glass. She has not changed her mind.

I feel something turn in me, tighten, all in one sharp click. The chatter of bugs in the grasses rises and falls around us. Fannie smoothes my flyaway hair under her hands. I like her face so much.

She says, 'Do not follow me.'

She waits for me to leave her. I walk to the graveyard and enter at the gate, stand with arms pinned at my sides, mute, betrayed. Does she see? Doesn't she?

There is a new stone this summer, marking another Smart son gone. The grass over his grave isn't new, as it hasn't been dug up, there being no remains to bury. The stone is flat, like the

18

others, carved with his initials and the years of his birth and his death: R.S. 1893—1916. I look at his initials and I think: *Robbie Smart*. I will never know whether his toes turned black or fell off.

I gather a handful of crabapples and throw them rapid-fire at a bird hiding in the branches of one of the trees. When I check, Fannie is gone.

She is out of sight, but I can see clearly the path beaten down by her steps, the weeds parting to show where she's passed, and so I do as she has asked me not to, and I follow. I crouch low, pretending to be a soldier in battle, a spy. Behind the lines. Or in no man's land, where Robbie was marooned when he got shot. The telegram said little of interest. It didn't say, for instance, where on Robbie's body the fatal shot caught him.

I think it must have been his head or his heart. I think it must have looked like a hole blown clean, like a pipe through which daylight could shine, one end to the other, and there he was fallen to the ground, one drop of blood sliding down his forehead, his eyes staring at the sky.

I've caught up.

I see Fannie, not so very far from me, and she is not alone. She's almost as tall as the corn in the field next door, and the man is taller.

I freeze like a rabbit hiding in the open.

He isn't one of the young men spit out of the war, missing a leg or an eye or wheezy from the gas. But he's not so old either. He's dressed like the farmer he is — and I know him, very well. I see he's got Fannie's hand in his. Her face is

19

inclined, hidden from me, her bunched hair brushes his shoulder, and they walk together into the corn. They're gone, like that, the tall stalks shifting, the tassels of brown gold thread drooping, heads hung low.

I rise like I'm going to follow. But I know that the field of corn is enchanted, its secrets held in tidy rows, and I do not follow.

I think that Fannie was right, after all: she is going on ahead without me, and I should have let her go. I shouldn't have seen her walk into the corn with a man who is family, our brother by law, if not by blood.

I can't name him, even inside my head.

All I can think to do is to run — away.

★ ★ ★

I am running over the crushed weeds.

I am running past the graves.

Tangling and scratching through the berry bushes. Choking in the dust raised on the lane. Our big black dog circling me in the barnyard, barking, confused. My breath comes harsh, my heart bangs, hair whips my face. But my feet scarcely graze the ground.

I had not known that I could run so fast — I can fly, that's how fast. Now I know. I know that shock can spin itself into something near exhilaration, by mere application of speed.

The brain is a primitive instrument. It plays its oldest, wildest songs best.

I fly into the barn — sweet with manure — and dart up the stable's ladder to the great wide mow.

Breathe. Climb. Breathe. *Sneeze, sneeze.*

I scramble through loosely packed straw, piled like a mountainside nearly to the eaves, where I know there is a fresh nest of kittens. Sharp straw, not soft, cutting fine red lines across exposed skin. My nose streams, and my eyes, and I'm almost blind with sneezing, but I stagger to the nest, rubbing my wet face hard with my wrists. The kittens are not even a week old, eyes like slits, little ears flat to their heads, a tumble of searching hungry fur. Without apology to the mother cat, I crouch and pull from the mass an orange striped creature, and I press its living body under my chin. It is mewling and blind, and I nuzzle its dusty fur until my heart quiets. Its ribs under my fingers feel like the bones of a tiny vessel, fragile as a boat made of sticks. Its darting heart. Its piercing cry and open mouth stills me, and I am myself again.

I press the kitten's soft skull into the soft spot under my chin. I coo to it. But I can't sit still for long. My legs are restless, always, my muscles twitch, my feet kick of their own accord. I've been known to kick my sister Cora under the table, not because I'm angry at her, simply because my foot leaps out and does it, can't be stopped.

'Ow! Aggie kicked me!'

'Not on purpose!'

'Off you go, Aggie. We'll have none of that.' It's Mother who puts me to rights; Father is slow to punishment, slow to tune in to the turnings around him. With Robbie dead, Father moves even more like a man living inside a dream. Only one subject captures his interest: a machine of his own invention, powered by a windmill, that he is building in the barn, even now.

'Off you go, and muck the chicken pen as you were meant to do this afternoon.'

'But — !'

'Not a word. Go.'

But Mother's punishment is gentle: she sets aside a plate of food for me. She won't let any of us go without a meal. She went hungry as a child, she has told us, and we are never to know that particular pain.

Mother is not one for stories, and does not tell more, even if I'd like to know, even if I ask: how hungry, and why, and when, and what did it feel like? She speaks rarely of her family, though her father and brothers are alive, and their homestead lies in the county west of ours. They might as well live in another country for all we see of them.

The kitten purrs against my neck.

Father is working nearby, somewhere overhead. I can hear him. It's likely that he's heard me too, clambering into the mow all in a scramble. He won't think anything of it. It is a broiling hot July afternoon, and Father should be busy with the haying, but he's hired men for the summer work now that Robbie is gone. Last summer and the summer before it seemed like Robbie would come home, eventually, if not quite soon. Edith's husband, Carson, helped, and Fannie too, and Mother, and even George was called on to drive the team of horses, while Olive and Cora and I made sandwiches and iced tea and carried them out to the field, three little girls in dusty dresses, our hair pulled off our faces under bonnets.

We managed without Robbie.

But not this summer.

Last summer and the summer before, we knew Robbie would be back soon enough. And now we know he won't be. There is absence, and there is vanishing, and these are not the same thing at all.

The kitten pricks my thumb with one sharp claw, like a pin piercing the skin. 'Ow!' It's small as pain goes, but I return the kitten to its mother, and stick my thumb into my mouth. I feel oddly recovered, and stride with wide leaps down to the swept barn floor.

'Hallo!' I call up to my father.

Father shakes his head in acknowledgement. He is erecting a staircase that circles to the top of the barn. When he has built the stairs, he will cut a hole in the roof and make a small house above, like a steeple, to shelter the windmill's gears. The stairs will climb right inside the little house, so he can mind the mechanics within.

Outside, on top, the blades of the mill will turn, powering Father's machine.

At mealtimes, Father drifts away from the ends of sentences. He goes on ahead in his thoughts and leaves us behind. But here in the barn, his purpose is visible. I am comforted by it, even though his plan lies in pieces — stacks of board — around which I carefully step.

'Can I help?' I call up.

'Don't try the steps,' he warns, even as he

climbs down them to the skeletal platform standing twelve feet above me. This is where his invention will rest: a machine powered by the wind that can be used as a lathe, or a spinning saw, or a grain grinder. The platform will double as a ceiling for a grain storage bin. I am quite sure that my father has thought of everything.

I've examined his plans, sketched in pencil onto the backs of flyers that come advertising cures for bloat or canker or colic. His measurements are mysterious and meticulous. I am sure of my father.

I watch him step silently up the circular staircase carrying an armload of roughly cut boards.

I love the smell of cut wood. I've forgotten about Fannie, here, amidst the ragged ends and sawdust and debris. I don't think of her at all. Working atop a table made out of two sawhorses and an old door, I hammer bent nails straight, the one job Father lets me do without question.

I ignore Cora, who has climbed up from the stable below to stand at my elbow, her breathing laborious.

'What are you doing?' she says.

'What does it look like?'

'You're not getting them straight.' She examines the nail I've just finished.

'Am too.' I snatch the nail out of her hand. The metal is still hot to the touch. I hammer it some more. Cora crosses her arms and observes. I can feel her judgement and the hammer lands wrong, bounces up.

'Stop watching me.'

'You've had your chance, now it's my turn. It's only fair.'

'Find something else to do.'

'I won't.'

Now that the hammer is silent, we can hear Mother calling our names. Father hears too.

'Go on,' he says, just that, no more. We must obey.

★ ★ ★

I run to the ladder ahead of Cora. She makes no appearance of trying to beat me, but steps on my fingers coming down. I've underestimated her.

We burst out of the stable door at the same moment, Cora calling sweetly, 'Here we are, Mother. We were helping Father.'

'Does he want help?' Mother frowns. 'You're meant to be working in the garden, Aggie. And Cora, there's laundry to pull off the line and ironing.'

'I finished in the garden,' I say, knowing that it is quite impossible ever to be finished in the garden.

'Olive's doing the ironing,' says Cora. We're the same height, though I'm younger by two years. I can see eye to eye with her. We've been told that we look the same, *like twins*, which neither of us takes as a compliment.

'I'm looking for Fannie,' says Mother, 'have you seen her?'

'No,' I say quickly.

'I saw her going down the lane with you.' Cora

25

stares at me hard, and I say, 'That was ages ago,' and Cora says, 'Well that's the last I seen her,' and Mother says, 'Saw her, Cora, saw her. That's the last you saw her.'

'Yes,' says Cora. 'That's the last I saw her.'

Mother waits. 'Well?' she asks me, and I shake my head to erase trouble from my face, a trick accomplished more easily than expected.

'You two can run an errand for me, in Fannie's stead. Take this on over to Edith's. Tell her: two teaspoons in a glass of water three times a day, starting now.' Mother hands Cora a small jar made of brown glass and stopped with a cork. Cora agitates the liquid like Mother's just done. 'Can you remember that?'

'Two teaspoons in a glass of water three times a day,' Cora says as I chime in a fraction too late on every word. I know Cora would like to kick me.

'If Edith looks poorly you must tell me,' says Mother. 'And stay and do her washing up.'

'She said to run,' I tell Cora as soon as we're out of Mother's sight, and I take off flying down the lane. I run past the graveyard, and past the place where Fannie walked into the corn, and I make myself not look at it. I make myself keep running.

Cora doesn't even try to keep up. It isn't much fun to best her when she isn't even trying. Maybe that's what makes me do it. Maybe. I don't know what makes me, but as I get farther and farther on, with Cora lagging behind, not even trying, I decide to hide in the corn by the side of the road. I'll surprise Cora. In a flash, I'm standing in the corn, listening to my own ragged breath and thumping heart and the whoosh of stalks swaying.

I'm excited, impatient. I try to hold my breath. I mark Cora's slow approach, measure her strides. Here she comes, proudly carrying the bottle of Mother's tincture, marching with her chin in the air — and why should Mother trust Cora with the bottle just because she's older? Here she comes, nearer and nearer, looking as if she's forgotten we are meant to do this together.

My exit could not be more perfectly timed.

Cora is opposite my hiding spot when I rush out with a thrilling whoop.

Cora shrieks. Into the air shoots the bottle.

'It's just me!' I laugh.

But she isn't laughing, and neither am I when we see where Mother's bottle has landed. It's struck a stone, and broken. We stare at the dark liquid leaking into the dusty roadway. We are each weighing our blame. Cora can say it's all my fault for frightening her, but she was the one holding the tincture, and we both know our mother assigns consequences evenly. If our mother is anything, it's fair.

Cora's eyes meet mine. We arrive at the same conclusion, at the same moment: we won't tell. No one will ever know. Together, we kick the glass into the ditch with our tough-soled feet, and sprinkle dirt over the damp spot in the road, as if we expect someone to come looking for evidence.

In silence, we continue to Edith's. This time, I don't run ahead.

As we're walking up the lane, Cora says, 'You play with Little Robbie and I'll do the washing up.'

I say, 'Little Robbie can help sweep. He's handy with the dustpan.'

It is rare for us to agree. I'm not certain I like it. I feel uneasy.

Edith and Carson's lane is bare, no trees, and there are no trees planted in the yard around the house either, not even young saplings. The grass is burnt away by the sun. I shoot a quick scanning glance, but I don't spy Carson anywhere, and I hope I won't; then I think, with horror, what about Fannie? I'm terrified of seeing them here, together, their presence like a haunting, like their languid selves might part the corn and float toward us, hand in hand. I'm shaky, almost glad for Cora's presence. Everywhere I look, I see what's been hidden, and there is doubleness layered behind what is, making a blur of the outlines, sickening me.

Little Robbie is playing by himself in the shade on the porch. He runs across the hard dirt when he sees us, straight into my arms, and he steadies me like the kitten did.

'Fetch your dustpan,' I boss him. 'We've come to play house. You can be the big brother and I'm the mum!'

He wriggles down, looks at Cora and tries to say something. He's only got a few words, and he sucks his thumb every waking minute. But I understand what he's asking even if Cora can't.

'Cora will be the wee granny,' I say, answering his question.

28

Cora doesn't like that one bit, and I'm relieved, like I've put something back where it belongs.

'Hello, Edith!' Cora calls brightly, going into the house ahead of us. 'Me and Aggie have come to visit!'

Edith says hello, but she doesn't get up to greet us. The kitchen door smacks shut behind us. There is no screen in it, and the house is stifling, the counter swarming with flies and no wonder: it's a jumble of dirty dishes and pots.

Cora and I work together to set things straight. Edith rocks in a chair in the corner, in her lap a little handiwork. She shows it to us: she is embroidering tiny flowers and vines around the hem of a white nightgown such as a newborn baby might wear. She looks the same as always, tall like Fannie, who is her full sister, but gaunt at the extremities, thick in the middle. She and Fannie don't look much like sisters, aside from their height, although both are very pretty, much prettier than Olive or Cora or I will ever be. Their mother must have been prettier than ours, that's the plain truth of it. But Edith's prettiness is faded, like it's been left outside to curl and shrivel in the sun. She is younger than Fannie, but you'd never guess it.

Cora and I stay as long as we can stand it.

Little Robbie doesn't want to let go of my hand. He follows me into the lane and I turn and walk him back to the porch again, and then again, and then I'm grown tired of it, and I speak sternly: 'Little Robbie, I'm going on now! You can't come!' I have to leave him crying and kicking his heels on the porch. I want to run to

29

get away, but I'm suddenly weary. I keep checking over my shoulder to see whether Little Robbie is going to follow me again. When he doesn't, I feel next thing to crying myself. He's given up.

Cora stays silent until we pass the faint traces on the road where the bottle broke, and then she says, 'Did you see the loaf of bread? Mouldy. I should have thrown it out, but I don't know if Edith has more.'

'I think Edith looks poorly,' I say.

Cora disagrees. 'Edith always looks poorly.'

I say, 'She didn't even get up from the rocker.'

'She's like that now,' says Cora, and she looks at me and frowns.

I'm about to argue, but Cora repeats herself: 'Edith is like that now, anytime we visit. You know that. There's nothing new to tell Mother.'

'I guess not,' I say slowly. I don't want Mother discovering what we've done — or neglected to do — any more than Cora does.

It seems Fannie's returned because we've hardly arrived when she calls us in to set the table for supper. I argue that I still have to do the chickens. That's a safe bet for me. I pretty much always have to do the chickens. I don't want to see Fannie just now anyway, not at all.

Cora says that's okay, she will set the table. We glance at each other and I think, *like twins*.

★　★　★

Here is the evidence against Cora and me: we do not deliver the tincture. We do not tell our mother what happened to the bottle. We do not say that Edith is looking poorly (more poorly than usual?).

But Edith is poorly, and she wakes the next morning in a worse state, a fact we learn when Carson arrives before breakfast and pounds on our door, like husbands do, shouting for Mother.

There's blood! We hear him say that, Cora and I.

Cora and I are making eggs and biscuits for the hired men's morning meal, and we don't stop in our work. Olive has been churning cream for butter, and she runs to the door that opens out of the dining room, the first to get to Carson. I'm hardly breathing. Is this my doing? Cora rolls and cuts the biscuit dough into squares, her head bent, eyes wide, and I know that she is thinking the same.

Fannie is not yet awake, but this isn't unusual. Fannie is the last to rise. She's not like the rest of us, but I don't know why, exactly. Maybe it's only that she's never hurrying to get somewhere.

My mother is a blur of hurry. She fastens her boots. She keeps a sturdy canvas bag with handles in the cloak closet by the dining room door, prepared for any sudden need. In her work, needs almost always arrive suddenly. She checks the kitchen: 'Good girls. Get the breakfast on for the men, and send Fannie to me when she comes down.' Her tone is serious, but unafraid.

I let Cora tell Fannie. I don't hear Fannie's reply, just her feet on the steps and the door slamming behind her as she rushes off — as

31

Fannie, who never hurries, runs now to help Mother, and Edith, and maybe too Carson, I think, and then I tell myself, *For shame*.

Father seems not to hear the uproar; only he doesn't touch his biscuits and eggs.

'You put too much salt in,' Cora tells me, of the eggs.

'You burnt the biscuits!'

Father retreats in silence to the barn.

After we feed the salty eggs and burnt biscuits to the hired men, who don't complain, and after we clean up, Olive says we should get going on the beans today, even with Mother and Fannie away. Cora says, 'Who put you in charge?' And Olive says, 'Fine. Aggie and I will do it. Aggie's a good worker, aren't you, Aggie?' None of us mention George. He is being deliberately slow over his tea. But he hears us arguing in the kitchen and comes in with his cup and saucer, and says, 'I'll help you, Aggie,' and I'm pleased, even though I expect little from George's help, and little is what I get. But companionship counts for something. After Olive and I have picked a mass of beans, George and I tail and snap them in the shade on the long porch that runs the length of three sides of the house.

Olive prepares the jars, and the hot water bath. George and I don't talk about what might be happening at Edith's. George tells me instead that he knows a boy who got into the army at fifteen.

'What'd he want to do that for?'

George says, 'It's better'n snapping beans.'

'You want black toes?'

32

'I'll keep my feet dry.'

'I'll tell Mother.'

'You won't.'

'You wouldn't do it,' I say.

George says nothing for a while. Then he coughs. His cough is ever present, a patient wheeze that worsens when there is chaff or dust around, or grass, or buds, or trees, or weeds, or hay, or animals, or smoke. He looks at me and says, 'Why wouldn't I, Aggie? Why'd you think I wouldn't?'

It will hurt him to say it. I hesitate.

'Why, Aggie?'

Because you're snapping beans with me. Because of that cough. Because you're skinny as a scarecrow. Because you like napping in the shade in the middle of the afternoon. Because they won't have you.

'Because you're not allowed to be killed,' I growl with an angry force that hurts my throat.

Mother says little when she returns, without Fannie, late in the afternoon. Mother is only stopping to gather fresh linens, and to prepare a tea from the dried herbs she stores, hanging, in the cellar. If she's noticed the absence of the tincture she sent with us yesterday, she doesn't mention it. In Edith's house items might be lost or misplaced quite easily; a person would not expect to find anything where it ought to be found.

But my hands start shaking at the thought.

Mother sends me to the cellar with a candle to fetch up some herbs. I close my eyes and select them by scent: calendula, blue and black cohosh, anise, chamomile, red raspberry leaf. When I bring the herbs to Mother, she reads the fear on my face, if not the guilt, and she thanks me, her hand gentle along my cheek.

'Your sister will recover.'

I can't ask about the baby that might have been.

I burst into tears.

3

Conspirators

We've reached the elevator doors.

Keep the nurse talking, distract her, there's a girl. This is the slowest damn elevator you're likely to encounter. I ride up and down on occasion. They push us outside to 'catch the breeze,' as they call it, arranging us all in a row like sale items outside a discount store. Who would want us? The young and healthy march past, determined not to be depressed by the sight of us, warning them of things to come — *if they're lucky*, I say, trying to pass the joke along to the crumpled crone in the chair beside mine, but as we've lost the ability to toss words through the air, I aim for psychic means, wondering whether she might hear me. Stranger things have happened. When she chuckles, I am certain she has. And then we are wheeled back inside to ride the slowest damn elevator in existence back upstairs again.

This happens daily in fine weather, and never for the rest of the year.

It hasn't happened in recent memory, if recent memory is to be trusted, which I am not so certain it is. If you were to ask me to name the month, I couldn't tell you. I could tell you the colour of the sky outside the window under which I was planted before the nurse woke me to

35

say you were here: It was white. That could mean anything.

The elevator doors open.

'Keep her blanket tucked, and if she seems chilled, bring her home right away.' Is she really going to let me go? 'Have fun, Mrs. Smart!' The nurse presses in to kiss my head, or more precisely, the woollen hat that is itching my nearly naked scalp.

I hear what she's said, what she's called this place: *home*. I'm enraged, though I can't think why. I've called worse places home.

The girl has taken over the pushing and we bump too quickly into the sighing elevator, my knees squashed against the back wall.

She doesn't think to turn me.

I can hear her hitting the buttons rather wildly, but now is not the time to panic. What's her hurry? A certainty sits happily with me as we descend in slow motion, that the pair of them are attempting a breakout. A heist. I smile to my dull reflection on the silver wall.

Am I conspirator or stolen object? How can I tell the difference?

She is whispering — to herself, I think, and not to him or to me — but I nod anyway, to reassure her as she pulls me backward out of the elevator. The wheels catch on an edge of carpet, and in her struggle she nearly manages to dump me out, prevented only by the belt.

I can hear the girl's breathing accelerate as she rushes us through the mouldering lobby.

The young man holds the door open.

Max.

There, I've remembered, and the girl is a green leafy vegetable like chard, but not chard. Bitter. I'm in my mother's garden, travelling the rows, darting from end to end pulling peppers and tomatoes and beans while my brother George lies in the shade of his hat beside the wide basket I am working to fill.

'Well done!' George crunches on a pickling cucumber I've brought to the basket. He's supposed to be helping, but I don't mind. I've got a job to do and I like a job to do; George likes not doing a job. So we're both of us happy, together. Green cabbage, red cabbage, broccoli, parsley, celery, scallion, kale. *Kale*.

Her name is Kale, or not quite, but close enough. Kaley, as I am called Aggie, not Aganetha; a pet name, a diminutive, most likely given in kindness, though not always. Depends who's speaking.

She's got us smoothly through the door and we are whipping down the ramp and into the brightness of day. The air is damp, but chilly. I am confused, struggling to remember the hour, the season, the whole of it, struggling to place myself in time. My hands fumble at the blanket over my knees, and I discover it is wrapped all the way to my chest. The sun stinging my eyes. The wind catching my breath.

I open my mouth to drink the heavy air.

Thirst. I am thirsty.

We cross a street without pausing, and the girl curses at a car that veers too near, though it's clear she herself is at fault. We crash up and over the curb. I grunt. She's got me turned on an awkward angle as she cranes to look behind, not ahead. She wants to be clear of the place from which we've escaped. Only when she's sure do we stop.

I think, *We are under a tree.* I think, *The tree has its leaves.* I think, *The leaves are young.* Clues abound.

I hear what the girl's saying, though it's not directed at me. She is speaking to the young man, to Max, whose name I have no trouble remembering while hers already eludes me, vanished among the garden rows.

She's saying, 'This is Aganetha Smart. We've got her! This is really her!'

★ ★ ★

Here comes Fannie down the lane.

I'm walking the fence rail, my feet bare, the skirt of my dress tied into a knot at the side.

The front field is a pasture for horses this summer, but today there's only the old mare and her foal under one of the shade trees near the fence. The other horses are working — the light-legged gelding is pulling Mother to wherever she's gone to help this morning, and the team is hauling the mower over the hay field, guided by one of the hired men.

Here comes Fannie, closer and closer.

I stop, one-legged on a post, but I don't bother to wave. Fannie's away inside her head, I can see it in her long stare, eyes ahead. She gives no sign of seeing me, passing right by, and turns toward the graveyard, though I think, perhaps, she's going farther, elsewhere, to Carson and Edith's. I feel invisible. Maybe I feel angry too.

I jump from the post to the fence rail, and run toward the road in a series of hurried steps that turn to stumbles, to hesitation and wildly flailing arms. *Watch me fall, Fannie, just watch me!*

George is lying under a shade tree near the mare and her filly. He has seen. He jumps to his feet.

But I won't fall — I'm only tricking. I bend over with laughter as he jogs anxiously toward me.

'Hey,' he calls. 'Aggie!'

I right myself. I'm pleased to have fooled someone: it makes me like George more. I turn the other way and sprint past him to where the fence stops, near the house, and I can see Olive hanging out a load of white sheets.

She sees me too: 'Have you mucked the chicken pen?'

I pretend not to hear, and run back toward George, who leans on the fence, grinning, feeding the mare a handful of grain from his pocket. 'How do you do it, Aggie?'

'Easy,' I say, and I mean it.

Motion comes lightly to me. Maybe this is how others feel about calculations and equations, or about words, or about their feelings, about choices, about right and wrong. Maybe this is how my mother feels when she's helping a woman bring a new baby into the world. Maybe this is how my father feels when he's building one of his inventions.

What I make can't be seen. It vanishes the

39

instant it's created. It can never be made in just the same way again. How can I ever grow bored of it?

'I don't think you'll ever fall,' says George.

'Of course I won't.'

The old mare is standing nearby, scratching her fat belly against the boards of the fence, and on impulse I step from fence to horse.

'Whoa, whoa, whoa.' George looks alarmed, and I like him even more. 'What are you doing, Aggie?'

'Watch me.'

But the mare shifts uneasily. She's ticklish. She doesn't like where I've landed. I come into a crouch and stretch out my arms for balance. Toes dig in, heels grip, arches rise. Her thin summer coat is slippery, oily. The muscles in her shoulders ripple under my weight. I can feel every flicker rising up from her body through mine, and I rise too, to standing.

'Come on, George! Get her going!'

George glances around, but who's to see the two of us playing, as we shouldn't, on this summer's afternoon?

He reaches his arm around the mare's head, firmly holding the bony frontal plate of her huge skull. A horse's head is as long as a child's torso, beautifully carved. George clucks his tongue, but his eyes are on me. We take a step and another and more, strolling into the middle of the grassy pasture. The filly keeps pace beside its mother's rump.

I don't look down.

George leads the mare in wide circles up and

down the field and I stand straight as a knife, and roll with her gentle stride. It's the next thing to magic. There's no reason for doing it, other than to do it. But it's too easy.

'Faster,' I say.

George stares up at me.

'Faster!' I command.

He is older, but he obeys. He urges the mare into a trot, but his lungs aren't fit for running, and in an instant he's behind us. I don't glance to see what's happened to him. I just want what I want, and now: 'Faster!' I gather myself into a firmer crouch and yell to the mare, 'Faster! Giddup!'

She breaks into a lumbering canter, her heavy hooves powerfully cutting the uneven turf. I won't fall. I won't fall. I won't fall. I am inside my body, and outside of it, watching us tear for the fence, our approach head-on and heedless. I'm certain the mare will leap. She will clear the top rail. I believe this with my entire being, and I prepare for it, my knees loosening to absorb the vault, the arc, the descent.

But the mare thinks otherwise. The mare is bound by the fence.

She shudders to a halt in three short strides. I cannot do the same. I sail on. My arms spread wide and I fly over the mare's lowered ears, over the fence where the grass grows thickest, like a thrown stone tumbling downward where I land almost gracefully — toes and hands, followed by knees and chin — in the soft manure pile behind the barn.

Ugh.

I can't believe I fell. I *won't* believe I fell. Already I don't believe it.

I'm on my feet, certain nothing hurts. I rub my chin, brush my knees. My dress is manure stained, that's all, though it will bring me some small grief when Olive sees it. No amount of scrubbing can lift a manure stain.

George wheezes toward us. Even at a distance, I hear air squeezing in and out of his chest. The mare is planted calmly, lowering her head to rip a mouthful of rich green grass. Her filly shoves its pretty nose under her mother's belly to feed. I climb the fence and stand on the top rail.

I watch George struggle. He makes it look like the field is a thousand miles wide, or an ocean through which he cannot swim. He slows to a shuffle, clutching his side.

I bow.

George laughs.

I bow again, deeply, to left, to right. I bow to the manure pile, to the house, to the wheat field, to the birds in the trees, to the chickens in their run, which needs mucking and which I have neglected to attend to. I bow to the garden. I bow to the linens flapping on the line. I bow to Cora, coming out of the house in a disagreeable way, and slamming the screened door behind herself. She doesn't see me, which is just as well, occupied by whatever task she is managing all on her own.

The old mare lifts her head and eyeballs me. Now, then, she says, enough with your bragging.

Here comes Fannie returning up the lane. She shades her eyes with one hand — she is at some

42

distance — and I think she might call out to me with a gentle admonition, but she walks on, swinging her sun hat by its ribbons, patient and slow as the day is long. I turn to George, as easily as that. George, who appreciates my efforts, who is taken by my tricks, impressed, says, 'I thought you were a goner! You just about flew.'

'That's right,' I say, fists to hips, like flight was my intention all along.

Well, wasn't it?

4

Speed

'This is her!' the girl is saying. 'Aganetha Smart! This is really her!'

This is she, I think.

'I knew we could do this,' says Max. I catch him gazing anxiously at me, and I pretend that I'm deafer than deaf and paying no attention.

'Do you think she'll say yes?'

'I'm not sure she'll say anything.'

'You're worried. Don't be worried, please, I can't stand it.'

'I'm not worried, Kaley. One step at a time.'

The girl pauses. Thinking. Trying to decide whatever it is she is trying to decide. It would be courteous of her to hurry up. I remember: I'm thirsty.

I open my mouth and I say, 'I'm thirsty.'

I see him peering at me, bent down, staring into my face in wonder.

'Did you hear that?' he says.

'Didn't you?'

Staggered by my production of a coherent sentence, she and the young man seem to be missing the point.

'I'm thirsty!' I roar.

'Give her a drink!' The girl panics, looking all around as if for possible witnesses.

'Of course, a drink!' Max fumbles inside the

large bag that he carries over one shoulder and removes a metal bottle with a black plastic spout. He thinks I can hold and lift it, which is flattering, but unhelpful. I paw his arm. He understands, sets the spout to my lips, and pours until I'm nearly drowned, but I appreciate the effort, I do.

I appreciate being heard, at last.

'Thank you.' My voice sounds hoarse, but clear, elated; there, I've thought *thank you*, and I've said it! I push my luck and try to make a joke, something along the lines of: I haven't put together a sentence in years, must be something in the water, but I hear myself wandering, and know I've already lost the way: 'My word, but isn't this . . . '

The girl leans over my shoulder to pat my hand. 'Mrs. Smart?' Her voice angling upward at the end of every sentence, giving her an innocence, her loose hair brushing my cheek. 'We have something important to ask you? A favour?'

'Not yet, Kaley.' He's talking over my head. 'Don't jump the gun.'

She snaps upright, away from me. Her tone is offended: 'Don't talk to me like that. I'm not a kid.'

I grab for her hand, and pull her back down. 'I know you,' I say, though I can't think why I've said it. I don't even remember the girl's name.

'Well, you do, in a way,' she says rather breathlessly. 'I mean, we do know you. We just never thought you would . . . '

I slump in my chair and hold tight to her

hand. I see my big sister Fannie walking past us on the sidewalk and I open my eyes wide to take her in. *Look at me, Fannie, look!* But she doesn't turn her face.

There is an electronic beep, a *woop-woop*, and lights flash on a dark blue car down the street. Reminds me of flashbulbs popping in a wall of cameras, lenses pointed at me.

'C'mon, Kaley. We don't have all day.'

'That's our car, Mrs. Smart. Let's go!' The girl tries to remove her hand from mine, and I struggle not to let her. But she is just like the rest of them. She pulls herself free.

'I don't think I know you after all,' I say, suddenly tired to the bone. This is harder than it seems.

* * *

'Good work, Miss Smart.' The coach's encouragement matches his appearance, brisk and casual. He is smoking a hand-rolled cigarette.

Hands on thighs, bent over at the waist, I'm too winded to reply.

'One minute's rest, and then around again. You've thirty seconds left, twenty-nine, twenty-eight.'

Around again? I can't speak it, but the coach reads the disbelief in my eyes.

'You think you're fast now? Just wait and see how fast you'll be when I'm through with you, sweetheart.'

Sweetheart.

'That's it, sunshine, do your job and burn a

path around the track. Three, two, one — you're off.'

Sunshine.

I almost hate him. How can I hate someone I've only just met? I haven't learned to recognize the subtleties of his trade, the way a good coach directs onto himself his athlete's frustration with her own limitations, distracts her from doubt, and gives her that extra flare of necessary rage, that compulsion to continue. He is good, this coach. He is good, but I don't appreciate his talent, not at this moment, gasping for breath, tucking my chin and leaning into my orders: around again.

The opening strides feel effortless, but by the first turn my breath has already caught up to my pace. My balance is off and I stumble, recover, aim myself at the back straightaway. Breath is now outstripping pace; pace has been lapped. My lungs rattle like a freight train — it's all I can hear, an alarming noise, ragged and out of control.

I force my feet to keep time on the ground like a drumbeat.

I run on my toes, digging into the strip of hard dirt at the tapered centre of the grass track, the strip that marks the most efficient route around and around. The skin at the back of my left ankle is rubbed raw — *why only the left one?* I wonder in a haze as I take the last turn.

'Not sure I can turn you into a sprinter,' the coach said after watching my first go around, which seems hours ago, a faraway memory fading against the glare of repetition, 'but let's see if you've got the guts for middle distance. Not many girls have.'

'Middle distance?' I imagine it might be like running down to the lake and back to the rooming house where Olive and I live in Toronto, which I do sometimes, despite Olive's concern: 'What will people think — a girl running the streets in broad daylight?' Olive is funny that way. She doesn't mind what anyone does, so long as it doesn't get people thinking. *Do not attract attention*, that sums up my sister Olive.

'Eight hundred metres,' says the coach. 'At the Amsterdam Olympics, that's as far as girls can go. And that's a helluva lot farther than nothing.'

'Eight hundred metres?'

'Twice around the track.'

'But that's so short!'

'That's short until you've raced it, Miss Smart. Then you'll find it long enough.'

'I could run around that track all day,' I boast. 'I could go until the sun goes down.'

'We'll see about that, lass. Are those the only shoes you've got?'

I glance down at my feet, heavy in black boots. I've got no others. Would it be better to run barefoot, as I did on the farm? Quickly, I bend and begin unlacing a boot, pulling it off.

'No, no, no! Don't do that!'

I freeze, startled. The coach takes an embarrassed stride away from me, toward the factory, three stories of red brick with windows staring straight at us. The rims of his ears flush the same colour as the brick.

A bared foot seems suddenly grotesque,

48

exposed, naked. There stand between us two blunt facts, which I've neglected to acknowledge: He is a man, and I am a girl.

I feel my face wash with heat too, and hurriedly jam my foot deeper inside the hard leather, tighten the boot's laces, as if that's what I'd been meaning to do. 'Does it matter what shoes I wear?' I mutter, crouched low, addressing the ground.

'Not today.' The coach keeps his eyes directed at the factory's back wall.

We are positioned at the centre of Rosebud Confectionary's sports field where the Rosebud Ladies' Athletics Club trains, sponsored fully by Mr. P.T. Pallister, owner of Rosebud Confectionary. In a flash, I see everything as if I'm suspended above the scene: red brick, chain-link, dying autumn grass, sandpits, wooden benches, a low set of bleachers, and the coach is a man of thirty or forty (I can't guess) with a pencil-thin black moustache, dressed in a well-cut pale-blue-and-white-striped suit and a white flat cap, and I am me, a girl in loose flannel pants and a man's cotton shirt, wearing black boots, long golden hair pulled into a tight braid, no hat, breasts flattened by layers of wrapped jersey (unseen, of course).

The peculiar discomfort of our situation feels suddenly acute, dire, quite beyond me. I'm attuned to a debt already owed to Rosebud Confectionary, which is not my place of employment, and by extension a debt owed to Mr. P.T. Pallister, on whose letter of invitation I've come, but my greatest debt seems owed to this man, this stranger, the coach whom it is my duty to impress should I hope to make the Rosebud Ladies' track team, should I hope to run and run and run.

Oh, how I hope to run.

'What do you want me to do? Run at night, after dark, so no one sees?' I can hear myself asking Olive in despair. The two of us, sisters, work at Packer's Meats, jarring and processing minced pork. Packer's doesn't have a track club, but for the past two summers I've played for their ladies' softball team: dutifully knocking balls out of the park, running the bases, and using my crabapple-trained arm to catch out opposing batters from deep in left field. Nevertheless, our team loses often. I hate losing. My skill, and the intensity of my efforts, has made me no friends among my teammates.

I've made no friends running in the city, either.

I run back alleys, disturbing chickens and dogs and mothers hanging out the wash. I run paved streets, dodging automobiles and horse-drawn delivery wagons and little boys on bicycles. I am occasionally pelted by handfuls of stones, by rotten fruit, once by a glass bottle that catches me behind the ear. I run along the curving lake going east past the concrete docks and warehouses, until I'm running in swamp and reeds, free from the city. It doesn't take all that long, really. I breathe in the big sky. But every time, I must turn around and run back into the city again. I can feel it settling all around me on my return like a physical darkness, a weight.

'You could go home,' Olive reminds me gently, but even if I wanted to — and I don't — I believe that I can't. I've left home.

The coach is waiting for me to fix my laces and stand.

When I do, almost hopelessly, he meets my eye. I'm as tall as he is — no, I'm taller. I have not the slightest glimpse of my own power or effect. I'm a girl who looks rarely into the mirror. The coach strokes his thin moustache with the fingers of one hand. He looks unhappy about something — he's sad, or grieving, or perhaps it is longing I sense in him, need, desire — and I feel a tug under my breastbone, a sensation akin to pity. I want, in this instant, to please him, to make him happy.

'Ready then?' he says, suddenly cheerful, clapping his hands together once and rubbing the palms in anticipation; perhaps I have read his expression entirely wrong. 'Let's put you through your paces.'

And here I am, paced so many times around I've lost count. Do I regret my boast? I do not. This is a different kind of running, and if I am to master it, I will need to suffer. I understand instinctively, and lean into it. I lean against the pain until I tear right through, coming around the last curve, legs lifting as if of their own will, not mine.

He waits for me at the finish, and he swings one arm in a wide circle to indicate I am to take a second lap. 'Let's see a full eight hundred, little lady!'

Little lady! Ha! My brain is deprived of

oxygen, cut down to the basics. I will trounce this extra lap.

You're too serious, I hear a voice telling me. *You're too tall. You're no fun. You can't dance.* It isn't a man's voice. It's a woman's. It might even be my own. *You've never been kissed.*

Would I like to be kissed? Why should I? I'm not like other girls.

I pour myself into the last turn. I can't actually feel my legs, yet they are rising and falling more smoothly than they have all practice. The choice seems to be to keep running or to drop dead on the ground, and I am aware of this man waiting for me at the finish. I think, *he's waiting for me.* He is waiting for me. It is possible I mistake his attention for affection. I hear him, feel him, willing me to finish strong.

Yes, he is a good coach.

I could cruise into the last few strides, but instead I run it right out.

He's gone a bit blurry. My head fills with blood as I stop abruptly.

'Next time, let's see you staying more compact through the shoulders. Less swinging, less movement here.' He moves his own elbows. 'Do you understand?'

I bend over, heaving, hands on knees. What I understand is that I might get sick. *Don't get sick, please, Aganetha, don't get sick.*

And that's when I see her.

I glimpse her in motion, in my peripheral vision. She must have come out through the back factory door and she is approaching across the bare field toward us, her step as light and natural as my own. I turn my head and there she is, running toward me. I have never met another girl runner, have never seen another girl running except at picnics and fairs, races that are too easy to win, against girls who are in it just for fun, as a lark, on dares, silly girls, I think them. Girls who pretend not to care, or who care so little that they need not pretend.

The girl comes right up to me. I am still considering whether or not I will be sick, and I'm afraid to stand up too quickly.

'What have you done to her, Mr. Tristan?' the girl scolds, but she's laughing. She pats my shoulder. 'I see you've met our taskmaster. Don't let him break you, even if he tries.'

I reel upright. The girl sticks out her hand. 'I'm Glad.'

Girls don't shake hands — we ought to curtsy to one another — but, then, neither of us is wearing a skirt. My tightly belted trousers belong to my brother George, who has told me to cut them off, but I haven't. It is 1926. There are no clothes made particularly for girl runners.

'Pleased to meet you,' I say, accepting her hand. She pumps it up and down.

She is dressed as I soon will be: in short black pants cut quite high above the knee, and a dark red shirt with a V-neck and short sleeves — black and red being the colours of the Rosebud Ladies' Athletics Club. ROSEBUD is written in white fabric letters, embroidered fast with black thread, across the front of the shirt. On her feet are lightweight shoes with rubber soles, and white socks that she wears rolled down to her ankles. Her hair is cut to her chin and she shoves a hank behind one ear.

'You must be Aganetha Smart. The new girl.'

'Oh — I haven't made the team, exactly,' I mumble. I'm soaked in sweat from my sprints around the track, and although the sun remains high overhead the wind has gone chilly.

'What do you say, Mr. Tristan?' Glad grins. 'I know I just met her, but I like her.'

'You might not like her quite so much when you see her run,' says the coach. I can feel the tension rushing out of me, out of him too. Glad's doing.

'Consider yourself a Rosebud girl,' the coach says to me, bowing ever so slightly. 'Glad needs the competition.'

'I do!' she agrees. 'Have I come too late today?'

'You're never too late for me, Glad,' says the coach. I blush, as if I've just seen him touch her face, but she ignores him and squeezes my hand once before dropping it, like we're already friends. I'm amazed at the idea of being friends with someone like Glad, who effortlessly commands confidence. She seems at ease being a girl and a runner, both.

'Let's go,' she says simply.

I am thirsty. I am dusty. My muscles are raging and torn, my feet blistered. I haven't eaten since breakfast at Mrs. Smythe's table, a woman never overgenerous with her portions, even when all she's serving up is a splat of grey porridge with molasses and a skiff of milk.

'Yes, let's,' I reply.

54

The coach gives me the inside lane. Glad stretches beside me, swinging her arms in circles, bending and rocking at the waist, kicking her legs out like a dancer on a stage.

'Twice 'round,' says the coach. 'On my go.'

And we're off.

I can feel her giving me the track. She is being polite, offering up space like some kind of bargain, letting me run ahead. Is she going easy on me? I don't like it. I'm offended. But it's good to race with a bit of gristle on the tongue.

As we enter the first turn, it comes to me that I've never raced like this before. My toughest contests have been in the schoolyard against boys, straightforward tests with no tactical underbelly. I'm either the fastest, or close to it, an accepted fact, as it is also accepted that the longer the race, the more unlikely it will be that even the fastest, tallest, strongest boy could best me.

I've never raced anyone like Glad — my match. There crackles between us an undercurrent of emotions that I haven't the experience to gauge, nor use to any advantage. All I know is that I've taken the first turn ahead of her, and I've stayed ahead, though she's on my shoulder now, pushing a little. I don't mean she touches me, I mean I can feel her presence, sapping me of will and strength, drip by drip, as if she's put a tap into me. I have to get away from her.

I open up a gap between us on the back straightaway, but on the turn, she taps me again, easily, and it takes a kind of fury to pull away as we pass the coach. I catch a sense of him as if in a still photo, his hands clenched into fists at his sides, his shoulder muscles risen up, his mouth open. He might be shouting instructions or encouragement, but I can't take it in.

I hear my own breath, chopping the air. The turn feels smooth. I haven't given way this time. She hasn't closed the gap. I'm ahead and sailing, and something in me loosens — and that is when she takes me. I don't even feel her coming, but suddenly I hear the coach yelling, and I know he's not yelling for me, he's yelling for Glad. He wants her to win.

It's like hitting a wall of water, like an ocean of resistance has risen up before me and I'm plunging into it. We are on the final turn and Glad is gathering speed ahead of me, seemingly without effort while I flail and churn through waves that come heavy and dark. I'm not sure I can stay upright for this last stretch.

She has me by an impossible gap. Still, I press. I finish on my feet. I have to walk in circles to stay upright. I feel like a fool, so easily tricked and beaten, battered, stolen of breath.

'Great run!' Glad dances around me, grinning, scarcely winded.

'Do another two of those, and then we'll work on starts,' the coach directs Glad, and she salutes him, heads out, alone, to sprint the track. I watch her take that first corner, compact and mighty, her stride coming short, leaning into the curve with a force I know I don't have.

'It's your first day,' says the coach kindly. 'Everyone has to have a first day.'

'I guess so.' I feel as down as I've ever felt; I'm

not a girl inclined to despair. What I'm seeing in my mind is the lane and the fields of my home, I'm seeing the path I ran through the backwoods, the shortcut to town.

'You'll catch her within the year.' The coach's voice is very low, very calm. 'And she knows it. She knows it.'

In stillness, we watch her glide past, her hair tucked neatly behind her ears. 'Once more!' he calls, and then says, just as low and calm, to me, 'She's a good girl, Glad. You're in luck to run with her. Her uncle owns this place.' Mr. Tristan gestures with his thumb toward the red brick factory.

I'm too in awe to reply.

We stand silent, watching Glad run, and then he informs me, briskly, clearing his throat, that I may use the ladies' change room, inside the building. It is near the back entrance, impossible to miss. I haven't noticed until now that my body is a mass of shivers in the cool breeze. He informs me that the team practices evenings when it's light, mornings when it gets too dark, and never on Sundays. When the snow is deep, the team uses a gymnasium inside the factory. 'It isn't much more than an underground bunker,' he says apologetically, as if I might object. I must make all practices, no excuse good enough. He will expect me to race for the team next summer. He tells me a job offer from Rosebud Confectionary will be forthcoming: this is part of the bargain, trading one alliance for another, trading greasy pork for waxy chocolate, trading cuts from flashing blades for burns from hot moulds, trading softball for track.

I know how badly I want Rosebud, not how badly Rosebud wants me, but I hear myself dare to blurt out a request.

'My sister — could she work here too, do you think?'

The coach says quite easily, as if it were nothing, really, that he will look into it, but he expects that will be fine. 'See you tomorrow?' As if he is the one who is uncertain, who does not know.

It washes over me, all in a shock, that despite my youth, despite my inexperience, despite just losing the first race of my brief career, which I desperately wished to win, he wants me. Rosebud wants me. Mr. P.T. Pallister wants me. I've done what I came here to do.

What I don't see, and fail to grasp, is that he might want me not despite, but because of, youth and inexperience and failure. I'm so sure of myself, of this track I'm on. I'm sure it will be as easy as muscles on fire and gritted teeth and learning to take the corners, as easy as responding to commands, as easy as running itself, which comes easily for me even when it is rough and painful and grim. I could run another lap right now, I know it. I could run until sundown, just like I said. I know I can't be spent.

5

Project

We've come to the blue car: nondescript, wouldn't stand out in police alerts.

The young man, Max, is opening a rear door, and the girl wheels my chair nearer.

I say, Are we going somewhere?

No reply.

The girl stops, fumbles with the belt: 'How do we get her in?'

Max bends and draws his arms under mine, and pulls, tentatively. I do not resist, though I'd like to know: where are they taking me? The chair squirts backward, out from under me, and I crumple against the young stranger with unwanted intimacy. The girl has neglected to apply the brake. Max is panting. 'Give me a hand here, Kaley!'

It's hardly a stretch to surmise they're unfamiliar with the elderly and disabled.

'If you get one of her arms around your neck — '

'Can you hold on to me, Mrs. Smart? With your hands?'

I can't. The joints of my extremities are swollen, fused.

'Turn her this way!'

'Hang on!'

Neither of them have the least idea how to lift

a person, and I wonder: will they drop me? And if they do, if I slap the ground wearing this old body will it flop like a rag doll or crack like a glass bottle?

'We're in, we're in.'

One on either side, they've maneuvered me through the opened door of the car, and heaved me, slumping, onto a plastic seat, listing like a house with a rotten foundation. Max struggles to haul me into position without dislodging what's left of my dignity, and his own. His scent, of rusty cologne, grows stronger the longer he struggles, bathing me unpleasantly. It's too much for my liking — he's covering something — but the girl's scent is familiar, of clean skin with a whiff of embedded salt, condensed sweat. She is shifting my legs tentatively, I feel her touch.

'There,' he says, and they both fall quiet.

I close my eyes and try to rest. The sound of birds.

'When should we ask her?' the girl says.

'I think she's asleep.' Someone is patting my hand.

I open my eyes with a grunt. Here they are, seated on either side of me, uncomfortable with my reptilian silence. But what have I got to say to them? Small talk is a wearying distraction. What do we know of each other? *What do you know of me?*

I must have said that last bit out loud, as the girl answers.

'I know you're a great runner,' she says, and I am confused. She is speaking in the present tense. *Are we having a conversation, then?*

'Aren't we?'

He says, 'Mrs. Smart, Kaley has something to ask you. It's important.'

I wait. I can be patient. I've become accustomed to thinking that nothing can surprise me — but the girl does.

'Mrs. Smart,' she begins, her touch light on my fingers and trembling, 'I would like to tell your story.'

My story?

'I'm not a reporter,' she adds hurriedly, as if this might be a possibility, as if I might mistake her for such. 'I'm a runner, like you.'

'Marathon,' he adds, taking over. 'We're making a short documentary — a film — about Kaley, about what inspires her. You were a trailblazer, Mrs. Smart. Kaley is following in your footsteps. But the point is that your story's kind of been, well . . . '

'Lost to the sands of time?' I burp out.

'Something like that,' he says, laughing with relief to hear my voice.

'Will you do it?' she asks. 'Please?'

I have no cause to trust them, quite the opposite. They want something from me, and they've gone to some trouble, that's clear, but I will figure them out. They won't get by me.

Let's begin with what we know, I say to them: precious little. You would like to do a story about me. Do you think this is the first proposal I've fielded on the subject? Do you assume I will agree?

★ ★ ★

Knock-knock-knock.

Cora is in the kitchen, warming a can of soup, nearest the door, and she is the one who goes to it and opens it.

I'm in the great room where we keep the beds, as we've shuttered off the rest. It's a draughty old beast of a house, and we inhabit only the rooms on the first floor, and only a few of them. We warm the great room with a wood-burning stove, which I installed. Father wouldn't have liked it. He admired form and function, and the stove is pure function, no form. It smokes. It sits crooked on slabs of rough stone joined by cement, which I laid and poured, respectively, myself. The stove ruins the lines of the room, but we don't care, for we sleep and sit in warmth. Cora busies her hands with work, knitting baby bonnets for African children, and I busy my mind solving puzzles and listening to the radio. We'll never agree on the station, me and Cora. Gospel and country for Cora, talk talk talk for me.

I leave her to it most days. I fill in the tiny squares of the puzzle with tiny letters, and then I burn it. Cora takes care of the house, and I take care of everything else, which explains why the house is in such a state. We are hardly in a position to accept visitors, and hardly any visitors come. When the occasional car ventures down our lane, we know it's not for us. It will be someone lost, asking for directions. Cora loves giving directions.

But not this time. This time, I hear Cora saying, 'Yes, that's she. That's my sister. Yes, she lives here. Yes, we're alone, just the two of us.'

Cora has less and less sense as the years swing past, takes after our father. I set my cup of black tea on the stove top and come marching out, wrapped in my old fur coat, drawing up to my full height, lips pinched.

'What do you want?' I ask, hiding my surprise at seeing it's a woman standing on our doorstep. She's carrying a heavy bag over one shoulder that looks like it will topple her. She is thin and pinched, a cigarette smoker, her hair sprayed into a professional pouf on top of her head, and coloured blond. I recognize what she is instantly, having occupied the same trade, once upon a time.

'I'm looking for Ms. Aganetha Smart.'

'You're a reporter,' I say.

'I am.'

'What would you want with Aganetha Smart,' I continue flatly. 'Aganetha Smart has nothing to say.'

'I'm doing a story on women in sports, pioneers, in advance of this summer's Olympics.' She names her magazine. It is a woman's magazine.

'Good for you. But Aganetha Smart has nothing to say on the subject.'

'Ms. Smart, are you aware that you're the last woman alive from the 1928 Canadian Olympic team?' She waits, but I won't take the bait. I am not aware of that, no, and the knowledge strikes me like a shovel to the chest, but I have no intention of betraying either my ignorance or my emotion. 'Ms. Smart, I understand that your speciality was long-distance running, and that you were prevented from participating in long-distance races due to your sex. Would you like to comment on the fact that female athletes will be permitted to contest the marathon at this summer's Games?'

I don't say a word. I don't know what this emotion is, flooding my body, but I feel myself going weak, quite suddenly.

Cora snaps to her senses. 'My sister has nothing to say.'

'I'm very sorry to hear it,' says the reporter. 'No comment? Nothing at all?'

'She doesn't talk about that time,' says Cora. Cora can rise to the occasion, and does when I least expect it. It's true, what she's saying, I never talk about that time. There is no reason to be bitter, to be anything but proud of that one damned race; only, it hurts me to talk of it. My reward burnt itself bright and quick, its ashes too precious to spoil with gossip, or nostalgia.

'Is that a lighthouse in the field over there?' the reporter asks us. She is switching tack, playing for time, maneuvering. I recognize her tricks, having perfected them myself.

'It is not,' I say, although it clearly is: denial easier than explanation.

'Why build a lighthouse in a field, nowhere near water?' the woman persists, as if this weren't a question Cora and I both asked our father repeatedly, and entirely in vain. As if our perplexing inheritance is any of her business.

Cora quietly pushes the door shut on the woman, turns the bolt. I should thank my sister, but I don't. She looks at me wearily, shakes her head, and shuffles in her slippers back to the warm room. We take up our positions once again across from each other at the stove. We wait for the sound of a car's engine turning over, the sound of a car retreating down the lane.

'I'll never know why you wanted to do it — go away, run away, run, run, run,' Cora says with irritation. 'Look what it brought us.'

'It had nothing to do with you,' I say with equal irritation. We are back where we started, and where we've spent our lives, locked in opposition.

'If you'd never gone,' she says.

And I say, 'Your problem is you're always looking backward.'

'Well, what's ahead for us, Aggie? Tell me?'

She's got me there. We're both of us nearly eighty years old. The answer seems pretty clear. I finish my tea and plot the last word into the last empty boxes of the puzzle, and carry my cup to the kitchen where I clatter around making noise, nothing more. Then I stalk past Cora to the frigid bathroom to get changed, and stalk past again, saying, 'I'm going out!'

Cora doesn't reply. I wouldn't expect her to.

The reporter's car is parked in the lane, turned around so as to make a quick getaway if needed. She hasn't gone after all. I follow her boot prints through the snow, dainty little marks with a deep point where the heel has stabbed through the crust. She can't have gone far in this footwear. I reach one arm over my head and pull on the elbow, then the other. I roll my neck to loosen it, and take several long low repeating strides to stretch out my hamstrings and calves. I jump on the spot, pointing my toes to ease the ache in my ankles that never quite goes away. I'm wearing a tracksuit zipped to the chin, thin gloves, a light toque, a windbreaker, double socks, and thin-soled running shoes.

I follow the reporter's tracks until I find her, behind the old empty barn, what's left of it, snapping photos of the lighthouse.

'What did you come for, really?' I ask, making her jump. My voice carries across the snow-banks.

'I came for a story, Ms. Smart.'

'Is that the story you came for?' I point to the lighthouse.

'I don't think so, but it may be.'

'It isn't,' I assure her.

'You're going for a run,' she says. 'May I photograph you, even if you choose not to comment?'

I shrug. I've never objected to being photographed, and it's been a fair while since anyone has made such a request. I rather liked having my picture taken, in my youth. My face, while never pretty, proved unexpectedly photo-genic, oddly haunting on film. I loved to see it in the papers. It never felt like I was looking at myself, but at a version of myself that might survive beyond mortality, a projection of the best of me. It was a vanity that served me poorly, and yet I'll admit I seem not to be entirely clear of the seduction. Who says we live and learn?

What happens to these photographs taken today, in the snow, if indeed the reporter snaps

66

any? I'll not find out. Cora and I aren't the type to subscribe to a woman's magazine, nor do we know anyone who might, with a thrill of familiarity, rip out a relevant clipping and mail it to us.

I set off for my run, but I say to the woman, in parting, 'You'll be gone before I'm back, and you'll not disturb my sister again.'

I follow my usual route, along the fields at the edges where dried weeds stand through the snow and wave their pale golden seed heads.

Today, I cross the land that belonged to my sister Edith and her husband. I don't know who farms the fields now, but the house stands boarded and empty in its barren yard. I check its perimeter for signs of breach by wild animals, or teenagers: it has stood empty now for nearly ten years. After Edith died, her daughter did not stay, and who's to blame her for wanting to take her girl and leave? Cora passed the rumours on to me, as she would — that Edith's daughter's girl had no father. Perhaps, wondered Cora, such qualities run in the blood? Perhaps, I wondered in return, it was sour old gossips such as herself who chased the young away?

I circle the house once, then cut toward the path through the backwoods.

My route shifts subtly with the season, or my mood, or my energy, sometimes aiming longer, sometimes shorter, sometimes looping over and over a favourite section. Much has changed. Seventy years gone by, and the woods through which I ran as a child are shrunken, though not disappeared. The town has eaten into the far side, so I rarely follow that path, or if I do, I turn back before the trees thin out to reveal houses situated on cul-de-sacs, monstrosities with gleaming backyard pools shrouded in black plastic now that it is winter. The houses and their yards look tidy, trim, and silent, as if emptied of their people.

But I prefer not to see anyone.

If I meet a dog walker on the path, or in the winter a couple on skis or snowshoes, I do not expect to recognize them. It is likely that they know who I am, in a general way. People in town do. Cora and I are known in the way that eccentrics are known, as curiosities to be avoided or peered at from a distance. One outgrows fame. Ancient fame carries a whiff of notoriety. People forget, or no longer care. One grows into another version of loneliness.

Even in summer, I rarely see anyone swim in the glistening, silent pools.

I would enjoy diving in myself, in fine weather, and I am reminded of Glad every time I run past and resist the temptation, as if I can hear her urging me to jump — and I miss her. I miss her with an ache, not with tears. It's the ache you feel when you leave a place you know you can never return to. Oh how I ache today. I can't run from it, I know that. I run with it. It sits inside me, at my throat, expanding across my chest. Before today, I did not know. I think of how the reporter has come to my door and told me, quite without guessing its significance, that Glad has died — though I don't know when, nor how, nor can I ask for details. Her obituary will go unwritten, at least by me. How have I missed the news? Its absence on our radio waves suggests that when I die, that news too will go unreported, and with it all that we accomplished, Glad and I.

I've missed Glad for so many years that it surprises me to discover that I can miss her differently, knowing she no longer walks the earth; the finality of it. I will never see her again, as she was. Perhaps I've lived until today thinking I might.

And what of Johnny? Is he gone too?

I am lost, I am running, lost in the running. My feet in my sneakers are damp with snow and sweat, not cold, though my hands are so chilled and stiff that I have to press them into my armpits, which makes my stride awkward. I pick my way carefully, reminding myself to take caution: roots, stones, invisible patches of ice. Hands thawed, or thawed enough, I swing my arms for balance and pick up pace, finding a rhythm that is familiar, two strides per breath, in and out, *tap tap tap* like a metronome.

The world is dim in winter's half-light, a heavy sky, the trees shake their boughs as I pass under their watch and care, and into the woods I creak, my bones not so different from the branches, absorbing light, greying and careful. We are old.

But we go on.

6

Going Home

'Mrs. Smart? What do you think? Won't you say something?'

They haven't heard me.

I peer into her face and I see an ordinary girl, perhaps no more than a teenager, fighting nerves; she is hiding something, some great desire. I am familiar with the scene. It loosens sympathy in me, and I reach for her hand. There, I've got it.

'Oh!' she says, misunderstanding my intent, wrapping me in an impulsive hug. 'Wonderful! Thank you, Mrs. Smart! Hey, we're making a movie!'

'Terrific,' the young man says, digging around in his black bag. 'Let's get moving. We need a few anchoring shots on the farm with the two of you.'

The girl launches herself like a small child would, over the seats and into the front, settling behind the steering wheel. 'Gimme the keys.'

'It's about a half-hour drive — that okay, Mrs. Smart?' Max asks, his body angled away from mine. I see he's got in his hand a small black-bodied camera with a stubby lens that reflects my own face, long and soft, like something coming undone. I am not afraid, because it isn't in me to be afraid. The truth is that I cannot feel tragedy's weight, though this is not a characteristic to be blamed on extreme age. It seems always to have belonged to me, carved into my bones at birth. It has cast me forward all of my life: a yearning for trial and test, an envy of extremity, an inability to understand in advance the consequences. Does this make me callous or courageous?

I hear my voice, frail but composed, asking politely, 'Perhaps you could tell me where you're taking me?'

'Home!' calls the girl, over her shoulder.

I'm silent. Home. I can see mine spread out before me, a patchwork quilt of cleared fields, stones picked and piled at the edges, the woods beyond. The house of stone. She must be very young indeed if she imagines it possible to go home.

★　★　★

When I leave my mother and father's house, I do not know that I am leaving.

I've never ridden the train before. Black coal smoke, the stench of acrid burning through open windows. I perch on the edge of a cloth-covered bench that feels like velvet against the palms of my hands, and I eat a sandwich that Mother has made for me. The juice of peaches fresh from the orchard drips down my chin. Am I being watched, my actions observed? If so, I am oblivious. I feel quite invisible, transparent, loose in the world, as if I could move entirely without consequence.

I am now sixteen, grown to my full height, slender and strong. My hair is tidy. I wear a straw hat with a blue ribbon. I would be giddy were there anyone here with me. I keep opening and reading the letters from Olive and from George. I'm not thinking of home. What I've left behind is like dust, but what is to come is impossible to imagine, and so I keep composing and recomposing myself, taking deep breaths — 'Be good, be very very good,' I whisper as the farmland rolls past.

The city is dirty, all grit and smoke and heat. But the noise. I step out of the metallic grinding noise of the train into the noise of the city, rich and miraculous to my ears. I suppose I stand gaping, overwhelmed: automobile engines, horns, the cries of children selling newspapers and shoe-shines, the hum of voices, and something I can feel in my bones, a rumble rising from the city itself, its paved roads and concrete trembling.

The city is as restless as I am.

'Aggie! Kiddo! Over here!'

It's George, come as promised to take me to Olive's room on a street called Bathurst. We will ride on the streetcar, but first he buys me a paper cone filled with shaved ice, red syrup drizzled over top, poured out of a tin jug by a man missing a finger. It looks like a childish treat, and though I eat it, I do not thank George for it — thinking, *I am not a child*. It has been five years since I've seen George, and a year since Olive left home. Olive couldn't meet me at the station. 'She's at work,' says George, and the phrase strikes me as strange. *At work*. At home we are never exactly at work, or at play, on or off, we simply go about our business, doing what needs doing. I'm not sure I like the thought of a split life, either bound or temporarily freed.

We jostle onto the streetcar. George steers me, holding my elbow. We ride west and then north and jostle off again. It is an unsettling and vaguely thrilling sensation, bumping up against strangers.

'Here we are!'

We've only just alighted. A small boy comes running toward us, chasing a slow-moving junk wagon. The child jumps to catch a ride on the wooden back bumper, but his legs are too short, his leap too late, and he falls to the paved road and strikes his chin hard. Behind him, coming fast, roars a motorized grocer's truck. The horn sounds like a pig's squeal. I am making a quick run to grab for the boy, but George catches me roughly and holds fast to my arm, and we watch as the child rolls out of the way — safe, but just — and slams against the curb.

'See here, he's fine,' George says, as if such incidents happen every day before his very eyes.

I yank free, and run to the boy and wipe his mouth with my handkerchief. 'Keep it,' I urge him. I'm reminded of my nephew, Little Robbie. Such defiance, no tears. His darting eyes. He scrambles to standing and flickers a bloody grin before shooting away, terrifically free, it seems to me.

'You're too nice, Aggie. You need to let people be,' says George.

'I let him be!' I argue back.

73

'You gave him your handkerchief.'

'I'll hem another, if I need one, which I don't.'

George doesn't show me where he lives, but this doesn't strike me as strange at the time. I suppose it doesn't strike me at all. Have we ever got along? I can't quite believe that we have. I dislike his porkpie hat and his thinly rolled cigarette. His jacket is made of a shiny fabric, and his hair is slick with oil, like he's trying to make himself impermeable. He seems to be pretending to be someone other than I know him to be.

We stand on the paved walk outside a row house covered in dark red-and-black tar paper made to look like bricks. The houses are attached one to the next, three stories tall, with peaked roofs and tiny windows. Behind us, a streetcar rattles by.

'I found this charming little rathole for Olive. The landlady came highly recommended for her rates if not for her soup — Mrs. Smythe. She won't mind an extra for a week or two. How long are you staying, Aggie? Want a real job? Real money?'

'Why would I want money?' I'm holding my bag myself. George hasn't offered to carry it, not that I'd want him to. I swing it lightly against my legs, tapping it on my knees.

'Everyone wants money, Aggie. Even the best of us.'

'Not me.'

'Hi-ho. In we go. Who do you think's paying for your room, kiddo?'

Yes, I kind of hate him. My own brother.

74

Mrs. Smythe shows me to Olive's room. It is clean: white walls, white board floors, and a tidy summer quilt atop a double bed. I like it instantly. I drop my bag on the floor and come downstairs to say good-bye to George. I flush when Mrs. Smythe tells me he's already gone. Am I to chase my brother down the street? I won't. It is hot in the entryway, dark even at mid-afternoon. I'm afraid to ask Mrs. Smythe if George has given her any money. I do not know what I owe, nor to whom, but I have money, a bit of it, entrusted to me by my mother. I know that it has come from Olive, who sends it home.

I excuse myself, deciding rather confusedly that I should give the money back to Olive. Olive will know what to do with it.

Despite all of this, I have a very odd sensation as I hurry up the steps and return to the clean white room: I feel at home. I spread myself across the bed like a long-limbed starfish and drift into a peaceful dreamy half-sleep.

The other girls in the rooming house are factory girls, like Olive. I wake to the sound of their voices in the hall. And then to Olive herself, coming in, crowing with a delight that seems out of character at home, but perfectly in character here in the city. She jumps onto the bed and onto me, kissing my cheeks.

'Um, hello,' I say, feeling shy.

'I can't believe you came! You really came!' Olive sits back on her haunches and folds her legs under her bottom. A girl stops in the doorway, leans in. 'Look! It's my little sister.'

'She looks enormously tall,' the girl drawls.

'Pleased to meet you, little sister. I haven't got any sisters myself.'

'That explains a lot,' says Olive. I understand, but barely, that Olive is joking, and that the girl appreciates it. Another girl leans in, and a third, and then they retreat. I need the bathroom, so Olive goes into the hall and bangs on the door.

'It's Mary Alice, crying over a boy,' says one of the girls walking by. 'She'll be forever.'

'Don't dirty your drawers,' says a second girl.

'Yes, don't poop your panties,' says the first.

'Don't dribble on the floor.'

'That doesn't rhyme.'

'Yours didn't rhyme. Are we rhyming now?'

This is all very hilarious. I am not doing it proper justice. I can understand, in my head, that it is funny, but I can't join in the laughter. Even Olive is whooping it up: 'Don't sprinkle your shoes.'

More banging on the door. The smell of boiled cabbage calling us to dinner.

I'm taller than the other girls in the house, taller even than Mr. Smythe, whose silent presence at supper is of a man removing himself, but reluctantly, from a distasteful, vaguely sordid scene.

One of the girls — not Mary Alice — is on her factory's softball team, and is playing in a game this evening. Mrs. Smythe has prepared supper early, and we eat quickly, shovelling our food, 'wolfing it,' says Mrs. Smythe, who also informs us that this mode of eating will harm our digestion and make us puff up like pastries. The girl, whose name is Joannie, dashes upstairs to change into her uniform: baggy pants and shirt, and white socks inside canvas shoes. Her hair is pushed under a cap. Of course we are going along, Olive and I.

We ride the streetcar to the field, a mess of noisy girls (though I'm quiet, hopeless at witticism and innuendo).

The light falls slowly through the thick air, humid, cooling as it blows off the lake, and there is the lull of constant noise that matches my own buzzing heart. The game is only a piece of it. What enchants me are the crowds who have gathered to watch and cheer on the factory girls, little boys peddling peanuts and popcorn, men pushing dripping ice carts, selling fizzy soda water that Olive buys to share.

I feel at ease in a brand-new way. There are so many people — no one will see me, especially, unless I decide to be seen. Unless I choose, like Joannie, to put on a uniform and stand at bat and hammer that fat round ball over the fence, or, in the infield, spring to scoop up a slapped ball and fire it into the glove of another, just ahead of the runner, to the cheers of the crowd. It's up to me. I can be invisible, as I am right now, or I can put myself forward to play the game and be judged.

That night, in Olive's room, I whisper, 'I love it here.'

But she's already asleep. I lie on top of the quilt, listening to the street sounds hush. The room remains hot despite the open window, as if the city's layers of pavement and concrete and steel and tin have drunk in the sun to hold for keeps, as if I have too.

I don't know yet that I'll stay. This is a holiday, a rare occasion. I believe myself content because I am content — immersed without thought of what will come next, without thought of return.

On Sunday, Olive and I ride the streetcar west to High Park. A huge white tent has been erected on the grass in a clearing that would remind only a city person of a field. Factory girls are dressed in their Sunday best, and a big canvas banner flaps in the breeze: PACKER'S MEATS. We load our plates with buttered buns and canned ham, and a sweet salad of potatoes and eggs, and we fill our cups with sugary iced tea. There is a giant sheet cake for dessert and it's someone's job to fan the flies away with a wide unfurled napkin.

Olive and I eat on one of the checked blankets that are spread on the grass, where we are joined by other girls who work on Olive's line. Life in the city seems captured by this moment — free food, free grass, free air to breathe, free roaming, free sunshine, free fun. Mine to splash around in, as I wish. Take it or leave it.

'It isn't always like this,' Olive says, like she's reading my mind.

I know what she means, but I erase it. I go and help myself to a slab of sheet cake.

'Aggie!' Olive finds me licking green frosting off the palm of my hand. She's excited about something. 'The girls are having a running race. You should join!'

'A running race?'

'They're doing egg-and-spoon, and three-legged, but I mean a real running race. Girls under twenty. Come on!'

Heaven, I tell you. Heaven will have a running race staged across a rolling plain of tended grass with start and finish lines marked out in white ribbons. Heaven will gather a crowd of girls standing at the start with one leg out, skirts lifted, ready for 'On your marks, steady, go!' Heaven will be lined on either side with little kids cheering and older folks too, but I won't be old in heaven. I'll be sixteen, the tallest girl in the field, and cheered by how easy it is to pull ahead, how I'm running almost alone across the spiky summer grass, how I catch, with a crashing burst of speed, this one last girl who fleets before me. How the white ribbon breaks free against my soaring and flutters to the ground, tangling my feet.

I'm hardly started when it's already over.

Who was that?

Olive is hugging me, saying she knew I would win as she lifts me right off the ground: 'Can you guess who that girl was, the one you beat? She's won the city championship two years in a row!'

The tone in the stranger's voice is admiring: *Who was that girl with the golden hair?*

I know right then. I'm not going home.

I compose a letter to my mother and father. I can't tell you what it says, exactly. I can tell you that Olive helps me to write it. She wrote one herself a year ago, but that was different. She was writing to say she had found a job, and here was some money to help at home.

I was there when Mother opened Olive's letter, and she flushed and pushed the money back inside the envelope. 'We don't need this,' she said.

I do not write, in my letter home, *I love you*. I may sign myself, *Yours sincerely*, or *Yours devotedly*, *Your loving daughter*, any of those. They know, I tell myself. They know I love them. Don't they?

7

Fall

'It's gonna be fine,' the girl announces over her shoulder, but it isn't clear to whom she is speaking, to me or to Max, the young man beside me fiddling with the camera. Besides which, this is hardly a reassuring declaration, as anyone with sense would know. Young lady, you should pay more attention to the road, I say. That was a red light. Here's another.

The car screeches to a halt and I'm launched against the seat belt with a groan.

'Do I need to drive?' Max looks up. He's transferred his attention to a different screened device, which he cradles between his hands, looking down as if in prayer. He can't leave it for more than a moment. He bows his head and taps on it with his thumbs.

'I'm good,' the girl growls through her teeth, pressing the gas pedal with more enthusiasm than necessary.

'Then drive like you know what you're doing.'

'You sound like Dad.'

'You drive like Mom.'

Ah. Siblings.

We're passing dull buildings, low to the ground, a huddle of ugly boxes that open, abruptly, onto wet ploughed cornfields and sky. She speeds up, and the fields fold one into

81

another and I think it unlikely that it will matter whether or not I pay attention. I close my eyes.

Some while later, I am jostled out of a rough sleep, tossed to one side as we take a corner precipitously. I press my hands to my cheeks. Warm. Am I sick?

'Roll down your window.' There is a young man beside me. He leans forward to get the girl's attention, pulling from one of her ears a slender white cord. 'Turn it off, she's awake again.' His thumbs *click, click, click*.

She cracks the windows, but I see she's disobeyed his other order. One of the slender cords rides up her hair and into her left ear.

Her hair is whipping in the wind, and she turns to grin at us. 'Do you recognize anything, Mrs. Smart?'

'Not far now,' says Max, as if to reassure himself.

'I'm getting butterflies!' the girl is shouting with some excitement. Her mood seems highly changeable.

The road we're travelling is freshly paved and looks to have been widened in the process. There are no trees on either side, just steep muddy ditches.

In answer to her question, yes, I think I know this road. I know something about it, but it's been changed from what it was, I think. Hasn't everything?

We are slowing as we pass a stony lane, with the little grey house beyond the bare field of mud. Someone's planted a few trees, must have been some time ago now, they're tall, but weedy, not full grown, and the yard is still bare. The yard is still bare. It always was. That hasn't changed.

They've put a swing set near the field. A dog runs toward us down the lane barking. I know this place. I know it. My throat fills up with dread.

★ ★ ★

The house is alert. The sun shines. The day is hot, for spring.

Mother stays upstairs with Fannie in the room Fannie shares with Olive. Father goes to the barn after breakfast, a cold meal of sliced bread, fresh butter, and the soft white cheese that Fannie makes from the cow's milk. Fannie herself heated and cooled and strained the milk to prepare this cheese she cannot eat, now. I scarcely swallow a bite. Cora and I carry the plates to the kitchen, cover the food. We stack the dishes in the sink but do not wash them, coming to silent agreement.

Father does not come back.

Cora and I pump water from the well, but it isn't cool enough to cool Fannie's fevered skin.

I stumble from the yard into the house in a daze. I stop to sit at the table, and stare. I don't climb the stairs to the bedroom where Fannie lies, thrashing and throwing off the bedclothes, crying out. I get up again to rip cloths with Cora and we place them in an enamel basin and pour water over top, and Olive staggers upstairs trying not to spill. She returns immediately. Mother has told her not to stay, not for one second. The danger is too near.

Olive boils water in the kettle.

Cora asks why? Why, when Fannie is so hot?

Olive says she will make tea.

Cora says, for who?

Olive says, for the doctor. For George. For you, if you want a cup. For Mother. For Edith if she thinks to come over and help. For anyone. For Father in the barn, you can carry him out a cup. For Aggie, look at her.

I can't see myself, but I see my hands laid out flat on the table before me, trembling, and I pull them into my lap and press them one on top of the other, changing back and forth, back and forth, trying to squeeze the fear out of them.

Stop your arguing, says George. He sits slumped across the table from me. We look at each other silently, me and George, holding fast for a moment.

Tea would be grand, he says, don't you think, Aggie?

I think I can hardly stand the noises coming from upstairs. The whole house is listening. The whole house is trying to keep Fannie breathing, to keep her wild rasps coming, the pauses between them growing ever greater. The fever has her and she is lost from herself. She is gasping out her sister's name — Edith's — and we are all pretending not to hear it. Mother's voice rising smoothly against the tide of noise.

I am only a child, but I know: I must never say what I know about Fannie. I must hold the terrible secret, because no one must ever, ever know. If Edith were to find out. If Father were to find out. Yet we hear it, over and over and over: Edith, I'm sorry, forgive me, Edith.

She can't know what she is saying. She's that far gone. The words drift, slurred. A blur.

Should we run for Edith, do you think? asks Cora.

Edith can't come here. She's weak enough as it is. The flu would kill her, says Olive.

George stands abruptly, shoving back his chair. Run for the doctor, he says. He is talking to me.

What good would that do? Mother's here, says Olive.

We have to do something, says George. That's my sister up there dying!

Then you should go, says Cora. By horse would be faster.

Aggie's quick as a shot, says George. She can go through the backwoods. Go, he tells me. Run, Aggie, run.

I feel the terror that has been pouring through my hands jerk back inside my body, suddenly useful and necessary. George is right. I'm quicker than a shot. I bang out the door and down the steps and around the back lane into the fields, my legs pumping like the pistons that power Father's machine.

The shortcut through the woods is narrow, a footpath rather than a lane or a road, and rarely used, not meant for horses. Tendrils of creeping vine cross it, and roots rise, and stones fresh from the earth. I am nimble and careful, my footsteps crisp, quick, and light against the darkness of the woods, its shadows casting down on me like a spell I need to break. I'm coming to the far side, bursting from dark to light, from narrow to wide. I scarcely hesitate, passing from one to the other.

The path gives onto a road that leads into town, and town is not far, not when you are running as fast as I am running.

I can't hear my thoughts over my breath coming harsh and regular. Running like this, this fast, this hard, fixes the strangest visions into my head. Glimpses become entire stories, full-blooded portraits. I see a groundhog waddle away from me, into the grass beside the road. I see a purple wildflower bend at my approach. I see the faces of three women standing on their front porch staring at me, their hair tucked beneath frilly caps, their mouths perplexed, their foreheads creased with disapproval. More houses, gone by in a rush. A stone in the road that etches the ball of my foot. A loose dog barking after me.

I see the doctor's son, who is my age and whom I know is named Peter after his father, playing in his yard with a ball. He is throwing the ball in the air and catching it in his hands.

I see him turn at my approach. The ball drops from his hands to his bare feet. Mine are bare too. I see them as I reel to a stop before him, and stare down. Dusty skin of my own bare ankles, dirt crammed thickly between the toes. I gasp, 'It's Fannie. We need the doctor.'

'He's out,' says Peter.

'But where?' I beg, blood rushing under my skin, flooding my skull, my hands on my knees, skirt swinging, bent over.

Peter and I know each other from sharing a classroom at school, all the way through the grades. Peter says his father is tending to someone sick, and he knows who and where: in town, at the far edge. 'I'll take you,' he tells me, and instead of expressing thanks, I shout with impatience, 'Well let's go! Now! Hurry!'

Peter's mother has heard the commotion and she comes to the door. She doesn't step all the way outside, and I can see a baby in her arms, one of Peter's little sisters.

'We're going to find Father,' Peter tells her.

His mother speaks sternly, or perhaps with fear. 'Do not go inside that house. Do not go near it. Call for him from the street, do not knock or enter. Do you understand?'

We nod.

We run, and I am faster than Peter, which is no surprise. I've beaten every boy my age at running and throwing games. But I am glad to have him with me, not just to show me the way, which I could figure out for myself, but also because the burden of my message is lightened by his presence, by his willingness to join me. I slow my steps to give him the pretence of showing me the way. And in a way, he is. My breathing comes freer; I almost forget myself as I watch his bare feet just ahead of mine, beating down an easier path.

Here we are, shouting from the yard. I see yellow quarantine papers hammered to the door, and the doctor coming out. He's afraid, I see, because his son is here.

87

'It's Fannie,' I cry. 'She's, she's . . . ' But I can't go on and say it. Peter keeps his distance, not just from the quarantined house, but from me. He is a step and then another gone from me.

Here I am, alone again, carrying my message alone, dragging it behind me like a stone.

Peter is watching me, the doctor is watching me, the lady passing in the street and her little boy are watching me, with pity. I have never before been aware of myself as a subject of pity, and I hate it so much that I might ignite.

'I'll come when I can,' says the doctor. 'I've got my horse. I'll be there within the hour.'

And at that, I turn and run, banishing Peter altogether, although I hear him calling after me. What could he say that would change anything?

I run like a hunted deer at the end of her race, my feet heavy and my legs weak, staggering with the effort. Nothing illuminates itself for me. All I see is the dusty street just ahead of where my feet slap down and rise up again. I enter the woods, and it is like stepping indoors on a brilliant day. Dimly, I see pulsing shadows, my eyes deceived by flickering sunlight, my toes catching as I trip on secret roots, my arms flying out to catch my fall. I stumble upright only to catch and fall again, again, running low to the ground in a crouch, bent over for protection.

The nearer I come to our farm, the slower my footfalls, the more pronounced my bent-over agony. A cramp between ribs. A feeling growing inside me: if only I can delay arrival, Fannie will live on, that it's my arrival and not her illness that will end her life.

And I cannot, cannot go home.

Instead, coming out of the woods, I veer away from the house and begin trailing around and around the back field, looping under the dark pines where fallen branches crunch and hurt my soles, curving down by the pond where little James drowned, and then behind the barn and away, out again toward the woods, past the woods, sliding under the pines, around by the pond, thinking again of James, to the barn where Father's new windmill turns brightly, and out on the path that climbs toward the woods, veering past and under the shadowed pines.

I will not stop.

I run and run and run until I've lost count of the loops, until my hair is wet all through its heavy braid down my back, my dress soaked with sweat. The bones in my hips and knees and ankles ache with every footfall into the soft dirt and early weeds, and my breath comes raggedly, harsh in my throat, in loud gasps that alert my father, finally. I see him as I round the pond.

Father is waiting for me to pass by the barn.

I've stopped thinking about anything, and I'm surprised to see him there. I'm surprised to see anyone. I would run past him like he's a tree or rock or weed, but he steps in front of me and catches me in his arms and I come to a sudden stop.

I collapse onto his shoulder, my eyes and nose streaming, my throat choked with mucus, no longer a valiant messenger refusing to arrive, but an exhausted child of ten. A daughter. The youngest, the baby, the hoped-for son who never was.

My father smells of wood shavings and rust. There is sawdust in his hair. I think that this is the closest I have ever been to him. It may be the closest I will ever be.

'You'll not be catching up to her, Aganetha. She's gone ahead.'

My sobs don't sound like sobs at all, but like a struggle to breathe. I go limp in his arms. Father does not bring me to the house, where Fannie's body is already cooling; perhaps he thinks this a kindness, or perhaps he is unprepared to go there himself. Instead, he carries me into the barn through the wide doors that roll open on oiled wheels so the farm wagon can drive up the grassy verge and onto the wide-planked open floor of the mow. My legs are long and trailing, bumping against his. He sets me down so that my feet meet the swept wide boards, and he waits for me to support my own weight, which I manage, heaving a shuddering cavernous sigh that drags me into myself.

He climbs ahead of me up his stair steps and I follow. I can feel the muscles in my legs trembling with fatigue. We stand side by side on the level deck he has built, home to his completed invention.

Wordlessly, Father shows me what he's been working on: boards smoothed to silk, just that, just boards. They might have been for anything. But now they are not. Now they are for Fannie. I recoil from his offering.

I see that we are speaking different languages, my father and I. Maybe we are saying the same thing, but it looks so different spelled out in the

90

air between us that we can't comfort each other.

My throat aches, my mouth gummy and dry.

'I'm going to the house,' I say hoarsely, and he nods his head, once, twice, and offers his focus to the plank he has been honing. I won't consider how many times my father has undertaken this task, how many times he has done what he can to help his own child rest easy in death as in life. How proud he is of the smoothness of the boards he has worked. How it is all he can offer, now. I won't let myself think of it, or try to understand.

The sight of those boards fills me with raw terror.

I come quietly through the summer kitchen. I pour a glass of water from the blue glass pitcher Mother keeps on the counter, and I drink the water down in great gulps, refilling the glass and drinking again. The sink is full of this morning's dirty dishes. I can't imagine ever caring enough to wash them clean. I stand over the sink and splash water on my face. Rivulets track down my arms, little streams rimmed with mud. I don't see George anywhere about, and I am relieved, though I can't think why. Only that I do not want to see him. I do not want to see anyone, except for Fannie.

She will be upstairs.

The house is so very quiet, as if everyone has gone to sleep in the middle of the day. I creep up the back stairs into the servants' quarters, tiny rooms over the kitchen and dining room that our family doesn't use, as we have no servants. My grandfather built this house with Father's help, and I don't think he kept servants or even a housemaid, so the rooms' inclusion in the design make no sense, and yet the rooms exist. I walk the narrow, dimly lit hall and open the door that separates these cramped quarters from our own bedrooms, which are vast by comparison, and bright, the windows wide, the bumpy plaster splashed with whitewash.

I hear the low voices of my sisters and my mother, and I follow their gentle pull. They hush as I come to the doorway and stop. At first, I can't bring myself to look directly at Fannie, resting on her back in her bed. But then I can't stop looking. Her eyes are closed. I wonder if my mother has closed them, or is this how Fannie died? How does a person die? Is it like a window gone dark, shuttered? Does a person keep looking at this world until the very last second of life, trying to take it in and understand it at last, or simply to hold it, to attend to it, to love it? Or does a person stare in dreadful panic at all she is losing?

I see that my mother is the only one who is touching Fannie. Olive and Cora stand at attention beside the window, shadows in the hot sunlight.

'Don't come near,' my mother says. 'You must not get sick.' She is rinsing a cloth in a basin and she smoothes it over Fannie's face, and around behind her ears, lifting her head with the hair flowing loose and damp all over the pillow so that she can wash the back of Fannie's neck.

'I went for the doctor,' I whisper because anything louder seems a disturbance.

'Thank you, Aggie, but he's been and gone.

There was nothing he could do but hammer up the quarantine papers.'

I am remembering something from my spent passage. I am remembering the white of hundreds of spring flowers, the spread of trilliums under the canopy of new leaves. Here it is, nearly June. Here is this terrifying flu that kills at random, stealing the healthiest, the most vigorous, as well as those who might be expected to succumb. Here is Fannie, aged twenty-three years, two months, and three days.

I stand in the doorway, my sisters by the window, I don't know for how long. For however long it takes to wash a body, and to dress it in clean underclothes and a fresh frock, and to brush and arrange its tangled hair, and to smoothe its brow.

And then a body is buried quickly, and deep, laid inside wood planed soft as silk.

F.S. 1895–1918

★ ★ ★

George says I'm only half his sister, not his full, not like Fannie was.

'Fannie is sister enough for me!' It has been two months since Fannie's stone was laid in our graveyard, but I can't bring myself to use the past tense.

'But it's better this way. This way, I can kiss you.' George nudges me in the ribs. I don't believe he'd actually try to kiss me, but all the same I wish he wouldn't joke about it.

There are things I don't like about George.

Have they always been part of him, drawn suddenly to the surface by Fannie's absence? How can I not have noticed? I observe him quietly, trying to puzzle it out. Why do I care so much what he thinks of me?

'What are you staring at, Aggie?' he says, catching me.

'Nothing.'

We're sitting on the barn roof looking out over the farm. Father's magnificent flight of stairs, finished in the winter months, lead directly into the belly of the steeplelike windmill. Father does not know, but inside the windmill, where the stairs end, George has loosened several boards so that he and I can climb directly onto the barn's slick tin roof.

'We're cursed,' George is saying. He's out to stake his bitter claim as one of the last living children of Robert and Tilda Smart — just George and Edith left, and Edith with a dead womb.

'Don't say that about Edith!' I beg.

'She can't be fixed,' he says bitterly.

'Mother's trying to help.'

'That's the problem right there,' he says, 'and Edith thinks so too.'

I fall silent. I don't believe a word he's said. Mother goes to Edith regularly. She brings us along too, me or Cora or Olive, to do the tidying and play with Little Robbie, or to scrub and hang a load of washing. Edith doesn't want to leave the house, but Mother urges her outside, helps her onto the porch and into the rocking chair. 'Some have a slow grief,' she tells Carson,

94

who edges around the house like it's not his own.

Does Edith grieve her lost sister, or is this a longer grief attached to the nearly grown stillborn baby my mother delivered her of last summer? Obediently, Edith swallows the tinctures my mother prepares for her, but even I would have to allow the medicine has had no effect. She remains a scattered housekeeper, a slothful cook, a pretty face with eyes fading onto a distant point. She seems to bear no expectations.

George refuses tinctures and teas. 'Potions,' he calls them, with scorn. None of us speak up to defend Mother, not even Mother herself. We stand aside and let his words fall to our feet, as if this could keep them from doing harm.

I don't know what's happened to George, but I wonder if it happened while Fannie was dying upstairs and he was downstairs listening to her die. This is not a question I can ask, but I wonder — did some loose pieces inside him slip into position that day, solidify, harden? I don't know. I wasn't in the house when it happened. It was George who sent me to fetch the doctor — did he do it not to save Fannie, but to spare me from knowing what it would feel like to listen to my sister die?

It's the middle of the afternoon, and the hot metal roof stings my bare feet, the sun slaps my cheeks, bleaches my hair, draws freckles across my nose. George looks like an entirely different creature: dark eyes and hair, and skin that tans deeply. For all his sickliness, he is tall, like we all are, and his shoulders stand straight, his carriage is graceful. We gaze over a sweeping countryside, the rich cleared soil, the work that continues, even as the two of us absent ourselves from the proceedings, even as we escape. I am content to believe that my family is prosperous, that our land will be ever giving, that all of this careful plotting and growing and harvesting will keep turning, no matter what comes.

The first Robert Smart to settle the land was a blacksmith from the old country: Scotland. The graves of his wives and children are not even marked, although his is. It was the first stone to have been set into the ground that became our family's graveyard. His son, Robert Smart, was my grandfather, who buried his father and built the original house, a square stone structure that was expanded and improved upon in the years that followed. My own father, also Robert Smart, worked with his father to finish the rambling fieldstone structure that I could see now, if I scrambled to the other side of the barn's roof.

My grandfather Robert Smart died before I was born, and my grandmother kept two rooms at the back of the house. Mother took them over when Granny died, which was after Mother married Father, but before I can remember. The larger room is our parlour, never used, and only rarely dusted. The smaller room — the Granny Room, we call it — contains a bed, and a mirrored bureau, and a washbasin, and sometimes girls stay there, but never for very long. We are not to disturb them, although occasionally

Mother asks Olive to carry a girl a tray with tea or soup and bread. She used to ask Fannie. Now it is Olive's turn to help.

The girls are ill and Mother nurses them back to strength. That is all I know.

But Mother couldn't nurse Fannie back to strength. I am anxious whenever my mind touches on that thought. I shove it away wildly. Mother didn't save Fannie. She was there when Fannie died, and she did nothing to save her. No, that is not the same thing, is it? She was there, helpless as the rest of us.

'I've signed up, Aggie.' George's voice cracks. He's spoken rather loudly, sneaking a sideways glance at me, and away.

'Signed up?'

'I'm going to the war, they need me, you know — boys like me.' He doesn't wait for my reply. He is angry, I see it in his hands: fingers curled into his palms, so tightly the knuckles have gone white. 'We're cursed anyway. What's one more dead Smart?'

'It was the flu,' I tell George. 'It wasn't a curse. Nobody could do anything, not even Mother.'

'Your mother is not my mother,' says George, but he's stopped on a cough.

'They won't let you.' I seize on the cough. 'Your lungs.'

'They will and they have. I'm going, and soon. So long, farewell, good-bye.' He sweeps his arm to emphasize what he's leaving, as if this isn't the most beautiful place on earth. I hear disgust in his voice.

What do I know of war? I'll never be a boy,

97

never be a son. War is never going to be my way out. But George — George is exactly that: a son, and a disappointment. Robbie died fighting for his country, Robbie, the brother George will never match up to, here on the farm.

I sense that the edge, the breaking-off point, needs to be jagged between George and our father, George and the farm.

'Keep it a secret, there's a girl, Aggie. I had to tell you, but the rest of them, they won't know till I'm gone.' He leans into me, awkward with eyes fastened onto mine, and I think he might kiss me after all. I hear my heart catch, then tumble to racing in my chest. George sways slightly like a tree in a breeze. And I'm up before he can horrify us both beyond repair, I'm scrambling to climb the roof to its top. A couple of good leaping strides, and I grab the peak and pull myself up. There is no higher point on our land: this is it, these are the heights.

It is easy to rise.

I am standing. My knees become springs, my toes point, my arms spread wide. I can feel the muscles in my back and stomach wrapping my spine like layers and layers of gauze bandages: stronger than they appear. The wind catches my untidy hair, and my skirt.

I can hear George wheezing, terrified down below me. Good. I'm glad. What do I care? I can't fall.

'Look at me!' I scream.

I take a step and another, chin high. The metal is imperfectly joined at the peak and hurts even my summer-calloused soles, but I dance, step

98

after step, all the way to the end, where I can see the barnyard, many stories below. I calm my breath and bend forward slowly, patiently, to look down on the cleared gravel where the wagons turn around. Our rat-hunting dog lies panting in the sun. He catches sight of my shadow waving to him, and jumps to his feet, turning in frenzied barking.

There is Cora, coming out of the house with a basket for gathering vegetables clapped against her side.

I wave, leaning toward her. 'Hiya! Cora!'

At first she can't find me. Something about this delights me: hiding in plain sight. She stops and stares around the yard while I holler and shout: 'Look up, up here!' She finds my shadow waving at her first, then lifts her eyes, shading them with her free hand. Her mouth is a perfect round O. I falter for half a breath, waver, steady myself before her sight. She drops the basket. Screams.

That brings our mother running.

Cora has fallen on her knees, hiding her face in her apron. She can't bear to see what might happen next. Why does she assume the worst? I could spit with irritation. Why doesn't she trust me?

I can do anything, anything I want to, Cora, just watch me.

'Lord have mercy.' I see my mother's lips shape the words a half beat before their sound arrives at my ears.

I make myself stand steady as a post. And then, as if I've been planted on the barn roof, attached like a weathercock to a whirling vane, I spin around once, twice, three times.

My mother's hand drops from her heart and she runs to find a better angle from which to see me — she climbs the pasture fence, as if by getting higher she will be closer to me, and then she climbs right up and into the branches of a maple that overhang the pasture fence.

Is she trying to save me? Or is she urging me on?

I feel birdlike, although I know I can't fly, nor do I wish that I could. It's just an act. I wave to my father, to the three hired men, to Olive standing on the porch, all of them summoned by Cora's cries. Cora herself peeks from under her apron only to resume her hysterics. 'Get her down, get her down, get her down! Before she falls!'

I curtsey, lifting my skirts and swinging them. And then I turn and run the peak to the far side of the barn where no one can look up and see me but the pigs in their rooting pen, and the cows pastured beside the mountainous manure pile.

I greet the indifferent animals. I salute the pond and pause for a breath to remember little James, drowned. And then I jog lightly back to my audience. I've forgotten almost everything, past, present, and future, but this — the line of hot metal, the sky over me, the waiting faces upturned. They are looking for me, hoping to see me again. They fall quiet at the sight of me, hushed for a moment.

My mother in the tree in her full apron and

skirts, her arms scratched by the branches, hugs the rough trunk.

I have one more trick. It seems, suddenly, a pity I didn't learn more last summer, when I practiced walking the fence hour upon hour — but this trick is a good one. It's the best I've got. I bend backward, reaching my hands for the peak of metal, and with one quick and forceful push, curve over myself, feet travelling overhead into a brief handstand that is meant to collect itself at the other end, and finish by coming around to standing.

But I've mistimed my push. My hands are not planted, my hips tilt off balance. I am coming down.

I hear them gasp. *No!*

I hear my mother's silence, her power. She would climb all the way up the tree and leap onto the roof and catch me if she could — if only the tree were taller, if only its branches brushed the barn.

My body collapses sideways, hip crashes vertical metal, the ridges, the nail heads poking through, the steep descent. Down is down. Down is hard dirt barnyard, broken stone, the rough unfinished roof of the never-occupied rabbit hutch, a pitchfork head, a rusted bucket, a broken plough, and God knows what: I am falling swiftly toward the side of the barn in which gathers the loose and lost elements of our farm's life.

I will not go there. No.

A grunt, a core reflex of refusal.

I snap my legs, my spine cracking like a whip.

101

Blindly, my arms slash out, hands slap the peak of the roof, fingers dig in. My face hits the hot metal, my legs slither straight. I hang like this, flat against the rough slide, flat against life. And then slowly, stiffly, I pull myself up, and mount the rooftop, like I'm climbing onto the back of a wild and unreliable horse.

All of this has happened in less time than it would take to say good-bye.

I gaze down on them.

They are silent. My mother is climbing down from the tree.

But I'm laughing, laughing like crying. Laughing like luck. Laughing like a child who knew she wouldn't, couldn't fall. I knew I couldn't. I turn to look down on George, who crouches behind the windmill, pale as a ghost.

'If you were Tilda's daughter,' he says in a low and angry voice, 'you'd be dead.'

I am not Tilda's daughter. I belong to the woman striding toward me across the barnyard, coming right up underneath so that her head tilts to an angle almost perpendicular, neck exposed, her face solemn with something that might — almost — be pride.

'Now you get down from there safe and sound, young lady!' my mother commands me.

'Yes, Mother! Right away, Mother!'

It is a relief to be commanded, and a relief to see her expression ease into a wide smile, even if she is shaking her head.

George holds his hand up to me, as if he could help me, as if I want his help, or need it. I swing my legs away from him, controlling this descent with my heels and the flats of my palms. We edge around the windmill on opposite sides and meet by the loosened boards.

This is our chance to say something to each other — this seems to be our chance. But we don't take it. So often, people don't. I can tell he wants me to climb through the hole in the wall first: chivalry, control. I give him that. The gesture is small enough, and I can do it. It doesn't hurt me.

I go on ahead of George, descending the windmill steps. I don't wait. On the way down, I pass my father walking up, nails and hammer in hand. He avoids looking at me. I guess he doesn't know what to say, what expression ought to cross his face, so he chooses to say nothing, his features blank.

But I hear him speaking to George. He doesn't sound angry, he sounds tired, defeated, almost. He can't find enough words, so he uses only a few. 'What is wrong with you, boy?'

I run across the mow floor and swing down the ladder into the stables below. I'm still running, across the spongy dirt floor and out into the yard. I still don't understand that what I've done does not look to everyone else like it felt to me. It does not look heroic or brave. It does not look thrilling and original. It does not look like an act, which is already what I believe it to have been, believing myself invincible, believing therefore that the fall and quick catch were as foreordained and central to the performance as the fine balance, the precision turns, the element of surprise.

They think I've almost died. They think I've risked everything for a foolish show-off's game. They don't understand what I'm doing.

The problem will persist.

There is life, as I see it, going on all around me, terrible in its uncertainty, frightening even. And there is me, as I see myself, preparing, practicing, anticipating a series of performances whose timing and discipline I can't predict in advance, but must be ready for at all times. These performances are not life, as I see it. They exist outside of what is real and dreadful. They arrive given an opportunity. I am in control of them. I shape them. I fold them into being and present them to an audience in order to give the audience pleasure, in order to show the world in its mirrored state, which is a state of perfect order, and the opposite of the world we're doomed to inhabit, dark with confusion and accident.

The supposed slip, the apparent fall, the heart-stopping thrill of a moment nearly stolen back by life and thwarted by artful practice: that is what makes the entire performance succeed. That is what gives it depth and meaning.

Why else would anyone care?

The appearance of perfection does not interest me. It is the illumination of near-disaster beside which we all teeter, at all times, that interests me. It is laughing in the face of what might have been, and what is not.

8

Cracks

There, we're past the bare yard, the grey house, and I can breathe again. Already I feel better, though the car is slowing, and I can see the weeds in the ditch waving slowly, taller than whatever's in the field beyond. We've only come a short distance from one property to the next. Do I know where I am? Don't I?

'I can't see the lane,' the girl says. 'Where is it?'

'It's overgrown — past that bunch of crabapple trees.'

With a sharp turn, the car bumps over the ruts and into the lane. I see the front field has been planted with winter wheat, rising faintly green and fresh from deep wet furrows, and I see the row of pines that hides the house from view. I always come back here. In my mind, I'm never really away.

The maples are dying, great wide spaces in between like a mouth emptied of rotten teeth. The raspberry brambles look like tumbleweed. I think I see the path we trampled, Fannie and I. See? There.

Stop! I want to see the graves.

They've heard me.

She's stopped the car.

They've loaded me like so much freight into the chair without dropping me, which is the best

I can hope for, with the pair of them.

Max directs: 'I'm going to film this from a wide angle. Bring her over to me, and then into the graveyard.'

'Are you ready, Mrs. Smart?' The girl stuffs the blanket up under my armpits. The white plugs dangle around her neck, emitting a distant beat, quicker than the heart, and the wad of bubble gum she snaps between her teeth pops in front of my nose.

How old is she? She looks like a child.

'Everything's good, I think,' she says. But she hasn't fastened the belt.

You haven't fastened the belt!

Max waves her onward: 'This is going to be a fabulous shot!' I feel removed from the scene, as if this is a long dream. I come here all the time in my mind. To be here, breathing the cool air and the wet soil, seems less real than a dream would be.

I can't worry over the details.

The girl knocks us through brambles, and we shudder into mud where the wheels sink, and she wrestles and curses under her breath until we progress. Max is backing up one step at a time, leading us closer to where the split-rail fence used to be (gone now, a blackened post and another standing out of the ground to remind us of how we stake our claim). We're really rolling, into the little yard, or whereabouts it used to be, hitting a clear grassy patch as the girl turns the chair toward the flat stones and we sink again.

Underground, the wheel strikes an unseen root, violently.

This is how I fall: flatly, in a state that recalls relaxation, into the dank spring earth, alive with thin green promises and the sweet rot of last year's roots and weeds.

I register nothing of their commotion.

I have fallen among the stones, but have struck none. One is quite near my head, the perfect distance for my eyes to focus on it with clarity. The stone looks soft, cushioned by moss, its edges crumbling and shot with rust-coloured veins, and it is sinking into the dirt, or being swallowed, pulled under.

A person might step on it and not see it for what it is; it is Fannie's stone, I'm certain.

* * *

The war ends, November 11, 1918, like that. I am ten years old. George is a boy soldier marching around the ruins of the Halifax Harbour, dreaming of going to sea. He is not quite seventeen.

I wait for him to come home.

Olive and Cora and I walk through the woods to town, carrying our lunches in pails. The low, brick one-room schoolhouse stands on the edge of town, and we enter through the door marked GIRLS. Olive will finish this spring. Olive and I are satisfactory students and haven't a hope (or desire) of attending the nearest high school, more than ten miles away; but Cora is clever. She won't leave her desk at recess, poring over her lessons in the poorly lit classroom.

I burn past Olive, who ignores me, one in a

clump of big girls near the door, all wrapped in coats and bright-coloured mitts, whispering together. They emit a shriek of laughter, their collective breath a frosty cloud. I scatter with the boys, heading for the playing field. I like boys. Boys say little, except what's necessary and brashly mocking. Boys talk about what they're doing, provide running commentary, try to make each other laugh. A boy would never shriek with inexplicable laughter when you pass by him. Instead, he would slide feet first into you at home plate in hopes of knocking the ball out of your frozen fingers. This makes sense to me.

When we return to the schoolhouse I separate and enter through GIRLS. I sit with Cora at lunchtime. I am not lonely that I notice, nor do I long for a best friend. I eat the bread and cheese and dried apple turnover, and listen to Cora and her best friend, Edwina, talk seriously about school and chores and what they'd like to do someday.

'There's nursing,' says Cora, 'which is better than teaching.'

'But sick people.' Edwina shudders.

'You can work anywhere,' says Cora. 'Teachers have to go where they're assigned.'

'I like children,' offers Edwina.

'I don't, not really.' Cora looks at me with mild contempt, as if I were so much younger.

'Children get sick too,' I point out.

'I'll specialize,' says Cora. '*Not* with children.'

When lessons are finished for the day, Olive and Cora and I walk home again, empty pails, town to farm.

One afternoon we arrive home to cracks of darkness opened, gashes in the ceiling, floorboards missing, an ugly pile of debris pushed into the empty space where the wall between the kitchen and the dining room has been. Father has knocked it down. He's accomplished the task by himself, drifting a layer of white dust everywhere in the house, even in the rooms upstairs. Our feet leave behind prints, our fingers too.

Father shovels the pile of debris out the front door and into a wheelbarrow, which he trundles down the wooden steps. He dumps it out behind the barn. It is up to us girls to clean up the rest of the mess; we do not put forth our best effort.

Father's new invention will be a floor-to-ceiling cabinet, with shelves going right through from the kitchen to the dining room. At the heart of the cabinet, a large double-decker lazy Susan will spin behind glass doors. Food will be sent from kitchen to dining room, and dirty dishes returned. We admire the drawings.

The weather turns cold, snow blows in and stays, and it seems that the dust from the broken plaster and sawn boards is snow too, blown through the cracks. I watch it float and descend upon our house, inside and out, and I wait.

George does not come home for Christmas.

I decide, privately, that this is for the best; Father's lazy Susan cabinet is nowhere near completion. I accept the circumstances in which our family is living, but I do not think that

George would like it. The table and chairs crowd against the far wall. The food we eat is gritty with sawdust — or do I just imagine it? We trip over the ragged ends of boards, catch our skirts on exposed nail heads, find screws stabbed into the bottoms of our shoes. In the kitchen, the hammer and the corkscrew drill lie side by side with the knife strop and the soup ladle.

Olive screams at the scampering mice, boldly scurrying out of the opened wall or gaping floorboards. Their droppings infest any food stores left unguarded. Sometimes Olive's scream is occasioned by a bat, winging wildly across the room.

What frightens me is the sight of the ceiling and walls and floor opened up, like a body cut apart, bones and guts exposed.

It is through the cracks, one lamplit evening, that I see my dead sister, Fannie, slowly appearing. She comes right into the room. I hold my breath, staring, the hairs standing up under my sleeves and at the back of my neck, but no one else seems to see her — neither my sisters, nor my mother, who are also in the room, entirely alive. I freeze, paused in the small actions I've been undertaking, the scratching of a pencil across a scrap of paper, the humming of a tuneless song.

I know it's Fannie even though I can't see her face. She doesn't look at me. She slips quietly past and up the back stairs to the servants' quarters.

I stand, knocking over my chair, pencil dropping from my fingers.

110

'Aggie? Are you all right?'

Without saying a word, I chase after Fannie. I'm running, stumbling on the steep steps, trying to catch up, but she's already gone around the corner and when I reach the cold hall, she has vanished.

'Aggie!'

My mother stands at the bottom of the narrow twisting staircase and calls me back, but I won't come. It's dark in this bleak hallway and I think that if I wait long enough, my eyes opened wide enough, I might see Fannie, she might emerge from wherever she's hiding. I hold my breath, squeezing my hands closed and open, over and over again.

My mother climbs the stairs slowly, her footsteps heavy, her breath slow and heavy. When she touches me, I shudder and spin away.

'What is it, Aggie?'

'It's Fannie,' I gasp out. 'I seen Fannie.'

'You saw Fannie.'

'But I couldn't catch her!'

'Aganetha.' My mother grabs my chin in her hand and directs my gaze to hers, though we can scarcely make each other out in the chilly blackness of the hall. Her voice is hard, and unlike her. 'You'll be more careful. You'll not be wanting to catch up with the dead.'

In this way, even as she cautions me, my mother tells me that she believes me.

Mother's solution is to brew me a tea prepared with dried rose petals, and to dose me with cod liver oil, but her medicines do not work. Now that Fannie knows she can squeeze through the

111

broken plaster, she comes when she pleases, not every evening, but often enough that I look for her expectantly, a shiver of excitement greeting her arrival. I see her shoulders, her neck, an ear, and sometimes the edge of her cheek, as if she were thinking of turning to me and saying something, but she doesn't. She never turns her face.

I, alone, watch her pass us by, my heart beating out of my chest.

Mother looks up from her book. 'You're restless. Go help your father in the barn.'

Olive and Cora study by lamplight at the dining room table. The dishes are washed and put away, the animals fed and watered. Father has returned to the barn to cut more boards on his lathe. Mother has cautioned him to use the oil lamp with care. His hands will be clumsy, thick-fingered in fat wool gloves.

I shake my head, no. I'm watching Fannie pass from the dining room into the unlit summer kitchen, cold and unused in this season.

Mother returns her attention to the leather-bound volume open on the table before her. Filled with handwritten notes and sketches, the book once belonged to her own mother, and is now hers. Its pages are unlined and their texture is rough to the touch, the paper tinged brown and flecked with red and green and blue threads and specks. I've inspected it closely. The pages in the back half of the book have yet to be filled. It is here that Mother records information she gleans from the *Farmer's Almanac*, and from her own experimentation and experience. She writes down the name and sex and birth date of every baby whose birth she attends, and every visit from every girl who comes to our door, identified by first name only. She writes down dates, and medicines tried, and dosages, and results. She keeps track of the moon cycles, and the harvesting of herbs. But she uses a kind of code, a shorthand that I can't interpret, though I've tried, poring over the handmade pictures and words.

'This will be a long winter, girls, and a short spring,' she tells us. How does the *Almanac* know these things? By the thickness of the bark on the trees, by the squirrels' stores, the shells of insects, the migration habits of the birds? The world around us is mysterious, but not unknowable — the physical world of living and dying.

We hear Father come into the summer kitchen, the door slamming with the wind behind him, his feet stamping on the boards. 'Help him, Aggie,' says Mother.

Father shoulders his way into the shadowed room bearing several small thin boards, veneers meant for the cabinet fronts. He brings the cold with him. As I'm shutting the door behind him, I glimpse Fannie in the summer kitchen and throw the door wide to be sure, but she's gone.

'Aggie! You're letting in the cold.'

Father arranges his little stack of wood pieces upon a larger stack with care, blows into his cupped hands, claps them together. 'Look at this grain,' he says. 'Look at the whorls. Look at the colour.' Beads of moisture glisten in his moustache and beard, the trimmed black hairs flecked with insistent grey. I go to look, but I'm the only one. I lift the veneer, pretending to be surprised at its lightness in my hands. But that is not what surprises me. What surprises me is that the grain has been painted onto the veneer by hand, the whorls too, and the hue is unnatural, a cherry-coloured stain.

It catches my breath, the care he's taken. I don't understand it — the artifice of beauty, the insularity of vision — and it frightens me.

Maybe I recognize it and do not want to. We're akin.

★   ★   ★

Dear Aggie — I might stop in Montreal for good if I can learn to parlay fransay. Not everyone has to work so hard as they do on the farm and thats a fact. They ride bicycles! They go out dancing! Sincerely yrs George

Dear Aggie — Toronto is the place for me I found work at the rail yards with the animals that come through horses especially. City folks dont know much about animals luckie for me. You would like it here. Yrs George

Dear Aggie — There is work for all that want it you could cut off your hair and be a jocky at the track. Tell them Im not coming home and thanks for the loan it comes in handy will pay back soon. Yrs truly George

★   ★   ★

As promised, spring comes late.

We start seedlings indoors in broken crockery and glassware and twists of brown waxed paper, balanced on makeshift brick-and-board shelves before the windows, wherever we can find sunlight. Spilled dirt clumps in the corners, mingled with sawdust. I find an abandoned nest of kittens and bring them inside, with Mother's permission.

Father gets to work. He frames in the cabinet. Instead of cracks and holes, there are only smooth boards, the smell of planed wood and dried sap.

Fannie stops coming. I think I know why: she can't get through.

We eat wrinkled potatoes and salt pork and the bright young dandelion greens that Cora and I gather from the front pasture. School's out now.

Spring comes late, but that does not prevent the day from arriving on which Fannie died, one year ago. The day seems so unlike that other day and the house too — so unlike the house that Fannie left behind. It's been emptied out, broken. I wonder whether the others are thinking the same thoughts as we bow our heads and eat warm biscuits with honey and butter. I eat and I swallow until the food is gone, but the feeling won't go, even as I clear the table, dry the dishes, escape the house — restlessness.

It's my job to muck out the horses' stalls and lead them to the front pasture. Even the old mare is feeling her grain and kicks her heels and rolls in the mud.

It's my job too to clean the chicken pen, and feed the squabbling, scrambling, brainless hens. I fight my way through the stinking pen with a pail of water, which spills down my dress and soaks right through to my thighs. The chickens peck and claw. I drop the bucket and back out of the pen, slamming the door.

Fannie isn't in the house. Fannie isn't here in the barn. But I believe her to be somewhere, nearby, just out of sight. I feel my heart slow with resolve. I will look for Fannie. I will find her.

Before I can think, I'm off and running, inexplicable excitement firing my limbs. I feel shaky at first, and my breath comes sharp. I run out behind the barn, along the field, to the woods. I run all the way to the edge of town. I look for Fannie in the early feathery green of leaves. I call her name, but quietly, under my breath. I figure she can hear me. When I don't find her in the woods, I run farther, across the fields, in the ruts at the edges, heavy with mud and churned-up stones. When I don't find her in the fields, I force myself to turn toward Edith's. But I veer off before I've arrived, and run, instead, along the stony road.

The graveyard.

I climb the split rails, catching and tearing my skirt, and swing over the fence.

'Fannie, are you here?'

I kneel on her grave, as if I expect her to rise out of it, my fingers scrabbling to dig a hole in the mud. I'm damp with sweat, and soon shivering. I speak down into the earth, my voice rising even as I repeat her stories, each of them, beginning at the beginning with the twins, and then the boy who was only six months old, and drowned James — 'It wasn't your doing, Fannie!' — and the first mother, and Big Robbie killed at war, and ending with Fannie herself.

'You went so quick, Fannie.'

I dig down deeper, but there is no reply. My fingers hurt.

'Aganetha.'

I jump halfway out of my skin.

She's come so quietly, I haven't heard; or perhaps I've fallen so deeply inside my own head that I've lost sense of the outside world going on around me. This happens sometimes. Sometimes I startle to the sound of someone calling my name — a teacher, a sister, my mother — as if I've been deep inside a dream, away, though I can never think where. Somewhere beyond thoughts.

'Aganetha, child.' My mother stands just outside the fence, open arms, calling me to her.

I feel my mouth crumple, my eyes sting. I run to bury my cold face against her neck. Her arms fold like wings around me and we are wrapped together inside her warm shawl. We rock like this. I want to hide my grief against her body, so she can't see, yet it isn't long before I'm too restless to hold, even inside her care, her heavy arms, her steady breath. I break free, wiping my eyes clean with the sleeve of my dress.

'Fannie liked to come here,' my mother says, but more like she's asking a question.

I nod.

'You liked to come with her. You came together.' More questions.

Yes.

'I would watch you go. I would think, how lucky little Aganetha is to have Fannie. And how lucky Fannie is to have little Aganetha.'

My mother stops. She doesn't go on and say more. She picks up my dirty hands and squeezes them. There is dirt from my hands on her cheek.

Pictures of Fannie stream behind my eyes, moving pictures, fast-motion, but silent. She is bending over the gravestones. She is walking away from me, waving me off, and I am following.

Mother watches me closely, as if she might be reading my thoughts — I believe she can. She lets go of my hands and kneels on Fannie's grave and gently covers over the hole I have dug.

Slowly she speaks, down to the ground. 'People we love do disappoint us, you know, Aganetha. We don't have to love them less for it. Maybe we have to love them more.'

I resist what my mother is saying.

I think that she is asking too much, that her demands are too steep, that she cannot possibly understand or mean what she says. But her words strike deep into me. I will think of them again, the years of my life unwinding in a whirl of hard-cast moments. I will think of what she is asking me to do. Can I do it?

'Come, let's eat.'

We walk up the lane, mother and daughter. I let her hold my hand.

9

Rosebud Ladies' Athletics Club

Here lies Fannie in her smooth wooden box. I can feel her beneath the earth, resting and waiting for this: for me to come home. I feel strangely peaceful. My breath comes deeply and slowly. I am aware of effort all around me, strain, excitement, but I let it go. The tiny muscles in my face and throat and neck and chest relax almost imperceptibly and my heartbeat slows.

I rest like I'm preparing for a race, one I didn't know I'd been entered in. I'll do my best. I'd never say no to a race. I take several unnaturally long breaths in order to steady my heart, to enter a place of stillness, a trick I learned as a young runner: how to conserve my strength, blot out disruption.

Don't disturb me. Don't try to move me.

She is a strong girl, but she can't lift me. I smell her fear, peppery and sharp. Her touch flutters, wary. She turns me, and I lie on my back among the stones like a beetle, exposed.

'Are you okay, Mrs. Smart? Is she okay? This is awful — we should just tell her the truth, just tell her everything.'

Oh, don't do that, dear. I won't if you won't. A rash confession is quickly a regret, believe me.

As if she hears me, the girl leans onto her heels, gone separate and apart. She no longer

119

touches me. I can hear the two of us breathing, or it could be the wind is picking up. It's gone cool.

The sky behind her head is a wall of grey. It looks like rain is blowing in: *April showers bring May flowers*, if this indeed is April. Might be May. Must be spring. I think I am quite all right, in fact. Whatever her motives, I would like to thank her for bringing me here, girl whose name I can't remember. Girl, who seems so familiar, though I can't place why.

She's got red hair, yellow at the roots, a long face, dark eyes. Clues, all clues. She moves gracefully, yet she's prone to clumsiness, if this fall is proof of anything.

'I'm really really sorry, Mrs. Smart,' the girl cries. 'After all you've done. You don't deserve this.'

I turn my eyes to Max, hovering indistinct on the other side of me.

What need have I for men bearing cameras? What need have you, young lady?

I move my hand by inches until I find hers, and I pat it gently.

'What should I do?' the girl asks me — I'd like to think it's me she's asking. She's calm enough now, I can read it on her skin. She'll carry me across the line.

★ ★ ★

On the grass track out behind Rosebud Confectionary our coach, Mr. Tristan, winds us up like toys and sets us loose, again and again. I fall inside a perfectly relaxed state for the few moments we have before he'll wind us up again. We are the lucky ones, recruited to train and race for Mr. P.T. Pallister's team. Everyone knows: P.T. has the best girls and the best coach; he has oceans of money, and he likes girl athletes.

Mr. P.T. Pallister announces in the *Toronto Daily Star* that he will personally guarantee girl athletes will win gold for Canada in Amsterdam at the 1928 Olympic Games. Personally guarantee it! He will personally spare no expense to see that it is so.

He finds Lillianna out in the Prairies and brings her by train to Toronto; Lillianna can jump like a gazelle. He discovers Ernestine at her high school near the lake. Glad is his own niece, but she earns her spot fair and square. Lucy comes from New Brunswick, but she will get homesick and drop out before the Canadian championships.

As for me, all I know is that a man comes knocking on the door at 445 Bathurst Street and leaves a message with the landlady, Mrs. Smythe, who informs me at dinner in front of everyone before serving up the gut-filling starter: a watery rice pudding, no raisins.

Olive and I slump at the table, aching and famished after the day's shift at Packer's Meats. Our hands and arms are rubbed raw and red, and our feet hurt, and we carry the scent of animal fat in our hair and on our clothes. I work as a 'runner,' which means filling in wherever I'm told to, while Olive works on a line, chopping pork into a fine mince. We wear tidy white aprons that are stained by day's end, and which we are obliged to launder ourselves. We tie our hair off our faces with kerchiefs.

We come to our landlady's table like ghosts of girls, too weary to speak, and we eat passively of her coarse black bread and cabbage borschts.

'This came for you today.' A letter at my plate.

'Oh?'

'A fellow in a suit asking for you.'

'What is it?' Olive wonders. She is busy saving her money for when she gets married. She will spend it on china and silver and linens, she says. She has not met a prospective husband, but I can imagine what he will look like. He will look like a fellow in a suit.

I rip open the letter and scan its typed-out contents.

'What is it? What is it?'

We share a table with three other girls, none of them older than twenty-two, also factory workers, and with the landlady's husband, Mr. Smythe, who irritably ignores us and reads the evening paper while eating. But everyone else is curious, even Mrs. Smythe.

'Has she got a beau?' 'Oo! Aggie's got a beau!'

'I have not,' I say across the table. Closer acquaintance has not brought me friendship. I don't like the other girls particularly, and they don't particularly like me. I think them silly and obvious, and they think me standoffish and peculiar. Perhaps we are right about each other, as much as we are wrong. We are all of us young, independent, hoping for more, but at different volumes. They are loud and declarative and crudely funny, cruel in a tribal sense, bonding against rather than with, and I am shy and bold and uncompromising.

Examine our hair for comparison.

They are constantly worrying over theirs. Washing it, drying it, tying it in rags and sleeping on it overnight, wrapping it around wooden curlers, brushing it, pinning it up, taking it down, trimming it, shaping it, asking each other to comment on the results, or to help. *Help! What should I do with my hair? What is my hair doing?*

I wear mine in a braid down my back for work. I can wind it and tie it into a knot at the nape of my neck if further tidiness is required. Otherwise, I brush it at night, as my mother taught me to do, and I keep it long. Olive trims the dead ends. I can sit on my hair if I tilt my head back. I wouldn't say that hair matters nothing to me, because I like mine, the colour, the texture, the weight of it, but I would say that the maintenance and care of my hair matters nothing to me. I can't be bothered, even knowing that not bothering sets me apart from the other girls.

'Well, what is it?' Olive asks again, of the letter, and I take a deep involuntary breath, almost like a sigh, startling everyone, even myself.

'Not bad news?' says Mrs. Smythe.

'Not bad news,' I say, disappointing her. 'Good news, I think. It's just, I don't understand . . . '

Olive takes the letter from my hand. 'Well,' she says several times, reading it over. I can see she doesn't know what to think either. 'It's private,' she says finally. 'I shouldn't think it's something to be discussed over dinner.'

Well, that gets the girls interested. Even Mr. Smythe rustles his newspaper in a way that suggests he's been listening in on the conversation.

'I don't think you should go,' Olive tells me in our shared room, in a whisper. 'You don't even know if the offer is real. What if it's a trick?'

'Why would it be a trick?' I move away from her and set my palm flat on the cool, warped pane of our window.

'To get girls, or, I don't know, honestly. That's beside the point. The point is, do you know this man personally?'

'Of course not.'

'Then you should not meet with him. It wouldn't look right.'

'I wouldn't be meeting with him. I'd be meeting with the coach of his team, and it's at the factory, and it's in the middle of the day.'

'And you'd have to ask for a half-day off.'

I'm silent.

'I suppose you'll do what you please.'

I lift my cold fingers to my lips, and then stretch my arms over my head.

'I suppose you always have,' says Olive.

'Have I?' I say slowly.

I stare out the window at the dark evening sky, pricked with windows like ours lit by oil lamps, or, others, by blazing electric lights. I keep my back to my sister.

When it comes to hair, that measure of a girl,

Olive is on the other side. She takes joy from scented hair creams and satin ribbons that I think make her look juvenile. Only recently, and somewhat alarmingly, Olive has gotten her hair cut to her chin in a newfangled bob that has been cause for many squeals and much discussion from the girls we work with and the girls we live with. I wonder: is it out of Olive's character to be in fashion? I decide it is not. Olive wants to be like everyone else. If you are like everyone else, no one will pay special attention to you. No one will notice that you aren't. That is Olive.

She is tolerant of me, loving, and we do not hope for the same things, but I trust her opinion.

'Oh, well, what would be the harm?' she says suddenly, coming to me and hugging me around the shoulders, so hard it hurts. 'You want to go, so go, and run. You're so fast they'll surely want you for their team, and you'll be wonderful. I know it.'

I kiss her cheek.

'And just think of making chocolates instead of canned hams,' she says.

Soon, that is just what we are doing, both of us: making chocolates instead of canned hams. The girls at Mrs. Smythe's are jealous and my popularity improves, ever so slightly, around the dinner table, especially when we pass around a box of broken candies to share.

'Ooo, what's this pink stuff?'

'Tastes like strawberries.'

'It's strawberry with coconut. Do you like it?'

'Not so much as the caramel. Is there a

caramel anywhere?'

'I'll eat it if you don't want it.'

'You'll all get fat,' says the landlady grimly, and quite seriously, prompting a tableful of girls to stare at her mid-chew, and her husband, newspaper at half-mast, hand hovering over the proffered box, to wave it away. Dessert has never been on her menu.

'Oh, won't you try one, Mrs. Smythe? So delicious!'

'Not me, no I will not, no thank you.'

There are other girls who run with the Rosebud Ladies' Athletics Club, but only a handful of us are believed to be Olympic prospects — only me, Glad, Lillianna, Ernestine, and Lucy, and we are expected at every practice, and exempted from work on the factory floor. I'm offered, instead, a secretarial job despite never having learned to type. That is my first assignment: learn how to type. Mr. P.T. Pallister arranges for me to attend secretarial school. It is Olive who brings home the boxes of broken chocolates, Olive who does, as Mrs. Smythe warns, grow plumper and plumper during our time at Rosebud Confectionary.

Me, I learn how to type and I learn shorthand and transcription and bookkeeping. My muscles grow leaner, my spine even straighter.

And I meet Glad.

★ ★ ★

Before I meet Glad, I'm the girl who doesn't bother with her hair, who runs along city streets chased by jeering boys on bicycles. Before I meet Glad, I'm the girl who perversely and in anger, in defiant defensiveness, does not care. I don't see the point of friendship, somehow, if it makes you pretend to be someone you aren't. Friendship looks calculating to me: a shallow alliance designed around exclusion.

After I meet Glad, I begin to care, and to take more care. I change in small ways to please her, even though she does not ask it of me.

Before I meet Glad, I do not know how to be a friend.

★ ★ ★

I like her almost instantly, but there is nothing amazing in that — everyone likes Glad. What is amazing is that Glad likes me in return.

On my second evening with the team, she comes looking for me after practice. I am hiding in the change room, sitting slumped against the wall, legs pulled to my chest, staring at my bared feet, blistered and red. The room is tiny, furnished with a wooden bench and a line of cabinets, and I have tucked myself into a small space between the cabinets and the wall. Directly across from me is a toilet perched oddly on a high concrete pedestal, and beside that a cold-water shower spout over a drain in the floor, blocked off from the rest of the room by a single floor-to-ceiling thin board wall. It is a dismal space, and I'm a dismal mess of dismal emotions: *I thought I was fast?*

'There you are!' Glad marches right over,

addresses me with arms crossed, head cocked. 'You need new shoes. Those boots are tearing your feet apart.'

I nod dumbly.

'You know what I do?' Glad puts out an arm and leans against the wall, tapping it thoughtfully. 'I swim. It helps with the aches. I like to go in the morning. Why don't you come with me.' But she doesn't ask it like a question. She offers it like an answer.

'I can't swim,' I say. 'I don't know how.'

'I'll teach you! It's easy. Everyone should know how to swim.'

In the YWCA on McGill Street the water is cold as ice, filling a tank sunk into a concrete floor. It's a dark echoing space, claustrophobic, slippery, spare. Water sloshes the sides of the tank. Girls churn back and forth, and it feels like there's not enough room to breathe. I panic. Glad's dark hair is tucked under a swim cap, mine is exposed and plastered to my head. Our black jersey suits are heavy, straight-cut across the thighs, scooped necks, no sleeves, and mine is borrowed from Glad and therefore too short, tight at the shoulders — 'Don't worry, I've got lots, I'm always trying out the new styles!'

No men are allowed.

My hair tangles in my mouth. I flail. I'll sink.

Glad's legs spin like an eggbeater and she bobs some small distance clear of me. 'Keep hold of the side.'

Shivering. 'You're turning blue, Aggie! You should see your lips!'

'This is not fun,' I mutter.

She laughs, yet somehow I don't hate her. 'You need to get moving. Here, I'll hold you.'

Glad's hands are under me, on my stomach, holding me in a float. She directs me as we edge slowly down the length of the pool. Face in, and turn, in and turn. Blow bubbles, and turn, blow bubbles, and turn. Float, relax, relax. Pull, pull, pull under the water. Kick with straight legs. Cup your hands. Don't crane your neck.

So much to remember!

Me: 'I can't do this!'

Glad: 'You'll be swimming laps within the week, I promise.'

When I float, when her hands come off me and I am briefly suspended, my face down in the dank greenish water, eyes wide open, I see little drowned James hanging atop the water in exactly the same posture.

I gasp and rear up.

'You did it!' says Glad, holding my elbows. 'Kick,' she reminds me. She thinks I'm trembling from the cold. I nod grimly. I try again. Again, I see James, my half-brother, his very small body, near to mine. This happens each time I put my face into the water, until after days and weeks of being near him, or feeling him nearby, I become accustomed to it, and I think of it differently. I think we are swimming together, in a way, until it is just another version of remembering him, as I promised Fannie long ago I would do.

I accept the shadow in the water beside me.

★   ★   ★

129

Glad bests me on the track, in practice, for the months of September, October, and November, 1926. When the snow falls and stays, we train indoors, in a wood-lined gymnasium, our rubber-soled feet squeaking on the floor. We work with dumbbells and ropes, and sprint from end to end, and practice a system of calisthenics devised by our coach, Mr. Tristan, who also urges those of us who are runners to go outside once a day to leap through the snowbanks around where we imagine the track to be.

I'm faster than Glad on these frigid dashes, but my long legs offer an advantage in the deep snow. I leap like a jackrabbit.

By April, we are back outside, training on the track. Mr. Tristan runs us in all weathers, and it is a chilly April, streaked with snow.

Glad bests me in practice for the months of April, May, and June, 1927. She bests me for most of July, but I am closing the gap. By August, it is a toss-up who will edge in front of whom on any given day, any given training run. We both know it, but we never talk about it. Never, not once. We meet to swim together three mornings a week. We meet at the track. We meet in motion, and speak sparingly as we prepare ourselves, and speak in shorthand afterward, spent and quiet.

'That was a good one,' she might say, and I will agree.

Or, 'Tired today.' 'Yes.'

This is friendship, as I understand it: a series of shared, parallel experiences that do not require elaboration.

Mr. Tristan tells me at the end of a hard practice: I've made the cut for the Canadian track and field championships at the Canadian National Exhibition — the CNE. He doesn't need to tell me this will be the biggest race of my career so far, my chance to prove, after nearly a year of dedicated training, that I belong. He places one hand on my shoulder and offers the other, to shake mine: 'You've qualified on time for the eight hundred. I knew you could do it.'

Holding his hand, I feel my face crumple toward tears. It's a struggle to hold everything inside, but I command myself to become stone.

'Aggie,' he says gently, patting my shoulder, 'this is good news. You're supposed to be happy.'

I am, if I could reach through the numbness and find it. I nod. My first thought is to tell my mother — for some reason, I see her standing in the treetop in her apron, watching me on the barn roof. I want to tell her the news. I wonder — could she take the train to Toronto?

But it is August on the farm, the garden overflows, the train costs money.

I send a letter containing only the barest jots of news, and none of the fear and joy. I can't ask her to come. She doesn't think of it herself. She writes back to me in her formal hand, the script in delicate circles across the thin page: 'Send us news of your race.'

I know it's me who left. But I'm young enough to think that my mother should be there for me.

131

I'm young enough to imagine that she might even surprise me.

★ ★ ★

Mrs. Smythe prepares eggs for breakfast — her silent contribution to the excitement. The other girls regret that they are working and can't come to cheer me on. They talk of skipping out. Merry laughter. Yes, I think it entirely possible that I will win a medal — haven't I caught up with Glad — so why should they not think so too?

'Will you be famous, then?' 'Won't she be?' 'Will you cut your hair and buy a pretty dress, if they put you in the newspaper?'

Everything I do not yet know, the hours that are rushing at me, that will crash down on me like a massive wave of salt water: the crowd like an angry buzz, the lean limbs and pointed elbows of my competitors, girls I've never seen before, girls who are not like Glad but are more like me, tight and twisted up inside themselves, sharp with nerves. My guts roiling, wishing I'd never seen those eggs like two undercooked yellow eyeballs wobbling as they stared up at me.

Are you feeling quite all right, Aggie? Glad, noticing. Me, wishing she hadn't. *Fine. I'm fine.*

I search and scan, but my mother's is not among the faces in the crowd.

Before I know it, it's over. Just like that. Quick as a flash, two times round the track. I've gone out too fast, I'm passed early, I hang on to second place as the metres stretch desertlike and unending before me until I'm caught on the final curve by two runners.

One of the runners is Glad, and she's sailing. She'll catch the girl in front of me too.

I watch her go, following her up the stretch, knowing we're in two different versions of the same story: hers is easy and mine is hard. This does not seem fair, after all we've shared. I feel as if she's grabbed something essential right out of me, a section of my heart or a lung, and stolen merrily off with it, leaving me crippled, drained of my powers. I know this feeling — it's betrayal, and I'm heavy beneath its weight, I must get out from under it.

As I approach the finish, I glimpse an open mouth in the crowd, jaw extended, veins popping from his neck. George, my brother — has he come to watch? If it is George, he does not seek me out afterward. I hope I've seen wrong.

I stagger across the line in fourth, out of the medals and the record books and the newspapers. An emotion that could be anger — though I don't claim it — swells out of me in stupid tears.

I force myself to approach Glad: 'Congratulations.'

I can hardly hear my own voice. I'm mumbling. I don't press near enough to give her a hug, my offering measly amidst the grand wild thrill that surrounds Gladys Wright on this brilliantly warm and breezy Friday afternoon. Gladys Wright, the 1927 Canadian women's champion at the 100 metres, with a surprise win at the 800-metre distance, too.

Mr. Tristan drives me home after the meet,

Lucy and Ernestine, too. None of us have achieved what has been expected of us — or, more precisely, what we expected of ourselves — although Ernestine made the sprint finals. We are hot and dusty and do not speak, clamping our hats to our heads against the wind blowing into the open-roofed automobile.

'Chin up, that's a girl,' Mr. Tristan says as I get out of his car.

I dread dinnertime. I dread telling Olive and Mr. and Mrs. Smythe and the girls what has happened.

But dinnertime comes and dinnertime goes, and I am required only to shake my head ever so slightly, *no, not good*, and the others leave me be. I need to be sad. I need to go to bed early, even though the day is still bright and hot, and I need to curl under the sheet, tuck knees to belly. I need to feel what I'm feeling.

It is a great kindness that nobody disturbs me with false assurances.

★　★　★

I wake to find Glad smiling out from the newspaper, waving a bouquet of white flowers and holding a big box of Rosebud Chocolates. Mr. Smythe must have shaken his paper open to this page, and folded it over, without making a comment on the subject over dinner. He must have kept the paper specially yesterday evening, he must have climbed the stairs when the house was asleep and quietly slid the folded newsprint under our door, because it is what I step on in

134

my bare feet on this brand-new morning, when I am still my ordinary self, and not the champion I'd let myself imagine I might be.

I rustle open the page, smooth it across the summer quilt on top of Olive, who is half-asleep.

I think Glad looks perfect.

I go for Olive's scissors and cut out the photo to keep. But my stomach hurts. I don't eat breakfast. I don't go swimming. I walk south to the lake, and west along the rocky shore, and north again through High Park and past the mineral pools where strangers are bathing. Eventually, it is time to make my way to practice.

Glad isn't there. Perhaps she is exempted today, given her victories.

I run strong. I run fine. I can feel my sadness running out behind me, like it's being spilled on the ground, and I figure that will be that. I won't be sad anymore, not over this. I have a sense of impermeability, of elasticity, of bouncing off of something hard, and believing in the first instant that I'd been hurt, then understanding the pain is superficial. It is already gone.

This is called recovery. I recognize the sensation from running. Under every layer of pain another layer of recovery lies in wait, the sweet, forever surprising truth of endurance.

If Glad was here, I decide, I would hug her and I would say, *Congratulations*, and I would mean it this time. I am sorry she is not.

The change room is emptying out. I rinse my face in the sink. I strip off my soaked training clothes, peel off socks, dry myself with a large piece of absorbent flannel. I powder my armpits

135

with soda and talcum. I dress. I unbraid my hair and brush it out and let it fall down my back, unfashionably long and loose, crinkled from the braid. I gather my damp belongings and fold them. I am the only person left, and the building is quiet and emptied out, the Saturday shift gone home at five o'clock, the cleaning shift not yet arrived.

I open the door, quite entirely inside my own head, and thoughts.

'I think I know what's wrong.' Mr. Tristan is waiting in the hallway outside the change room.

My heart is a runaway horse, spooked into a gallop. I try to hide my surprise. His hand on my upper arm, gently, steers me to the little room that is his office. 'Now, then. Let's talk.'

I refuse to sit, even though he points me to a chair squeezed beside his desk.

I'm wearing a dress made of summer-weight fabric with a plain collar and short sleeves, belted at the waist, and a skirt, like most skirts, that is too short on my long legs, and falls to just below the knee. It is a yellow dress, pale yellow, approximately the same colour as my hair. There is nothing fashionable about it, nor about the straw hat on my head. I carry my valise, with the sharp-smelling training uniform folded inside, over my left shoulder. I will take it home and wash the uniform and hang it to dry in the room I share with Olive. By practice on Monday it will be dry, but usually, at most practices, the fabric is still slightly damp when I put it on again. I will pull on the shirt and the short pants and the socks and something about the dampness, the odour of sweat and lanolin, will bring me comfort, or nearly.

'Good showing yesterday?'

I stare dumbly. Is he asking a question?

'Are you happy with fourth?' he presses.

I shake my head. No.

'You know you can do better. I think I know what's wrong,' he says, again. He takes a seat behind his desk and narrows his eyelids, scrutinizing me. I have the petrified feeling that he can see through to my thoughts.

'I've been watching you,' he says.

I feel as transparent as glass, open as a wound. What has he seen?

'You're tough as hell in practice, but in races you let her get past. You know who I mean. Glad. You ease up.'

'I don't!' The fury of my reply shocks me. I'm shaking.

Because even as he's saying it, and I'm denying it, I know somehow he's right.

Yesterday's race washes over me, a series of short sharply illuminated frames, glimpses. Out of a too-quick start, a nervy start, I'm burning, falling to second, but holding on. The pace as we enter the second lap a little quicker than I prefer — can I hold it? I don't question, just push.

Here is where I'd like to make my move — on the outside turn, back straightaway. I glance over my shoulder.

Never look back, I hear Mr. Tristan saying as if he's running beside me, in the race, saying it into my ear. Too late. I see what I see.

Glad on my heels, grinning. Glad pulling me

137

back, pulling on me. Like a tide. Like rope. Glad like a stone in a slingshot zinging past my shoulder, brushing arms. My fingers fold into my palms. I let her go.

The finish line, fluttering tape, one two three four strides behind first, second, and third. My head turns, left shoulder dipping. Too easy, I think. I've got too much left in me. This is not what you want to feel at the end of a race. You do not want to finish a race and know you could have given more. You want to pour everything out. You want to be emptied.

Mr. Tristan is watching me.

I'm back in the tiny office with him, back with the sharp sunlight angling through the dusty windowpane. It's hot in here, airless, like a closet. His expression is unguarded, as I am unguarded too. I shake my head violently to shake away the sensation of losing. To shake off the emotions flooding me again, fresh as yesterday: jealousy, envy, shame, and worst of all, betrayal.

'You like Glad,' he says simply.

I flush hot.

'You'd do well to like her a bit less.' Mr. Tristan speaks coolly, thrumming his fingers on the desk. 'Her uncle pays the bills, mine included, but that won't stop me from telling you the truth, because the truth is I like you, Aganetha Smart. No, don't go all coltish and startled. I'm speaking as your coach. I like your potential, always have. You work harder than anyone else out there. Harder than anyone I've ever seen. You've earned your place on this team the hard way. That's what I like about you. You're like me. You come from nothing.'

I do not, I think defiantly, hardly hearing what he's saying.

'You like Glad,' he continues. 'What's not to like? She's a friendly kid, she's got the world on a string, happy-go-lucky, always gets what she wants, always has.'

'Stop,' I say.

'I don't think Glad is who you think she is,' says Mr. Tristan. 'Be careful, that's all.'

I'm breathing like I've been through a race.

'She's quicker over the short run,' says Mr. Tristan, standing and coming to the door, holding it open to indicate that our conversation is coming to a close, 'but you've got endurance. The only way she can beat you is up here' — he leans in close to me and taps his temple — 'and don't think she doesn't know it.'

10

Golden Girl Runner

I hold out my arms, and the girl leans down. I must weigh next to nothing, muscle and fat vanished under loosened skin, even while I remain a long woman, long bones, long spine. My feet drag behind me, a huge breath leaving my lungs, and hers, almost simultaneously, *ah*, as she settles me into the chair. She's forgotten about the belt, but the complexity of expression necessary seems hardly worth the effort. I can't remember the word for *belt*, though I can see it like a picture in my mind.

'This isn't my fault!' She yells at her brother, but she's angry at herself. She shakes out the blanket, which has fallen into the mud, adjusts my ridiculous knitted hat, tucks me in. 'Don't even talk to me,' she orders him. He hasn't lowered his camera, nor said a word against her, as far as I've heard. She's rattled.

Well, she's young. She's young and she's ambitious. When you're young you think you invented the light that shines on you. You think it arrives at your bidding, and you would not claim the shadows that blot this sun of yours. I'm the one who fell, but she's the one hurt by it.

She's pushing me out of the graveyard, forcing the wheels of the chair through the muddy ruts and brambles, and back to the lane, which is smooth, bare of gravel, worn shiny and slippery like a pair of old corduroy pants.

'There.' The girl's breathing comes purposefully, but the *click click* sound of the rubber wheels slows as she pushes me closer to the line of pines planted long ago to hide the house from view. Her brother hurries to get ahead, the shuffle of his shoes scuffing the dirt. He searches for the best angle, a tall figure crouched into a ridiculous position as he crabs himself backward, away from us. We follow.

I can see the scene this will make in their movie: I am a wizened, gnarled, crumbling creature tucked into a wheeled chair being pushed along a bare farm lane toward a place I can't recall, not perfectly, but I know that I'm coming home. I suspect the boy would frame this as a sad scene, even pathetic, and he would score it accordingly, with tinkling piano music. In the movie they say they're making, I'm a helpless being steered by a strong girl, a teenager clad in fitted, gaudily patterned athletic clothing, a girl who is perpetually prepared to take off running. The girl's muscled calves are the same circumference as her thighs. Her regimen is different than mine was. I've heard they bathe in ice these days — the blithering television is occasionally good for something. On foot, she covers a distance of 200 kilometres every week in intervals, sprints, tempos, and hills. She swings weights. She crunches. She planks. She stretches. She dreams of gold.

But it is I, the muttering, bewildered creature in the chair who does not dream, who has no

141

need to. Gold is already mine.

Once upon a time, I crossed an ocean to catch it and bring it home.

I wonder, would it be a kindness to tell the girl what it weighed, like a warning, or a promise? It was so much heavier than I imagined.

★ ★ ★

1928, Amsterdam. The first Olympics at which female athletes are permitted to compete in track and field events.

I don't know what I'm doing, not really, nor what it means. I'm pleased as punch to pose on the steps of the pension in Amsterdam with the other girls, all of us dressed identically in the team uniform: white jackets and skirts trimmed in red, with a maple leaf over the left breast, and a cloche hat to match that Glad says suits me better than it does her. I'm happy to do as I'm told, to arrive where I'm taken, dress in what I'm given, eat what's before me, and run without complaint on the spongy track where the Canadian girls have been assigned to practice in the days leading up to our races.

The news is broadcast in occasional static flares sent up from the ground. I won't see my own photo until I arrive home weeks later: my mother cuts out copies to save. Black-and-white, reproduced on newsprint, hawked by shouting boys in the streets, beneath words three inches tall, wide and black: GOLDEN GIRL RUNNER!

I wonder, do I remember the photograph itself, or do I remember living inside of it?

The photographer must have placed himself ahead of us on the track, crouched down for the best angle. He snaps me in motion, crossing the line in front of the German girl, though just, her expression stern, mine disbelieving and pained. My head is angled. I am glancing over my shoulder as I lean for the finish, but I'm not looking at the German girl, as it appears. I'm looking behind me for Glad. I can't understand why she isn't running beside me. I am sick that she is not here too.

I am also just plain sick.

I wear a short-sleeved white tunic, cut into a V at the neck and emblazoned with a red leaf under which my nation is declared: CANADA. Two tight undershirts layered beneath the tunic flatten my breasts to my ribs. Loose black shorts swish around my thighs and are too ample for my waist — I've dug an extra notch into the thin leather belt. I'll have red marks on my stomach afterward from cinching it so tight. Little white ankle socks tucked into inflexible black shoes. My number on paper pinned across my hips: 692. Glad is 689.

Flash. I am front-page news in Canada, tomorrow.

I run out of the moment, unable to slow my stride immediately. I keel sideways, collapse to the ground, holding my head with both hands, flat on my back. Mr. Tristan and Miss Gibb, the manager of the Canadian girls' team, are with me in the next instant, pulling me to my feet.

'Brilliant finish. World-record time,' says Mr. Tristan. 'Walk it off, walk it off.'

'Where's Glad?' I ask as stars explode behind my eyes. Miss Gibb wraps me in a scratchy woollen blanket.

'She's chilled.' She is talking to Mr. Tristan, not to me. 'It's this rain.'

'Keep them away.'

'Coming through, give us air!'

Glad darts into focus, ahead of me, and she turns. Her grin is a mile wide. I can't believe it, not after what has happened. She swings her hand for mine, shakes it wildly. 'Kiddo!' she yells. 'I knew you had it in you!'

I am crying, snot streaming. Glad responds as if she's decided everything I do is a lark. I love her for not letting me spoil my own moment. She's pretending to spar with me, her fists up, her feet dancing, her mouth laughing.

Miss Gibb discreetly daubs my face with her handkerchief. 'You should be happy,' she says sternly.

'She shouldn't be anything other than what she is,' says Mr. Tristan.

'She needs to pull herself together. Throw your shoulders back. Now.'

'There's a girl.'

'I'm sorry, Glad,' I'm blubbering.

'What for?' Glad pushes through the others to hug me tight. 'It's just a race,' she whispers in my ear while I fold my head down onto her shoulder and weep until I'm done.

Here is the medal ceremony: I am handed a bouquet of white and red flowers. I stand on the top step, already the tallest girl in the crowd, so tall they'll remark on it in the foreign papers.

'What are they feeding those long-legged Canadian girls?' As if we're all the same. *God Save the King*.

Mr. Tristan helps me down from the podium. He has a tender expression on his face that makes me sad, though I don't know why. It's as if he's saying good-bye, as if he knows something I don't about this being the end. We've gotten what we came for.

Miss Gibb falls in on my right, holding firm my elbow. I lean away from Mr. Tristan and into Miss Gibb's trim figure, demure in jacket and long navy skirt. My legs are water and my lungs are underwater, and it is too loud under the drumming stands to speak, and they are walking me out into the Amsterdam morning, into the fine drizzle, and they are delivering me into the backseat of a humming black motorcar.

'Hot broth,' says Miss Gibb, climbing in beside me. She shuts the door on Mr. Tristan. 'Hot water bottle. Sweat it out. You've caught cold, that's all.'

★ ★ ★

It's just a race.

Funny Glad would say that. I wonder — could she mean it? I hide in my room at the pension, huddled under the sheets, laid by with fever and chills. If I am honest with myself, I will allow it is not a fever of the body, but a fever of the mind. I am twenty years old and unprepared for the experiences of the past weeks, all except for one, of course, which was the race itself. For that, I was sublimely prepared; not so, Glad.

145

It is Glad I can't get out of my mind.

Glad, who goes into the 100-metre dash as the favourite, who breezes through the semifinals with the fastest time, who wears her confidence like a feathered hat. Some brood under the weight of expectation — you see them at meals picking at their food and snapping at any approach — but Glad seems instead to glow. We are dining on cold potatoes, fat slices of ham, and bread with preserves, the day before Glad's 100-metre final, when Miss Alexandrine Gibb asks to sit with us — although it being Miss Gibb, her request sounds more like a command. 'I'd like to write you up in my column, if you'd agree,' she says to Glad. 'I think readers would be interested in how you prepare for your race, the little details. What you eat and drink, and what exercises you do to keep strong.'

Glad laughs. 'I run with Aggie. That's all I need to keep me strong.'

I blush and hack at my slice of ham with a dull butter knife. I should say something in reply, demure, make light, offer a compliment in return, but my mind is blank. This is what I mean when I say I'm unprepared for these experiences. I'm empty, I think. Fill me up. All I've got are these legs, trained for speed, this mind, trained to conquer a circle of track.

But that is not entirely true. What I lack isn't knowledge, of which I have more than most girls my age on subjects unmentionable — what I lack are ordinary social graces. I don't know, yet, how easy these are to learn. They are strategies, nothing more.

On the morning of the 100-metre final, I watch with the other Canadian athletes, crammed into the stands as close to the track as we can manage, leaning over the wooden rails to holler to our girls, as Glad lines up at the start. She looks over at us, and waves, flashing her grin to the newspapermen with their cameras, before settling into position, one foot on the line and the other ready to push, arms cocked, knees bent, spine angled forward yet upright, prepared to leap at the gun.

On your marks, steady, *BANG!*

They're off. But just as suddenly, the pistol fires two shots into the air to call the runners back. There has been a false start. And we all know who it was, flying a half-step ahead of the others like a bird frightened out of a bush. Glad! We are holding our breath.

The change in atmosphere is sudden, like we've stepped off a precipice into the unknown, we're falling.

Glad shakes her head, her arms, her legs. She walks a tight circle back to the line. She isn't grinning, and she doesn't look over to us, watching in the stands, calling out her name. I hear my own voice, its pitch frantic even to me: *Glad, Glad, Glad!* There isn't time for Coach Tristan to speak to her, to try to steady her. The race must go on, and the girls line up a second time. Germany, the United States, France, Canada, Holland, Canada, Japan, Italy.

The pistol fires. And again, almost instantly, fires twice more to stop the race.

No.

The crowd gasps, falls to silence. My hands clap my face.

Surely there has been an error. Surely the judges will recognize that Glad twitched early but held off, that it only looked like she started ahead of the others. It is only that she's so quick, she got the leap on them. Isn't it? Give her another chance! Mr. Tristan is running onto the track, protesting, but he is blocked, held up, talked back by other men from the Canadian team.

An official dressed all in white escorts Glad off the track, to the side. She has been disqualified. She will not run.

Glad sinks to the grass in disbelief. She kneels, her hands buried in her hair, and bends her head to the ground. Rises up, only to stagger and sink again. I have never seen Glad in such pain. I have never seen her down. It is like watching a solid building crumble before your eyes. No, it is worse. It is like seeing a horse in a race suddenly snap its leg and tumble, confused, dazed, uncomprehending, trying to stand and stumbling to the ground in pain.

The girls are lining up again. They avoid looking at Glad. But they can't avoid hearing her animal cries.

The pistol fires. They're off, and almost just as soon, they're done. Canada, thanks to Ernestine, has earned a surprise silver behind the American girl, a sixteen-year-old who can't believe her good fortune. She leaps in the air with a shout. Such a sharp turn of luck; none of us can grasp it. Glad, the favourite going into the final, watching in agonized weeping from the side, and

148

the pretty little American, her hair in two tight schoolgirl braids, lifted to the podium by teammates, biting her gold medal, behaving in a way not fitting of a sportswoman, as Miss Alexandrine Gibb will write in her column telling of Glad's sad turn.

We know not what goes through the mind of an athlete who works so hard only to see her dreams crumble before her very eyes. Miss Wright alone could tell us, and she has chosen, wisely we think, not to speak on the subject.

Solace, perhaps, will come in the form of another chance, in another race. Miss Wright is among those who will line up to contest the 800-metre final on Thursday morning, along with her teammate and friend Aganetha Smart. These plucky girls finished first and second respectively, both breaking the former Canadian record, in what could only be described as the closest race of the Olympic qualifying championships in Halifax earlier this summer. Both girls earned the opportunity to compete here in Amsterdam proudly wearing Canada's colours.

Could another one-two finish be a possibility on Thursday? Canada can only hold her breath and hope!

★ ★ ★

Miss Alexandrine Gibb raps on the door of the room I've been assigned to share with Lillianna,

149

the high jumper, who is lanky and reserved, keeps to herself. She's gone out and won't be back all day. Miss Gibb knows I'm alone and enters without waiting for a reply. She carries with her a newspaper.

'You've been hiding in here quite long enough, Miss Smart. It's time to get up.'

I cough feebly.

In silence, she passes me the newspaper and I peer at the words on the page, the black print smudging my fingertips and the bedspread. The meaning of what I'm reading does not immediately register, entering slowly, like thick muddy water. This is not the story I suppose I'm halfway expecting to see: a flattering report about myself. This is quite another story altogether.

It's news that burns, that clouds, that pollutes: the Olympic committee has voted against girls competing at the 800-metre distance in future Games. The committee has met and come to an immediate decision, argued for and supported most strongly by the Canadian representative. It is written that the collapse of runners after the final proves the distance is too taxing for a girl's inferior strength.

'But — they're talking about me! I fell down at the end. You were there, you saw me. I was on my feet in an instant! Can't you tell them I was sick?'

'This isn't about you. It's not personal.'

'But — oh! Didn't the boys fall down after their races?' I twist the bedcovers between my fists. 'I saw them! They were rolling in the grass too, practically dead.'

Miss Gibb perches on the bed beside me. 'Men don't have uteruses,' she says. 'Don't tell your mother you know that word. I am supposed to be guarding your innocence.'

'My mother taught me that word.' I sink against the pillow. It has been so long since I've seen my mother, so long that I've accustomed myself not to think of her at all, to turn away from her in my thoughts, yet as soon as I recall her to Miss Gibb — her voice, her words — she's present, as if waiting. I fall backward in my memory through years of separation that seem accidental, not deliberate, and yet impassable. The weeks spent in Amsterdam preparing for the races. A week spent on board the ship crossing the ocean. The train ride from Ontario to Montreal to Halifax. The qualifying races. Nearly two years spent training in Toronto. Two years before that at Packer's Meats. It adds up to four years gone.

Here in a strange bed, in the city of Amsterdam, I remember myself at the age of sixteen leaving by train to visit Olive and George in Toronto. I am promising to be home again in two weeks.

'Be good.'

'Yes, Mama.'

* * *

My mother.

Her first name is Jessica, her middle name Eve, her father's name Liddel.

151

I know my mother as part of the flow of the household, part of its noise and bustle, part of the air I breathe. That is how well I know her, and how mysterious to me she is and ever will be.

There is a knock on the side door after dark. Upon hearing it, one of us calls for her: 'Mother!' We politely avoid scrutinizing the supplicant too closely, leaving the girl waiting just inside the door for Mother to come. It makes sense to me that anyone in trouble, in need, would come seeking my mother, if only to hear her soothing voice, to be bathed in it, and reassured.

When I am a child, I do not know exactly what my mother does. And when I discover what it is, I enter a new room in my life. I am no longer a child.

My mother is twenty-six — old for her first marriage — when she accepts my father's proposal, which comes with four children ages nine and under, including an infant. Her own mother has recently died. Because my mother is never done, because her work stretches and spreads ahead and all around her, and even through the night, she sometimes falls asleep sitting at the supper table. Her head tilts, she begins to sigh, her breath slow and settled as she passes from wake to sleep without struggle. My father raises his hand to alert us. He retrieves a small pillow from the rocking chair, and, standing behind her, tucks it between her ear and shoulder. This is a silent task. His hands brush her temples for a fraction longer than is necessary for the job.

Her breathing is regular and sound. She is relaxed, at peace.

My father resumes sitting and eating.

If this happens before dessert, Olive or Cora dish it out instead, and we eat and talk as we always do. It is quite impossible to disturb Mother, and in any case, she will wake within the half hour, and rise and go about her chores as if she's never been away. She says she can hear what we're saying, the whole time, woven into a kind of dream.

It is not fashionable to sift through one's dreams to hunt for clues, but my mother does. She is fascinated by animals that enter a dream, and by people who shape-shift and become strangers, or strangers who shape-shift to become familiar.

She speaks freely, if infrequently. I know that I can ask her about anything.

'The mind is powerful strange,' I can hear her saying. 'Powerful, powerful strange.'

This is before she changes.

I am remembering her as she was when I was a child. I try to keep her there. I want to keep her as she was, before I left home — which I believe, when I am eleven, that I will never do. I still believe this when I am twelve, when I am thirteen, when I am fourteen.

George has written to invite me to come visit him in the city, and I am showing her the letter, just a little bit afraid, and she asks, *What do you think about this, Aggie?* And I say, *I would never go, I would never leave you, Mother.*

I am insisting, adamantly, in the kitchen, and she folds the letter and pulls me into her warmth. She smells musky, perhaps a bit unbathed, and she smells of the lavender which she keeps crumbled in drawers around the house. We will all smell of lavender, so long as we live in our mother's house.

You may wish to go, my mother says. Someday.

No.

And if you go, you may always come home again, no matter what happens, my mother says, I promise.

★ ★ ★

In a hot curtained room in Amsterdam, that is the mother I make up in my mind. I make her up and seek her out, suddenly weak with missing her, sick for *before*, though before what, I do not know. I can't go far enough back in my memory to find the perfect resting place.

'You must have an unusual mother,' Miss Gibb says.

I nod. I can't tell Miss Gibb more, specifically. There is too much to tell, and none of it belongs in this room.

Miss Gibb picks up my hand and strokes the knuckles soothingly. 'A girl who has an understanding mother is a fortunate girl. Perhaps I could stand in for your mother, just for now.'

I remove my hand from hers, suddenly wary.

How I like Miss Alexandrine Gibb, how I

admire her. She is far and away the most independent woman I have ever met. She writes newspaper articles for the *Toronto Daily Star*, and she is our manager, in charge of the girls on the Canadian Olympic team. She is unmarried, perhaps fifteen years my senior, her hair sleek and black in a tightly wound bun, the lines of her fitted suits crisp and sharp, and such dramatic hats. I have never seen Miss Gibb out of sorts or uneasy, but I have seen her cause others to become out of sorts and uneasy. I don't want to be her, exactly, but I study her, curious to locate the source of her power.

'I think I know why you're hiding away,' she says in a low, steady voice. She is making me uneasy. My eyes flit away from hers, but only for a moment. Somehow she draws my gaze to hers. I read sympathy there, but it is cool, appraising, purposeful.

'You're well enough, aren't you, dear? It's just that you're afraid to face someone — you think you have put your friendship in jeopardy. I suspect you believe you oughtn't to have won that race. Now, I'm not going to tell you what to do, but I'm warning you to be careful. If you believe something, it will be so. Don't make it so. Here in this city are people who want to take your photograph and write about you, and back home in Canada are people watching to see what you will do with yourself, now that you are a Golden Girl, as they say.

'If I were you,' says Miss Gibb, and she takes my hand again and squeezes, powerfully, inducing pain, 'I would put the race behind you.

155

Do not think of it. Do not reflect on it. Your friend has run her own races. You owe her nothing.'

'You mean — Glad?' I whisper.

She nods but doesn't say anything further, gazing at me. It's her silence that pulls it out of me — this is a good trick to learn, as a reporter. You can ask all the questions you like, but it's the awkward pause, perfectly timed, that will net the biggest fish.

'Didn't you see the race?' I blurt and blunder.

'It wasn't mine. I was going to lose.'

'But you didn't, did you?' she asks, examining me intently.

I shake my head, flooded with shame, avoiding her eyes.

'Then you won, fair and square.'

But I didn't, I think.

I look at Miss Alexandrine Gibb, and she says, 'You won and she lost. She's been more than graceful in defeat. It's your turn to be graceful in victory.'

★ ★ ★

It is thanks to Miss Gibb that I'm here in the stands to cheer when our Canadian girls win silver in the 100-metre relay. It is thanks to Miss Gibb that I'm screaming so fervently that the next day I'll wake up with a sore throat. Glad runs the third leg, Ernestine the anchor. There are no errors. I jump from the stands, dash onto the field, barge into the crowd to greet Glad with a hug. I swing her into the air off her feet — she's so tiny.

156

'We've matching medals, now, Aggie,' Glad says, and I believe she means it.

I hold this moment, shining, in my memory, when all things are equal between me and Glad, when our rivalry on the track is scratched out by friendship, or so it seems, in the great balance of the world. When I love Glad and Glad — yes, I'll say it because I believe it, despite everything to come — loves me.

11

House

The girl won't stop pushing me up the lane, awfully determined she is to deliver me here. The house is hidden; not for long. My hands begin to knot themselves together.

'Mrs. Smart, we're taking you home, like you wanted. Remember?'

This is what I wanted? I remember like I am washing down a raging river and on the banks the past is standing, waving to me, trees bending in the wind. But I can't see everything, not all at once like this, and it isn't lined up in order, and it flashes past as I flail.

The wheels cease turning.

We've arrived, or so the girl says: 'This is where your house used to be, Mrs. Smart. But it's all gone.' She sounds like someone affecting to sound sad, who has never been dealt a blow of real grief. That may not be fair. It may only be that she is a bad actress and being filmed turns her stiff and implausible. I can sympathize, having been a lousy actress myself. As if to prove it, my hands fly to my face, smack-dab over my mouth. The boy's camera will recognize the posture: melodramatic disbelief.

But I do believe, and I see, and she is wrong, quite wrong. The house is not gone.

It is smaller, I'll allow, without its walls and its

158

roof, stripped of its dimensions. It is not what it was, but neither am I.

Everything stands back from this place, even the trees, their limbs damaged, trunks blackened — or do I only imagine it. The stones are smeared with black. A sunken pit. A small ruin. The ashes long since blown away.

'I did this,' I mumble.

'They said she didn't suffer — your sister, I mean. They said it wasn't your fault.'

Whoever they are.

I consider the parallels: my body like the body of the house, slumped and hollowed out, an apparent ruin. Everything stands apart from it, even this girl; especially her. I can't explain why this should cause me such a deep ache. A long slow leak of sadness spilling between my ribs.

I gather the clues, apparent and invisible, one by one. This girl and her brother do not know what it means to suffer if they think my sister — Cora — did not. They do not recognize culpability if they think I am innocent. They would like the world to bend to their wishes, to absolve them, and they think I need the same things too, but they know nothing about how to comfort a body.

No, nor do I. It must not have been what we were put on the earth to do.

★ ★ ★

After Fannie dies.

After George leaves home.

The house closes in on those of us who remain

159

— Mother, Father, Olive, Cora, me — my father's second family, whole and complete. But we do not feel whole or complete because we belong, also, to the first family, to the stories buried in the graveyard, and to our sisters and brothers from the first mother. Maybe the house tries too hard to keep us. Maybe it is hoping for the past to curl around and return us to the fortune it has been built to hold.

It is a magnificent house. Sometimes I walk around it in my dreams. Sometimes I am wide-awake, and can see everything as it is, as if I am eleven years old. Yet even at eleven, the house cannot hold me, no matter how it tries. I am walking around it only to walk away.

Each section of the house has its own season.

The sun's heat beats on the board-and-batten summer kitchen, on my mother's flourishing herb garden.

But already it is shadier as I pass the dining room. Sunlight never penetrates this far, and I shiver, an absence of grass beneath heavy pines, a soft carpet of fallen brown needles under my bare feet.

Here is the Granny Room with its peaked tin roof, a den or nest, sheltered by banks of blown snow.

It is spring the moment I come to the back of the house. I hurry through a grove of fragrant lilacs, the path to the vegetable garden beaten down in fresh, muddy grass. Oh, I am restless. Just past the laundry line is an orchard of pear trees and apple trees in fragile bloom, and beyond that, a lane that leads to the field on the

160

western side of our land. I am leaving the house behind, cutting through the orchard to the wide back lane, which slopes toward the western field. Black walnut trees on either side. I pass like the ghost I am, unnoticed.

Here is the field's edge.

I can see Edith and Carson's back lane, although theirs is exposed to the sun, parched and bare, and leads to the stinking manure pile behind their barn. I might cross the field to visit. Or I might not.

If I am eleven, Little Robbie must be five, and his affection grows wilder, more demanding with each passing year. He leaps on me, wraps his arms and legs around me, squeezes my cheeks with his hands, with a frantic need to touch and be touched. I can see him now. I am leaning down so that our faces are very near, and he is pressing my cheeks between his hands, hard.

Stop! Little Robbie, I don't like that, it hurts!

But he can't stop. He can't let go, when he's got something to hold. His eyes are shining, fanatical, and he's making a strange noise in his throat, almost a growl.

So I don't cross the field to visit Little Robbie.

Instead, I continue on to the backwoods, stepping off the dusky trail to push a path through tangled undergrowth. I play that I am lost; why does this please me so, to imagine slipping out of reach? I am startled, then, to hear footsteps scuffing along the trail I consider all mine.

I dart farther into the brush, but I stop, hold my breath and crouch down, wait to see who is coming.

161

Edith?

She hurries with her head tilted at an angle. No, her gait is quicker than hurry. Edith is running, her skirt lifted, her breath harsh. I follow, but she stops where the trail ends at the edge of our back field, out behind the barn. I wait while she waits, wondering if she will see me or hear me, holding my breath, watching her. But the only disturbance is in her mind and she turns, her face blank, eyes stark and inward. She retraces her steps away from my hiding place.

I listen for the dull sound of her feet in their laced black boots coming this way again, but she is gone to wherever she is going.

This could belong to a dream, or it could be a story I've made up to tell myself, though I can't think why it should be. Why shouldn't it be true? Why shouldn't Edith run, even if she only travels home the way she came, her hair damp and stuck to the nape of her neck?

My mother's cures aren't working. Edith has only Little Robbie, and what will become of him, his clawing grip, the way he pushes on me even while squeezing, like he wants to break us both? What of him, grown to the size of a man, with that growl in his throat, those shining eyes? He will make a fine killer, fighting for his country in another war.

And what of her, Edith, aimless, fasting and counting days and swallowing tinctures, bounded by these trees and fields? And what of me? And what of this house? Of all we can't hold, and won't, and didn't, and couldn't. In my dreams, I am walking around the house, through its seasons

162

and weathers and magnificence. I walk until I'm out of sight. And then the house is gone.

MILLER, ROBERT C. Born January 7, 1915, New Arran, Ontario, died June 3, 1943 in Italy, aged 28 years. The son of Edith and Carson Miller, Corporal Miller served with the Ontario Regiment. 'Little' Robbie's outstanding bravery in battle was remarked upon by his fellow servicemen and this gives comfort to his parents, sister, and extended family, who survive him.

★ ★ ★

I see the house: alight and disintegrating, its shape visible as a darkness behind the flame. It looks like a model cut from cardboard and set aflame. A paper house — stone and masonry and plaster and lathe turned to paper. Crumpling.

I should be watching Cora, so clumsy, so stiffened with arthritis I have to carry her to the toilet, though her weight is almost too heavy for my own weakened arms, her legs dragging on the floor; so cruel too. We hardly speak without visiting her litany of accusations, which I will not repeat. She tells the truth, does Cora, but it isn't a truth we need to drag between us till death do us part.

I don't know who is to blame. It tires me to consider it. What does it matter?

I say to her, *I'll be off for my run, then,* and she says, *Go on, begone with ye,* and I say, *You're tucked and cozy, so you are,* and she says, *Like a baby, poor baby, poor soul*, and I say, *I'll be back*, and she says, *Don't leave me*, and I say, *I'm sorry*, and she says, *You should be*, and I say, *Here's your tea then*, and she says, *You should be sorry shouldn't you shouldn't you*, and I bend to tie my shoelaces. I want to go and I will go even knowing I should stay here with her, so clumsy, so angry, so stuck.

Cora, everything that has happened in your life up to this moment has been of your own damn choosing.

But I don't say it. I'll not say it. Is it kindness or cowardice? Am I a good woman, or do I fear confrontation? (No, I don't fear it. I dislike it. I find it distasteful. I've seen its harm and how its harm can't be undone.) I don't say what I'm thinking, not to Cora, not to most, not to anyone. On this morning, I dress myself in jogging trousers worn thin with use, and cap my head with a woollen toque, turning away from my sister, grateful that I can remove myself from the stale warmth of our shared room, with its patched and greasy walls, its blackened ceiling, its blankets and slippers and cups stained with half-drunk tea.

The air outdoors will be clean, it will wash me clean. If only I could drag Cora outside from time to time. It's like she's nesting in her chair in a ragged heap of blankets that she picks at and plucks at with her bird claws. She needs to breathe. She can't think straight in our smothering room — I can't think straight in here either, my thoughts scrambling, racing to escape.

I've been seeing a lot of Fannie in the walls,

but when I report this fact to Cora, she tells me I'm a crazy old lady. Yes, I agree, *we're two crazy old ladies. But Fannie's still a girl, and she'll watch over you while I'm out. Just look for her, Cora, do it for me. If you need anything, just tell Fannie.*

Cora doesn't like to hear of Fannie.

I heard Fannie was a bad woman, says Cora. *Now, now. Don't go repeating gossip,* I say, and Cora says, *I'm glad she's gone.* But that last is the sickness talking. Cora is losing herself, moment by moment, in each breath that much less herself than in the breath before. I wonder sometimes whether the sickness is stripping away a veneer to reveal her true and exposed under-self, that voice in the head that all of us have, that we none of us would want to share. Is that the true self?

I told Carson it wasn't me, but Edith won't believe it, she declares. *I'm not someone who speaks ill of her own kin. I'll tell him again, next time I see him. I'll go over there on purpose just to tell him.*

That is when I crouch, creaking and aching, and tie my laces with fingers too stiff, knuckles too swollen to bend. It takes me a good long while to pull and push the soft laces into tidy bows, my head pounding as the blood rushes to it, and Cora on and on all the while. *It wasn't me, you know. Everyone's speaking of it in the town. And Edith blames me. Mother blames me too. So do you.*

I don't, I say. *Nobody blames you for anything, Cora.*

It was all your fault. We were happy till —

Cora, I say, *everyone's dead. Mother's dead.*

165

Edith's dead. Carson's dead.

I can be cruel too.

She bursts out it was Fannie killed Carson, and I say no, and she says then it was Edith, but no, I remind her, it was Carson's own bloody heart. Blocked-up arteries, years of bacon and butter sandwiches, stopped up and keeled over, gone. And Edith outlived him by two decades, sickly through the years and plagued with miseries till the very end, when some ailment finally did as promised and killed her.

Remember? I tell Cora, knowing she doesn't. I suppose it comes as a shock every time. I suppose that should make me kinder in the telling. I suppose I could spare her, rather than breaking the bad news over and over again.

I embroider the stories, each time told with different details. *We didn't go to Carson's funeral, out of respect for Edith's wishes. She didn't want us there, she sent one of Carson's cousins to take Father to the service. I came home to stay that weekend — remember? We never had such fun — we played cards, and Father joined in when the cousin brought him home again. He remembered the rules to 'Pit.' He couldn't tell us one useful detail from the afternoon, except he hadn't liked the pickle sandwiches. 'Pickle sandwiches?' We laughed, you and I. 'What on God's green earth is a pickle sandwich?'*

I don't add that the news of Carson's death did not affect me greatly at the time. It does not affect me greatly now. I was never enamoured of the man. He had a soft face, pouting lips, a man who thought highly of himself in the mirror, and honed his skills as a flirt, even practicing on a young girl like me: 'Aggie, those big blue eyes could send a fellow the wrong message.' A man likely to suffer when his hair began falling out. No, I was not an admirer.

Edith's funeral, now that was different. I stop.

That was different, yes, agrees Cora.

Do you remember? I ask her.

Don't I?

The way she says it, so hesitantly, like she's touching her tongue to a sensitive tooth, testing it for pain, assures me she's lost track of the memory just as soon as it was found.

Well it wasn't much of a funeral, I say, although I wasn't there to see it. Maybe Cora doesn't remember that, either. *She was an old woman. She kept to herself. She had few friends.*

Like us, says Cora.

Just when I think nothing stays in that head of hers, she goes and surprises me.

And then she's lost again, looking me up and down like she's seeing me brand-new all over again. *What are you dressed up like that for? Leaving me again? Run, run, as fast as you can, you can't catch me, I'm Aganetha Smart.*

I laugh. I'm wrestling with the laces and my back is pinched with pain.

She is like Father was, at the end, emptied of all but the most persistent fragments of original self. Like I may be too, losing myself without even knowing it. I wonder: what is the meaning of what's left behind? I don't think, not really, that what's left behind is the true self revealed. I am not that cruel. It seems instead an accidental picture of a life, and true to the way life is lived — not as we may wish it to be lived, but as it insists on being lived.

A man like my father can vanish almost entirely while he wanders the house and the fields, handling objects as if they are artifacts from an impenetrably foreign world, stumbling, searching for what's been taken from him. I remember that Cora told me it was a relief when Father fell and broke his hip, and could no longer stray. I was living in the city and I thought her cruel beyond all measure. I stayed away, myself. And now I wonder how she managed, the two of them, alone here. The simplest actions painful, laboured rituals of baroque effort. To eat. To toilet. To bathe.

To sleep. No peace.

The shoes are laced, at last. I have a dozen pairs, all as worn as me, simple rubber soles and canvas uppers, splitting along the seams. But when could I get to the city to buy another pair — and how? Our groceries come delivered from the store in town. We have no telephone, so I run to the store to put in our order and run home again, every other week, more or less the same items. Not on this day. On this day, I will travel the woods and the fields. I've seen children playing in the woods, and it cheers me. I've been hearing their shouts, seeing evidence of forts built and wrecked and rebuilt just off the path, jumbles of sticks and rotten leaves pushed into piles that make sense, if you recognize in them a plan larger and more elaborate than can be seen by the eye alone.

Someone's living in Edith's house these past few years. I saw a large metal rubbish bin out back for a while, and thought maybe they'd tear the place down, but that never happened. It must have been three summers ago, a woman brought over a coffee cake, but Cora sent her packing, so she said; I was off running at the time, and have no evidence whatsoever of the exchange. I've seen a grey car in the drive, and lights shining out of the windows after dusk, shedding puddles of orange and blue light. We don't need anyone's coffee cake. Cora and I have got a recipe we favour, old as the hills, to make for ourselves, if we care to. I leave the neighbours be, whoever they are. None of my business, not anymore.

Go ahead, go on, leave me like always, here, alone!

Do I answer my sister? I wish it so. I may, instead, go quietly, part without a word, without protest, in silence, as is my habit — only afterward wishing a kindness from my mouth.

I'm away.

Breathing in, breathing out. Ninety-five years of age and running yet. I call it running — it is what's left of running. My pace shuffles, my gait as stiff as my joints, my breath thin, whispered. Yet I run and run until my chest warms and my lungs warm and I can feel my lips peeling into a smile. The ground is not yet hard.

I hear the crunch of leaves on the path. I see fallen colour over a darker mulch, a light wind picking up and moving the tops of the trees. I am running. I remember this.

169

How can I forget? I will not run again.

On this last run, this last day of this life that feels like it might go on and on forever, I smell smoke from an autumn fire. I tell myself it is the good scent of humble chimney smoke, or that it arises from a burning leaf pile, but I think perhaps I am worried, just a little bit, that the scent is too pungent for either of these.

I run out of the woods and past the row of pines along our back field, their branches thinned by age. I run past the empty lighthouse that towers over the pond, and I avert my eyes, as I always do. The scent of smoke comes sharp and acrid, it flowers in the crispness of rattling weeds. Still, I can see nothing until coming around to where the barn used to stand whole and tall, like a ship in the great wide field. Parts of the barn remain. Skeleton. Bones. Cavernous underbelly.

And I see as if I've seen it already, as if it is a dream I've dreamed before, the mind striving to make sense of the insensible.

There is the great house, down the little slope: black plumes of smoke rising, choking. I am running. 'Cora, Cora, Cora!' I am inside the smoke, throwing open the side door, stumbling into the kitchen where I am blasted backward by a wall of heat. I am staggered, staggering. I cannot believe what is happening, nor what I'm losing, I can't believe that our lives together are coming to a close, and in this way. I can't believe the evidence of my blistered palms.

I am turning circles in the lane, making a noise in my throat that hurts, later.

I am running the shorn front field to Edith and Carson's, searching for their names, struggling to call for them, confused, now. Time telescopes. Where has everyone gone?

Near Edith and Carson's bare lane, a big black farm dog lopes up to me, challenges me at field's edge, barking and barking, hackles high, head angled oddly over outstretched paws, as if prepared to leap for my throat.

I lose the ability to calculate my own age. Suddenly, I become so very old, as if age is an extremity I've been searching for, as if I've scaled its heights, stumbled upon its limits. I stare down at the dog, down at my soft pants and sweatshirt hanging loose around scaly, shrinking limbs, rickety and frail.

I don't know the woman who opens Edith's door.

She hollers to call off the dog. I try to explain, to ask for help, but my throat is raw and I can find no words. The woman sees the rolling smoke behind me, rolling into the thin blue sky, blackening and spreading across the afternoon.

She waves me closer, frantically, to come, come into her house. The yard is little changed and now is not the moment to express curiosity, but I can't help looking. A child's plastic picnic table is tipped over in the wind, a scattering of scraggly spruce bushes sprouts around the cracked stone foundation where nothing ever agreed to grow without complaint. Maybe it was always in the soil, this infertility, this refusal to thrive; maybe it was nothing to do with poor Edith after all.

I am not to call her poor Edith, not ever. I hear my mother's mighty tone.

'Come in, please,' the woman calls me, the stranger on Edith's doorstep.

I'm chilled, shaking, but I refuse to enter. I haven't stepped inside that house since Edith carried her lovely daughter — such a big, bonnie girl, already talking — through the door, and left me standing in the yard, as I stand now, feeling then as now frail and spent and bewildered, calling after them.

Am I never to visit, then? Am I never to say hello, never to talk, never to love you and yours, Edith? Never?

I turn away.

Against the wind, now, fighting, I move out of the yard and across the field, dragging a terrible weight behind me, so heavy I pause and look around to see what's there, but it's nothing that can be seen. I'm chilled through. I drag myself all the way across the field, up the lane, stopped by the heat. This is where I stand to watch the burning of my family's house. This is where I hear the smash of windows breaking, witness the sudden caving of the roof, the retreat of the men who have arrived with hoses hooked to a tanker truck, sparks cascading. Heat like a vicious sun, like my face might suffer a sunburn. A crinkling silver emergency blanket thrown over my shoulders. A ride to the hospital rocking in the rear of an ambulance. My sister's name, saying it.

Can we notify your next of kin?

There is no one, just her. We lived alone. She

172

died alone. I should have cleaned the chimney. I should have blown out the candles and the lamps. No, the house was never wired for electricity. No, we have no telephone. I left a pot of soup simmering on the stove for our suppers, nine days old, pease porridge hot, pease porridge cold.

SMART, CORA. Suddenly, in her ninety-eighth year, at the home of her birth, New Arran, Ontario. Respected daughter of Robert and Jessica Smart. Affectionate sister of Olive and Aganetha, and half-sister to eight. Predeceased by all but Aganetha. A faithful nurse to many, she will be remembered. *Think not of the coming night, but of the days we shared.*

12

Homecoming

Voices drift around me. This is how memory works. I could be looking intently at the tiniest detail and not realize it, losing sense of the larger landscape in which the detail rests.

'Remember when we tried to build a fort out of these scraps? We were always building forts.' The young man digs around in the debris. 'Remember when I was babysitting you, and you cut your hand on a nail and it was bleeding, and I wrapped it up in my shirt. I paid you two dollars not to tell Mom, and I threw out the shirt because I couldn't figure how to get out the blood. Like it was a crime. We worked on that fort the whole summer. Bet it's still here.'

'Two dollars!' The girl laughs. 'I kind of remember that. Not really.'

'We came over here all the time. Looking for treasure.'

'Did we find any?'

Rustling noises. 'I think the fort was over here.'

'What do you think she remembers — Mrs. Smart?'

'She's clear, sometimes.'

'Don't you feel sorry for her, Max?'

'Why should I?'

'She was this amazing runner, amazing — and

look at her now. I can't even imagine.'

Slowly I open myself to her, to him, I let them leak through my skin, her pity and her need, his camera lens, their youth.

I've known my body well enough to recognize its limits, and this chair is only the most recent diminishment in a long descending line. You never run again like you run as a child: without pain. Later, you reach a point at which you've run the fastest you will ever run — the pinnacle that goes unrecognized at the time. I remember whispering the word 'indestructible' as I ran or as I approached a great grief, but I only chanted it because I knew I wasn't. I never ran because I was strong, if you see what I'm saying. It wasn't strength that made me a runner, it was the desire to be strong.

I ran for courage. Still do, if only in my mind. *Why do you run?*

'Did she say something? Mrs. Smart?'

'Why do you run?' I pronounce each word as if it were standing by itself.

'She's talking to you, Kaley.'

The sunlight is particularly piercing and cold.

'Why do I run?'

'Excellent question, Mrs. Smart!' The young man and his camera approve. 'Why do you run, Kaley?'

The girl is struck silent.

'I don't know,' she says slowly.

'Are you trying to run away from something?' her brother asks, genuinely curious.

'I don't think so.' Very slowly.

'Then you're running toward something?'

175

'Well, obviously, I've got goals. I want to break the Canadian women's marathon record. I want to make the Olympic team. Obviously. But — ' She stops altogether. She looks at the camera, then at me. 'I think I would run even if I knew I would never win another race again. It's weird. I can't explain it. It's like something I can't turn off.'

'Good girl,' I say. I reach for her hand — there, I've got it — and I squeeze until she squeezes back. I would like to think she is not afraid of me right now. I would like to think, also, that she does not pity me.

The girl feels me shivering: 'She's cold.'

Well, so much for that.

'This is a nice frame,' says Max, the stubby lens between his face and ours. 'Let's get one quick shot. Follow your script, Kales — the opening.'

The girl inhales deeply, sighs it out, and launches into her lines. 'My name is Kaley' — her voice gone declarative and unnatural — 'and this is my story. Let me introduce you to my inspiration, Aganetha Smart.'

Max gives her a silent thumbs-up.

'You might not guess it from looking at her,' she continues stiffly, doggedly, 'but Aganetha Smart was once the most famous woman runner in Canada. Weren't you, Mrs. Smart?'

The burying past tense. I've never liked it. My teeth are clamped and I won't reply.

'How did it feel to win gold, Mrs. Smart? I want to know.' Her voice goes breathy and anxious — genuine — greedy, almost. This is not an idle question, and perhaps, I think, off-script.

But I can't answer the girl's question, much as I'd like to. The details I remember most clearly stand apart from my own emotions, as if severed from feeling altogether: the sounds of voices ricocheting, and suddenly a quick clear cast of words in my ear, in Glad's laughing tones: *You won! You did it! I knew that you could!* And then her voice is gone, and I can't reproduce it nor hear what comes next, or came before, and the truth is I can't set straight whether that happened, or whether it's a story I've told myself until it might well have happened — but I hear it happening. I hear and almost see a buzz of sound and the quick focus in, the clarity of her joy. But not my own.

I shake my head and reverse back inside myself.

'She's really shivering, Max.'

'Good enough. Let's go.'

★ ★ ★

Reports have it that Miss Aganetha Smart, age twenty, of New Arran, Ontario, is the most photographed girl at these Olympic Games. With her golden hair and flawless skin, she cannot help but attract notice wherever she goes. As the Canadian team prepared to board ship for the journey home, Miss Smart seemed almost to be blinded by a series of flashbulbs, and her name was shouted repeatedly by members of the foreign press. Accompanied by the team's manager, Miss Alexandrine Gibb, Miss Smart never faltered. She smiled and

posed naturally for photographs.
   Could a future in film be far off?
   *We only wonder: will Miss Smart prove
too tall for Hollywood's leading men?*

★   ★   ★

The most interesting story of my life it is not. It is quite ordinary, really. And yet it is the story that makes me swoon, forever after. I fall into it in dreams — no, I fall into him. In dreams, he is unchanged, as am I. Or, we are older, but not aged. We remain ourselves. We find each other and we grin, *Oh, it's you, you've come again.* How happy we are. We meet clean and unformed, at the beginning of our story, without pasts, our lives as they happened to us vanished. Dreams are lovely for this.

But in dreams we never quite manage to come together. If we do, if our lips meet or we find ourselves climbing with ravenous hunger into some makeshift bed, we are interrupted, parted by a silly detail that intrudes, a task that must be completed, another woman walking into the room, or, occasionally, by shame. We are caught and found out by our futures, our original intentions, our desire, dissipating into nothingness.

I wake and insist on returning to the best part. To before.

But a dream will not be commanded, no more than life will.

I think I must want to keep us here, forever in a state of meeting. I want to preserve the surprise of being desired, and not knowing why, the

178

mystery of being wanted and of wanting, the tangle of possibility — suspended on the verge of being fulfilled. I don't want to fall through to the other side. I don't want the mystery to collapse. I want not to know anything.

I want us to meet, forever, as we were, and never after that.

I am twenty years old and Johnny is twenty-two. He makes his living as an automobile mechanic. He would like to become a doctor, like his father was before dying an early and unlucky death — blood poisoning. And Johnny is an athlete. If he'd have won, he says, he would have found a way to use his fame to pay for school. As it is, he'll have to work his way there by old-fashioned means: hard labour and careful saving. His father is dead, and his mother lives on the Prairies with his younger brothers and sisters. There are grandparents too. Johnny sends money home.

We meet on board the ship from Europe to Canada, or rather, the ship is where we find each other; we are not then meeting for the first time. I know who he is — the hurdler who stumbled over the final jump and fell out of the medals — and he knows who I am — everyone does. We belong to a select group: Canada's 1928 Olympic team, with its large contingent of young men, and much smaller, special group of girls.

'We can have our pick,' one of the girls says — the young swimmer who failed to get through to the finals.

'Aw, who needs 'em,' says Glad.

I quietly agree with Glad. I am thinking myself

quite sophisticated. I don't need a boy, and besides, we girls are chaperoned up to our ears. Picture this: nearly seventy young people in top physical form confined on board a ship for a little more than a week. Some of us have won and many more have lost. Our fitness is a useless energy we can't help but trail around. We are firecrackers crying for a match. We run morning laps around the decks in good weather, and a large room has been set aside for calisthenics and stretching and, in the evenings after supper, a whole lot of foolishness that comes awfully close to dancing.

But if ever a girl gets too intimate with a boy, here is Miss Alexandrine Gibb shouldering in between, ticktocking her forefinger.

Glad earns the most ticktocks, but it is only because the boys like her so — like one of their own. She could have any boy she wants, I think, and it's because she seems not to want or need any of them. She is in no danger of being discovered in a broom closet kissing a discus thrower, as happens to the young swimmer. That isn't Glad, not at all. If she throws her arm around a boy, it's to say, *Hey, pal*. That's all. Hey. And the boy knows it too.

I wish, in this way, to be like Glad.

But I'm not like her. It isn't just owing to my height, or my long golden hair, my angularity, my lips that look to have been stained red though I never paint them. It is the way I hold myself apart. I watch, I observe. When approached by an interested party, I stiffen as if offended or, worse, threatened: 'What do you want?'

180

Johnny doesn't approach. His manners are not like the other boys'. Like me, he stands stiffly, holding himself apart. He is focused on maintaining his strength and speed, as if he hasn't already raced and lost. He does not enter into the frothy atmosphere in which we sail across the ocean blue.

We find each other on deck.

I am running slow laps in the early afternoon, breathing the sea air, feeling the chilly spray on my face. I have a terror of falling overboard, and yet I can't bear to lie in my bunk paging through magazines, any more than I can bear to laze around gossiping with the girls. Johnny falls in beside me. He doesn't say a word. I suppose I appreciate that. For a few rounds we keep our thoughts to ourselves, and it is only the sound of breath that speaks. I am running beside a boy very nearly my own age, something I have not done since my school years.

But when I was near those boys, it was not the same.

Up until this moment, I've imagined that I understood romance, a state to be scorned. I understood love, a curse, of sorts, that binds women to men, weakens them. But as we run together, Johnny and me, I forget all of that. My imagination has failed me: it never took into account the flesh and blood awakening of desire.

Johnny is as tall as me, slender but sleekly muscled. I can feel myself appraising him as we jog, and not coolly — with rising tension. It is as if we're protected inside a bubble that contains only the two of us, with room for nothing else. I

181

am suddenly and acutely attuned to the smallest particulars of his person: his dark blue eyes, dark curling hair, his long jaw. Still, we haven't spoken a word. As if we are of one mind, we slow in tandem, come to a stop. We do not look around to see whether or not we are alone. We know we are alone. Our hands graze each other's, gravely. Behind him, a red door, shut. I see his eyes, their kindness, their surprise.

I like you, he says.

No boy has ever said this to me. The only words I can think to describe what I'm feeling are ridiculous as a trembling swoon, but swoon it is, and trembling, flushing, quickening.

The roar of the engines. His hand on my cheek, over my ear, our mouths in silence meeting. My hands covering his eyes, as if I can't bear to have him see my desire.

We kiss and pull away, kiss and break apart, and kiss again, the sounds of the ocean and the engines roaring around us. He doesn't need to ask me to be his girl, because it's all settled there against the red door. I'm his girl. (Aren't I? I'm too shy and too proud to ask, too uncalculating, too satisfied on evidence alone. The way he kisses me is proof enough. The way he came looking for me, in particular. The way he holds my hand, later, when we walk in the parade down Yonge Street, the air over our heads thick with ticker tape. The way he brushes the bits of shredded paper from my hair, his hands on my temples as gently as my father's on my mother's. I remember. And I think I know enough to be sure.)

It is an ordinary story. A very ordinary story.

But I don't care. It's mine.
It's all I've got.

A crowd of one hundred thousand cheered as our Canadian Olympic girls were welcomed back to Toronto with a tickertape parade. Marching and smiling and waving to their fellow citizens, the girls looked shy and sweet, clutching bouquets of flowers given them by adoring admirers.

There can be no doubt that the prettiest girl of them all is New Arran, Ontario's, own Miss Aganetha Smart, age twenty. But sorry, boys, it may already be too late! Rumour has it that Miss Smart has become engaged to one Johnny Tracy. Yes, the one and the same! Mr. Tracy represented Canada in the hurdles, and although he failed to medal, it appears he may have caught himself another prize.

★ ★ ★

I do think, briefly, that I shall never have to work in a factory again. I take a leave of absence from my bookkeeping job at Rosebud Confectionary. Rosebud pays me, instead — oh glory, oh thrill! — to pose with a box of their gold-dusted chocolates. I do think, briefly, that I shall never again have to do work that I do not find amusing. I am in love with being loved. Here is my photograph in the newspaper on the fold-out 'Society Page.' Here I am arm in arm with Johnny, smiling for the camera.

Here I am, coming home, again. A visit to the farm seems easy, suddenly. I'll just leap over the years that separate us. I will go home.

Olive and I take the train. It seems perfect. Return as I left, complete the circle. Am I even thinking in such terms? Well. I suppose not. I suppose I think it's perfect because I'm so sweetly satisfied with myself. I suppose I think I've become someone quite different, a new and improved Aganetha Smart.

On the train, we eat green grapes and drink tea with milk, dipping crumbling cookies into the lukewarm liquid in the fancy dining car with the red swag curtains.

We are greeted at the station by a small crowd of cheering schoolchildren. The local newspaper has announced my visit in advance. Upon stepping off at the small station in New Arran, I am surrounded. I lead the troupe off the platform and around to the front of the station where more curious onlookers have gathered. I can sense my parents and sisters standing apart from me, watching me move among the children, signing autograph books. I can sense my hair keeping its sharp shape around my face, held in place by a waxy substance which I've carefully worked into the strands before combing it to perfection. But I haven't changed so very much: I wear no makeup, no adornment save for the medal around my neck.

People like to pick up the medal and hold it in their hands, to feel the weight. It seems a strangely intimate gesture. It ties me to a stranger for a brief moment, as if I belong to them, as if I am their pet, their possession.

I do not know what to do with the love and admiration of strangers. I mistake it for something personal. I believe that it is I who am loved and admired, rather than the girl in the newspaper photos. I don't understand, yet, that I'm not really that Aganetha. That no one is. That she is a simple and finished idea to whom everyone can relate. She has no edges, no catches.

The children for whom I sign autographs mistake me for being her, and no blame to them — I am her, I guess, just for now, smiling and waving, expectant of welcome, sweet as a lily, polished as glass.

'You're wearing that well, Aganetha,' my mother says, offering me a cup of tea as we stand in the kitchen at the farm. She reaches out to touch the medal, and I flinch, which surprises us both.

'Of course, you must,' I say quickly, and pull the medal over my head, holding it out to her by the ribbon.

She sets the teacup on the countertop, which has been painted white. All the cupboards in the kitchen are now painted white, clean as bone.

I open a cupboard door and see on the wide double-decker lazy Susan the covered butter dish, the salt and pepper shakers, and several cut-glass dishes for serving jams or pickles or relishes. A loaf of bread wrapped in cloth looks less attractive. I spin the Susan slowly. Through the glass doors on the far side, the dining room can be seen, wavy behind the warped panes.

My mother tries to hand me the medal and the cup of tea at the same time.

I accept the cup, but not the medal. She inspects it more closely, and I watch her as I lift the china to my lips and sip. I am as tall as she is. I think of everything my mother does not know about me. Everything she never will. Yet I fail to consider everything I do not know of her. Everything I never will.

My mother holds out the medal, flat in the palm of her hand, the ribbon dangling down. I swallow the last of the tea. 'Thank you,' I say, and gather the weight into my own hand, hesitating. What to do with it? It seems wrong to wear it around the house.

'You'll be staying in the guest room with Olive?' My mother's voice lifts into a question.

'The guest room?'

'Your old room. Yours and Olive's. Cora repainted it and sewed new curtains.'

'Do you have guests often?'

'You and Olive are our guests, of course,' says Mother.

'Oh,' I say. An ache in my throat, the hollow where sadness fits. I don't really like this, not at all. We are not guests, we are daughters. But I understand that my mother is giving me something that she finds painful to offer and that she thinks I desire — she is giving me space, freedom, the ability to walk away from this place and take no responsibility for it, or for the people who live here. As if she could do such a thing. As if I could take such a thing.

I lift my small suitcase, which has been sitting

inside the door, to carry it upstairs.

'Let your father do that!'

But I just keep walking, carrying the valise through the empty main room, piled with boards and nails and the detritus of Father's latest project — what could it be now? Something involving coils of wire. I skip upstairs, taking every other step at a leap. My mother follows to the bottom of the staircase, protesting. Here is where she lets me go. It's the golden light I'm giving off. I can feel it, sending people away from me. I make people a little bit afraid, as if I weren't quite human.

'I'm a parasite,' I tell Olive, who is napping atop the clean pressed quilt in the so-called guest room, lying in a patch of sunshine.

She only half-wakes, like a cat, stretches, rolls onto her side. 'You mean, a cockroach,' she mumbles.

We last two days before escaping back to the city.

13

Young Love

'Let's go.'

The girl is wheeling me down the lane, away from the burnt house, past the treeline that separates the yard from the front field. My mother planted the pines herself when automobiles became popular and our dusty side road transformed into a byway for people from town driving out to the lake for picnics. The house was hidden from view, perfectly private. Later still, a new highway diverted traffic away from our road, and our privacy was assured, pines or no pines, but the pines stayed. They've grown enormous, thick and foreboding, their untrimmed branches sweeping the ground.

Our secrets are so old now. What have we to hide? I don't want to go. But the girl keeps rolling me down the lane. The boy opens the back door of the plain blue car, and together they load me in, like a parcel of dry goods.

'Mom's waiting,' the girl explains. 'She'll make you a cup of tea, warm you up.'

It isn't far, I see, as we drive. One field's length, no more. The same field. The field of pale green winter wheat, freshly broken through the dirt, a haze of brightness across a drab landscape.

This lane is bare and stony. We've come to a

stop outside a framed house weathered grey with age. A dog circles and circles, barking wildly.

The girl leaps out to greet the dog. Without a backward glance, she slams the car door and runs for the house, calling. 'Mom! Mom! We're here!' The dog follows and disappears. Max climbs out of the car and I see him stretching. I'm alone with my dread. I can't hang it on to anything particular, so I look around for Fannie, who isn't here. I hear thumping from behind. A slam, the car rocks down and up, once, and Max comes around to my side, awkwardly pushing the wheeled chair only partially snapped into position. He opens my door.

I say again, 'I won't go,' but he misunderstands, trying to fix the chair.

'Hang on a minute,' he says. 'Mom's a nurse. She's better at this than me.'

A tall broad-backed woman in sensible beige clothing strides through the mud, hair cropped short, like she doesn't care. I smell the scent of her as she leans in to say hello, how are you, her arms cradling me as she pulls me nearer. She smells of soap. I think of my sisters, Olive and Cora, who were not so very alike in most ways, but who both smelled of soap, and nothing more, and I am briefly lulled. I forget myself and do not fight.

'There, we're settled.'

I clamp my teeth down hard against the dread that twists inside me, squawking like a hen about to lose its head for our dinner. It's this yard, its bareness. I'm somewhere I shouldn't be, a place that wants me gone.

We bump up the porch steps backward, and I am pulled in reverse into a cramped entryway, then swung around to view the room. My eyes strain to adapt to the dimness. Papers sloping off surfaces, peeling linoleum, dinged plaster, the smell of cat. Funny how houses hold to their character, just as much as people do. Here I am. Where I'm not meant to be.

'I'm sorry, Edith,' I say with stern regret, because surely she can see I didn't choose to intrude like this; and everyone in the room stares at me.

★ ★ ★

I tell Olive I intend to look for better rooms for us. Olive says she's perfectly content in the room we've been sharing ever since I moved to Toronto.

'Well, I'm not — Mrs. Smythe doesn't like me, never has, and there's never enough food. And besides, I can afford to pay for better now!'

'Well, I can't,' says Olive.

'Olive,' I say, 'I'll pay your share too. We're sisters! After all you've done for me!'

And so it is agreed. Glad will be our third. We are three young women living freely in the great city of Toronto without the scent of a chaperone on the premises. Don't believe it when you hear that Toronto is a staid old maid of a city, that she's stuck-up and cautious and dull. She has us. She is quite the going thing.

We rent a double-storied apartment over Yonge Street with windows almost as tall as the ceilings, and a grand fireplace that fills the rooms with choking black smoke. On the bottom floor, at street level, is a butcher shop, which draws mice and rats. Johnny brings us a kitten, a male tabby that grows fluffy and fat, feeding off the premises.

We take turns cooking. Glad is the worst, a rich girl born and raised.

'What's this supposed to be?' Johnny teases her.

'Chops,' she says. 'Fresh from the butcher.'

'Chops and what?'

'Chops and chops! You don't have to eat with us, don't forget.'

'I like when Aggie cooks,' says Johnny. I've just come into the kitchen.

'So marry Aggie,' says Glad, who knows as well as I do that the newspaper reports are mistaken — Johnny and I are not officially betrothed.

'Maybe I will,' says Johnny.

'Well, why don't you, then?' says Glad, and I almost hold my breath. She says it so lightly that surely he will think it a joke, rather than a question I dare not ask for myself, though it twinges occasionally, pinging like a pulled muscle.

'Might be I'm not good enough,' says Johnny, as if I weren't right there in the room with them.

'Not good enough for Aggie, you mean? Or not good enough to marry a girl whose reputation is yours to ruin?'

'Well, what do you figure, Gladdie?' he dares her. 'Aren't I a good boy?'

191

'Aren't you? You tell us.' She turns on him with a wooden spoon, points it directly at his chest.

'Come, now,' says Johnny. 'Who says Aggie wants to get married?'

'She's standing right here. Ask her,' says Glad, her eyes sparkling. Is she enjoying this? She doesn't stop but turns the spoon on me. 'Do you want to marry him or what?'

If I were to imagine our proposal — and truth be told, I have — it would not be like this, not at all, with the pair of us badgered into an engagement by means of a greasy wooden spoon.

'I don't see what's the rush,' I say, surprised to hear my voice sound so calm against their heated ones.

'She doesn't see what's the rush,' Johnny reports to Glad, as if Glad might not have heard. 'She doesn't see what's the rush and nor do I.'

'Doesn't she?'

'No. She doesn't.'

'Sit down, all of you,' says Olive, who has been pretending not to listen. 'I've laid the table and your chops are set to burn any second now, Glad, so I'd say it's past time to eat them.'

But Glad won't be shut down cold. 'Don't you dare break our Aggie's heart.' She frowns at Johnny, but prettily. She *is* enjoying this, I think. I glimpse the whisker of a smile cross her lips, and something hurts inside of me, a new hurt, like I've got a body part I never knew about before, invented especially for the purpose of feeling this pain.

192

★ ★ ★

We are fortunate to have a back entrance. No one sees Johnny coming or going. I've shocked myself with my own casual ease given our situation, which is, I tell myself in serious talks before the mirror that hangs behind my door, a dangerous business, though we've not yet, it must be added, gotten ourselves into any kind of serious trouble.

Tonight, we're playing dominoes, legs crossed, facing each other on my neatly made bed. His fingers stretch to stroke lightly down my arms and I shiver. 'Don't make me go, back to my cold dark room,' he says.

I laugh, but uneasily. Has he already forgotten the conversation before supper, and the uncomfortable silence that followed, as we tore through Glad's offering of gristly chops?

'Maybe you should find yourself a warmer room,' I say.

'I like this one,' he says, looking around, and I blush because that wasn't what I meant to imply — I'd been speaking literally, thinking of his cramped space over the garage where he works. 'Well. It's already mine,' I say.

'Don't you care to share?'

'No,' I say, and it's the truth. 'I don't.'

Now he laughs.

'You're a funny girl, Aganetha Smart.'

'I wouldn't know, I guess,' I say, because it's hurting again, the part inside of me I've only just discovered.

'You're right, you know,' he continues,

193

seriously. 'What's the rush? I've got nothing.'

'Don't say that.' I frown. 'I've got nothing either.'

We play another game of dominoes sitting across from each other on my bed. But the dominoes fall to kissing, and we are lying atop the quilt, now rumpled, and he is heavy on me, kissing my face all over.

'Tell me something, anything,' I say, pulling his hands from where they are exploring the zipper on the back of my dress. 'And then go home.'

'I'll spend all night thinking of you,' he says.

'That's not something.'

'I miss the Prairie,' he says agreeably, distractedly. Johnny is not from here. He comes from out west, from flat fields I can't imagine, though he's tried to describe the huge prairie sky.

'The Prairie.' I'm trying to imagine it, wishing he'd go on and tell me more, but he is busy arguing with my zipper. I roll out from under him. We are the same height, though he is denser in his bones and muscles, and if it came to it, he would win a physical fight. I'm afraid he might try; no, I'm afraid I might want him to try so that I may give in to him, beneath him, one of these times.

'Tell me something else, more, please,' I say. I can hear my own breath, rapid and shallow, and feel his body lying beside mine, wired with desire.

'Too much talk.' His teeth on my collarbone.

I jump to standing, quick as a strike.

194

'Go home.' I point to the closed door, where the mirror hangs. I glance to see myself, tall, cool, hair a mess. I move to settle the loose strands into place with the flats of my palms.

He is calloused hands and a smooth jawline, dark wavy hair that he lets grow too long down his neck and over his ears. His lips have a humorous tilt that fool me to thinking he's on the verge of laughter. I do not think he would ever whistle at a woman in the street. He does not use foul language. I sense in him no bitter edge, no rotten pit at his centre eating away at his youth and determination, yet he's deeply competitive. He will get what he aims for, I'm certain.

He smells of black grease and metal beneath bought bar soap and ironed cloth. His skin tastes of salt. His eyes are ink blue. On a glance, you could mistake them for black.

I almost can't imagine knowing him better or more. What would I do with the knowledge? I am afraid that I might hurt him. That I might not love him enough. That I am playing a game whose rules I'm inventing, while he is dead serious — kiss and push away, kiss and part. He looks so clear to me, needing me from the bed, the muscles in his arms like twisted cord. He is handsome in the way that men are traditionally considered handsome, ruggedly, toughly good-looking. I am surprised whenever I see us together, passing a storefront window, reflected in the same frame. The kind of man that I've observed other women watching, even Glad.

If I send him away, will he come back tomorrow?

195

Don't be silly, Aganetha, I think, and the peculiar pain inside me stops.

And he goes.

★   ★   ★

Glad and I are taking acting classes together. She is attending for a lark — her father has money enough and the willingness to support her — but I am going because I intend to earn a living. I've made the mistake of believing what I read in the papers.

Hollywood beauty specialist thinks Olympic Golden Girl has chance in movies!
From the gruelling realities of athletic triumph to the glamourous inventions of the screen: will this be the journey undertaken by Aganetha Smart? According to Miss Aria Morrison, a beauty specialist formerly of Toronto, now of Hollywood, the choice will be of Miss Smart's making. 'Does Miss Smart love the spotlight? To that only Miss Smart can reply, but it is apparent that the spotlight loves Miss Smart,' declares Miss Morrison, who adds: 'Miss Smart is tall, slender, and agile, and there is nothing artificial about her appearance. In photographs, one can see that Miss Smart projects a special type of beauty — she is a most Canadian sort of girl — altogether fresh and new. Given Miss Smart's capacity for hard work, I predict no end of success in the pictures, should she so choose.'

I've never met Miss Aria Morrison. Can there really exist the occupation of 'beauty specialist'? I imagine Miss Morrison, beauty specialist, contacting me — through what means, exactly, I can't say — and offering her expertise. That she does not fails to discourage me. It is only October. I have only been Olympic champion for a few months, and already I have posed with a box of gold-covered chocolates; my hopes are keen.

A letter has arrived, though I choose not to show it to Johnny. I sense he will not like it. It is from Miss Alexandrine Gibb, who has been asked to contact me on behalf of a third party interested in hiring me to pose for a magazine advertisement for women's undergarments.

'I will not advise you, other than to warn you to guard your reputation closely,' she writes, requesting, also, a visit. 'How are you? Flourishing, I hope.'

The evenings are growing dark earlier and earlier.

We've fallen into a pattern, Johnny and I, of wrestling around on my bed. Tonight, the lingering smell of supper's already eaten bacon with biscuits and eggs (my turn to cook) rises to my room. His hair smells smoky. I touch his head, pull him against me, imagining his hands coming under my dress, imagining myself —

'You have to go,' I tell him urgently. We are both breathing hard. He fights only briefly to stay. I hear his rapid-fire descent down the stairs and far below, the slam of the door, which opens into a back alleyway. I wonder what he does when he goes. Does he leave me easily, jog directly home to his tiny rented room? Or does he circle the blocks in the harsh city wind, his desire uncoiling like a long rope behind him, still attached to me?

I wonder, if he catalogued his desire, pinned it to me by name, would it make it more real? Would I trust him, as I feel I should, but don't?

Slowly I rise, dizzy in the head. Slowly, smooth my hair, arrange my dress. I pull the letter from the drawer where I've hidden it, but I don't open it to read it again.

What do you want, Aggie? I ask myself in the mirror, but I don't know what I want, only that I haven't got it.

I find Glad in our main room, reading a magazine, legs crossed on a chair beside the fireplace that does not work. The ceilings in the rooms are tall, shadows thrown wide and high from the bare electrified bulb that shines above her head.

'Miss Gibb sent me this.' I show Glad the letter.

'Undergarments aren't quite Hollywood,' says Glad. She unwinds herself from the chair and strolls around the room, waving the letter thoughtfully, letting the paper brush her lips.

'Rosebud Confectionary paid me lots to pose with chocolates,' I say. 'And it was easy!'

'You're too sweet.' Glad turns and sizes me up. 'Come here. Let's play out a scene. I'll be the director, you be you.'

I approach.

'In your undergarments, please,' says Glad, adopting a directorial tone.

'Pardon me?' I stammer.

'Well how do you suppose I shall photograph you for my advertisement, dear? Undergarments, now!'

'Well I won't,' I say, but I'm hedging, hesitating. Should I? I can feel my shoulders folding protectively over my chest, a tall girl's instinctive cower.

'You're wasting my precious time. I shall rip up your contract now!' She raises the letter dramatically.

'Wait!'

'I'm waiting.'

Slowly, I straighten my spine and reach my arms behind my neck and tug at the zipper on my dress. My hands shake. A rush of strangeness washes through me. I think that I might begin to cry, or to laugh, I can't tell which. I am terrified that my sister Olive will come in from the kitchen and find us, standing like this before the fireplace that doesn't work, in the harsh light cast by bare bulbs that stick out of the wall and toss our shadows against white plaster.

Glad seems very near me, although she isn't, not really. We are staring at each other and I can't read her eyes. They aren't laughing, like they almost always are. This does not seem, suddenly, to be a joke.

Slowly, the zipper unsinks its tiny metal teeth until the fabric begins to loosen and gape and my fingers pull open the neck of the dress, sliding it down over my shoulder, exposing skin. I feel myself moving deliberately, slowing down, scarcely breathing.

199

'Stop.' Glad sounds angry, and not as if she's acting.

'You see,' I say. 'I could do it.'

'But don't. Don't you see? I agree with Miss Gibb.'

Glad turns away, flushed, and goes to stand by one of the tall windows that overlook Yonge Street. I don't understand her anger — are we playacting, or is this real? Have I hurt her in some way? When I put my hand on her arm, she pulls away harshly, crossing one arm over her chest, the other flying out, finger raised and pointed.

'Out, out, out of my studio!' She is back to being the director, acting again. It must be said that Glad is a much more natural actress than I will ever be, even if the newspapers haven't promised her a Hollywood career.

'Glad!'

Her look is hard, appraising. 'You're too sweet, Aggie,' she says, repeating her words from earlier. 'You should never trust what a person says to you. Would you really take your clothes off for a man with a camera?'

My face burns with shame.

Glad is laughing again, brushing my bare shoulder with her cool fingertips. 'It's just that I love you so, Aggie. Don't do the advertisement.'

'Zip me up.' I flick her hand off my shoulder. 'I suppose you're right. You're always right.'

But her fingers on the zipper light a mutual shock, a spark of electricity that stings for a second. 'Never mind. I'll do it myself.' I walk away from her, my hands behind my neck,

200

struggling with the zipper.

'What are you doing?' Olive asks when I come into the kitchen. 'I thought Johnny left ages ago.'

'This zipper is broken,' I say, dropping into a chair without further explanation.

'I'll mend it for you.' My big sister brushes aside my hair and takes a look. 'It's not broken, it's jammed. Just hold still . . . '

I sit at the kitchen table after Olive's gone, under the blazing bulb, listening to the sound of mice scrabbling through the walls, and I compose a letter in return to Miss Gibb.

Please, on my behalf, explain that I am not the right girl for an undergarment advertisement, even if it is in a magazine, and ever so tasteful. (Would it be tasteful, do you think?) No, I must not. I think it's best to say no.

★ ★ ★

I have not yet sent the letter. I can't say why, exactly, but it waits on my vanity in an envelope, addressed and stamped, and unsent.

'You're writing to Miss Gibb?' Johnny picks up the envelope and looks at it.

'She's a friend,' I say.

'I don't like that woman.'

I've heard other men say it, boys on the team, even Mr. Tristan, who resented her authority over 'his' girls, as he called us, but never have I heard this opinion from Johnny. I can't say that I like it.

'Why ever not?' I frown.

We are about to launch into our first fight.

'She thinks she knows everything.'

'She knows more than you.'

'She isn't a real woman.'

'What is that supposed to mean?'

'You know what it means.'

I know he's talking about sex, and I'm familiar too with the slur of 'mannish woman' that gets attached to sporting girls, and suddenly I'm furious, rent up inside with rage. The right words don't come to me — well, this is no surprise. I'm not made for pithy speeches pouring from some deep well. In their weakness, I hear my own lack, and failure: 'I thought you were nice, Johnny. I don't like you right now, not at all.'

'Then I'll go.'

'Yes. Go.'

A little while later there is a knock on my door. Glad pokes her head in, even though I've chosen not to answer. I'm lying on the bed, staring at the ceiling. 'Everything okay?' she asks.

I'm not made for this. Conversing about my feelings? Parsing my emotions? Being in love? I'd sooner jump out the window. 'I need to run,' I tell Glad, and instantly I feel better. Just the idea of it. 'Or swim.'

'We'll swim in the morning,' says Glad.

'I miss training,' I say.

'We'll get back to it in the spring.'

'I have to run.'

'So run, who's stopping you?' She comes into the room, and stands over me with her arms crossed. 'People fight,' she says. 'And then they say I'm sorry. You should know these things.'

'I'm sorry?' I say, looking up at her. Maybe I'll see her forever, as she is, looking down at me, compact, impatient, shaking me free, if only she can, from my own special form of blindness.

She laughs, almost sadly. 'Not to me, dummy. To him.'

Oh.

'You don't want to, but you have to. Now get up and come downstairs and have dessert. Olive's made some kind of lemon cake thing and it smells like heaven.'

This is the night our brother George turns up. Maybe he smelled the lemon cake from across town — I wouldn't put it past him. He bangs on the door at the bottom of the staircase. Olive doesn't want to unlock it, but Glad marches down with me close behind, and hauls open the door, stands there with her arms crossed.

'Are you trying to scare us to death?'

George stumbles across the threshold, rubbing his bare hands. He doesn't know how to say he's sorry either — a family trait? I'm thankful for the fight if only because it means that Johnny has left early this evening. I do not want George and Johnny to cross paths, not like this, maybe not ever. George gazes at me owlishly before beginning to climb the stairs.

I glance at Glad, ashamed of my brother, and she shrugs. *Not your fault.*

We have nothing to drink in the house, which is for the best, with George.

'Nothing at all?'

'I'll make you a cup of tea,' offers Olive. The three of us, Smarts, stand awkwardly clumped at the entry to the kitchen, neither in nor out.

Glad observes us from where she's gone and curled into the comfortable chair beside the fireplace, like our half-grown kitten.

'Tea is it?' George's tone is sneering. 'Mother's special tea?'

And Olive takes one step backward in order to have room to hit him with a bright shocking slap. The sound of it seems to hold.

Nobody moves.

The tea on offer is, in fact, mailed to us by our mother, tea she has prepared with herbs grown in her garden, and dried, and carefully blended. She supplies us with several different boxes, each marked with its special purpose. After-Dinner Tea to soothe the troubled stomach. Woman's Tea to ease the pains of a difficult cycle. Every Day Tea, with a mild laxative. And the tea I assume Olive has intended to serve George, which is our favourite, a mixture of mints and lemon balm, called Tea for All Occasions. Now this is an occasion — I almost want to laugh, thinking of serving it now.

Glad rises in slow motion out of the chair. I catch her eye and shake my head, one short *no*.

'What's that for?' George rubs his jaw.

'Leave Mother be,' says Olive in a low voice.

'I've no interest in your mother.'

'What did you come for, George?' I ask quickly. I can hardly bear to hear him say 'your mother,' as if she hasn't raised him as her own, from infancy. As if she isn't the only mother he's ever known. As if her love is not worthy, somehow. But it is my own pity of my mother that haunts me most, and I know that George is not to blame for that — it is only that his dismissal makes me feel doubly traitorous. I've given up on George. I can hardly remember the brother who believed I could fly.

'I'm short,' he says bluntly, to me. 'I thought of you.'

I stare at the floor and chew the inside of my mouth.

'I'll pay you back,' he says. 'You know I will.'

'You never have yet,' counters Olive.

'Not just for me, Aggie. Please.' George tries to catch my eye.

'Not for you,' Olive says, disbelieving. 'If not for you, George, then for who?'

For whom, I think, knowing perfectly well of whom my brother speaks, but George has sworn me to secrecy on the subject, and I see no reason to break my silence now, to pull the complication of Tattie, the woman who is not his wife, and her children, who are also his if not by law, into this room, into our lives.

'Business is tight,' says George softly. 'You win some, you lose some. I've got a chance to invest in this horse. Finest filly I ever seen. I always bet on the fillies, Aggie, you know that.'

'How much?' I say.

In my head, I'm tearing up the letter to Miss Gibb and writing a different one.

I will say, *If it's not too much trouble, could you explain that I'm a modest girl. I hate to turn them down. Perhaps they will understand. Perhaps they would like a modest girl, anyway. What do you think? I will come for a visit on*

Friday, after my acting class, if you are available. Please write and tell me where we shall meet.

★ ★ ★

Johnny says he's sorry. Therefore, I don't have to. This is probably bad for me, but good for us.

I decide not to tell him — or anyone, including Glad — about the undergarment advertisement until after the photographs have been taken. I am photographed as modestly as one can imagine, fully clothed — demurely clothed, even. I tell myself that this is fun. I pretend that I am having fun. But I am discovering that modelling is tedious work. The lighting is hot, the greasy paint on my face is thick and sticky and looks unnatural, I perspire and my feet ache, my back aches, my shoulders crunch, the clothes are ill fitting and pinned all over. I throw every effort into not looking or feeling anything like myself. I do understand that part of the job: it isn't me the photographer wants, sweating and irked and dull, it's a girl stripped of her visceral qualities who is willing to suspend herself in amber.

'Smile, Miss Smart, there's a good girl. Less teeth, there's a lass. Just a natural smile, like you're catching the eye of a boy you like. That's better, Miss Smart. We'll get it yet.'

'It' is a version of me gazing airily into space, a vapid expression upon my features, chin on folded hands. This girl, who is not really me, can be found widely in newspapers, flyers, and magazines, lost in happy reverie. I suppose I'm meant to be thinking about my underthings, dreamily, 'as one does,' as Glad remarks, sending me and Olive into fits of giggles around the kitchen table. I pose, 'as one does,' while Glad narrates an imagined inner monologue on the cascading charms of undergarments. 'Oh, lacy loveliness, my heart doth flutter to think of you, folded into colourful stacks, one upon the other, in my secret drawers.' Her voice drops low on *secret drawers*. 'What wouldn't I give to have an armful of your satiny softness pressed against my pillowy bosom?'

'Glad,' Olive clicks her tongue in warning and indicates with a shake of her head Johnny's presence at our otherwise feminine table. His lips twitch, and he gazes at the ceiling and blinks hard.

'I've gone too far.'

'You have,' agrees Olive.

Glad wonders: 'What were you thinking of, Aggie, when the photo was being taken, for real?'

'Nothing,' I say.

I'm mildly troubled by the emptiness of my expression in the photograph, even while I recognize its appeal. Its blankness makes me restless, makes me want to run.

Atop my neatly made quilt, upstairs, Johnny repeats Glad's question: what was I thinking about — really — when the photograph was taken.

'They told me to think about you,' I say honestly.

He seems to find this arousing, and it occurs to me, for the first time, that perhaps he doesn't know me at all. That he thinks I'm someone quite different from who I am. Why should he want a girl with eyes so empty to be thinking of him?

★ ★ ★

After the undergarments, I am offered a job modelling a fur coat for a department store. In this photograph, my gaze is distant but somewhat sterner, as if I am dreaming of icy mountaintops, my hands clutching the collar around my neck. The advertisement is a success, and I am invited to continue the promotion by wearing the coat at the department store while signing autographs, and as the department store has locations in several cities across the country, an early winter tour is arranged by train, although I only travel so far west as Winnipeg. The train struggles along its iron tracks through a stark, naked, snowy landscape. I am billeted in the home of the department store's manager, chaperoned by his wife. I am not unhappy. It is as though I'm living a life that belongs to someone else, a borrowed life.

Yet I tell myself it is mine to keep. There are things I like about this life, things I want to keep. The fur coat, for example.

Home again, I describe to Johnny the sky I've seen, the one that belongs to his past, and how it has not frightened me, not at all, in its endlessness.

He tells me he's imagined me wearing nothing but fur.

The department store wonders whether I might model their new swimsuit for women, for their summer campaign. It is sleeveless, cut in a curve on the upper thigh, and made of a new fabric that promises not to trap and hold water like wool does.

The photographs are taken inside a studio in early spring but are made to look like I'm posing on a beach with a child's sand bucket and shovel — playthings — nearby. I have perfected the dreamy gaze, I think, oddly pleased with the effect, when the newspaper falls open to reveal this latest campaign. My eyes appear to address something exquisitely attractive just behind the camera. It makes a person want to turn around to see what could be there. I don't really notice the rest of me, exposed on cheap newsprint.

'Ooo,' says Glad, leaning down for a closer inspection. 'You look . . .'

But she doesn't finish the sentence.

'I look what?'

'Bosomy,' she says. 'Or something like that. Your legs look very long, even for you.'

'Is that a bad thing?'

'You've got lovely legs. Which everyone will now know.'

I feel myself go uneasy, slightly unmoored by her comments, though she seems to jest.

'You've got great gams — that's what the boys will say. You're a real doll. A babe.'

'Ugh. Stop. Please.'

'Isn't she?' to Johnny who has just come in without knocking — he has a key — taking the steps to our apartment two at a time.

'Isn't who what?'

'Isn't your girl a doll.'

Johnny glances at the photograph spread across the table, but quickly averts his eyes. I flush hot. He won't look at me either, not directly, and leaves the room.

I stand, leaving the newspaper open on the table, and I follow Johnny out of the kitchen without a word to Glad from either of us. I chase him up the stairs to my bedroom. I am terribly unsteady inside myself and he sits on the bed and looks at me, but I see that he's not angry or upset. He looks at me like I can suddenly imagine boys looking at the photograph of me in the newspaper, and I don't like it, it frightens me, like I'm made of paper, like I'm a printed picture, all surface, all skin, no depth, no muscle, no heft.

'Say something,' I demand of him.

'You've got great gams,' he says, and he breaks into a grin.

I feel safe, then. 'Anything else?'

'Why do you have to go and be photographed like that,' he says, sincerely.

'Well.' I feel defensive. 'It pays for this apartment for one thing. And I'm saving up.'

'For what? You'll just be married someday.'

'Will I?'

'Won't you?'

'Well maybe I won't,' I say defiantly. 'If this is a proposal, it stinks.'

'Who says it's a proposal?'

My breath catches and I flood with humiliation, like I've been slapped. This is our second argument. Neither of us apologizes afterward. We pretend, instead, that it never happened.

* * *

The newfangled bathing costume is indeed more revealing than some decent people would like, and some decent people take time to compose and send letters expressing shock regarding modern levels of decency and morality to the newspapers that run the advertisements, which gives me a brief taste of notoriety before the newspapers do, indeed, pull them. Almost immediately I am offered another undergarment advertisement, but this time I tell Johnny, and he says simply, *I don't like it.*

* * *

Johnny and I have seen our photographs paired in the newspapers again this summer, Johnny as Canadian champion in the 100-metre hurdles. I'm a fading fourth in the women's 800 metres, a distance now virtually defunct for girls — Glad does not choose to compete, focusing her training on the 100-metre sprint, which she wins cold.

Mr. Tristan is too merciful to chastise me. He's gone soft with me, and I don't respond well to softness. Perhaps, in truth, I don't respond well to winning. I need to run from behind. I need to tell myself a story in which I'm not the best or the favourite, and no one is watching me too closely — no one believes I can win. The other story doesn't work for me.

I should regret my poor showing at the Canadian championships, but I don't seem to care.

'Your heart's not here,' Mr. Tristan tells me, calling me into his office. 'If you want to consider retiring, I would understand.'

'Retiring?' I'm only twenty-one.

'You've got other things on your mind,' he says with a wink.

I do? I stare at him feeling stupid and dull as his meaning washes over me. Girls become wives — it's what happens, it is the trajectory of our lives. Am I to be an ordinary girl after all, like Olive intends to be, when the right man asks her, like the girls at the factory, like every girl, everywhere? Am I to wind my fate up with the fortune of a man, and leave it at that?

'No thank you,' I tell Mr. Tristan stiffly. 'I have no intention of retiring.'

'Then I'll expect more out of you, as will Mr. P.T. Pallister, your sponsor,' he says, his tone changing fractionally, hardening. 'You are not to skip any more practices. You are to work your hardest, as I've seen you do and know you can. Do I make myself clear, Miss Smart?'

I nod and pull myself up to my full height, shoulders back. But secretly, like a slow poisonous drip entering my bloodstream, I begin to know he's more right than he is wrong in his assessment. I can't pretend to feel the same urgency, the same desire to fling myself around the track, mile after mile, day after day, nursing aching muscles and blistered feet, chasing something I've already got.

My heart isn't here.

★ ★ ★

I don't like it, I can hear Johnny saying. I've just told him about my burgeoning career as an undergarment model.

'I don't like it,' he says. I can hear him. 'You're mine.'

'Am I?'

'You should be.' His voice goes rough with emotion, quite out of character, entirely unlike him, and the rumble of it sets me off like a starter's pistol. It is a hot August evening and the windows are open to the street sounds below. We have the apartment to ourselves. I want to believe him, and in the very same breath don't care if I do. My body whirls with a mess of emotions, tangling me up in the only sensation that seems to matter at all: to be with this man who desires me, who claims me. I fall onto my bed and look up at him. I think I know what I'm doing.

'Lock the door,' I say, and he does.

★ ★ ★

No offers follow.

My modelling career, which I like to pretend is the forerunner to my acting career, settles into a small lull — I assume it will be small.

It has been a year since I won gold at the Olympics. Miss Gibb hosts an anniversary party

213

at her own apartment for the girls on the team of 1928: seven of us, excepting Lillianna, the only one who does not attend. She's gone home to the Prairies. The swimmer has graduated from high school and is visibly pregnant, her wedding ring tight on her swollen finger. Of the girls who swept to silver on the 100-metre relay team, Ernestine has become engaged to a man in the dry goods business — she came in third this summer at the Canadian championships — and Sarah Jane and Beth, the other two, have chosen not to compete.

Sarah Jane is newly married. And Beth's mother has begged her to stop running, please. 'She says she wants grandbabies.' Beth laughs. 'Someday.'

'Oh for God's sake,' says Miss Gibb. 'The ignorance of some people.'

'My husband too,' confesses Sarah Jane. 'I mean, it could be true, Miss Gibb, the doctors say so.'

'What about you and Johnny?' The conversation turns on me like a spotlight catching out a comical character in a silent movie. I'm holding a slice of Miss Gibb's carrot cake on the palm of my hand, eating it like a horse. Where are my manners?

'What about me and Johnny?' My mouth full of crumbs.

'Aren't they just the darlingest couple?' Glad jumps to my rescue, and everyone is forced to agree.

Miss Gibb corners me privately, offering a cut crystal glass filled with red punch. The liquid is spiked with something alcoholic, and as the afternoon sinks into a wane, we've all taken several glasses more than we ought to have. The pregnant swimmer is crying happily on Miss Gibb's sofa, while the other married or engaged girls surround her like acolytes, offering handkerchiefs, their own eyes filling with tears, a soft drawling hum of 'I know, I know, you're so lucky!'

'What will you do next?' Miss Gibb asks me quietly. 'Oh, please, please, don't be predictable. I hate when a girl like you becomes predictable.'

'I was thinking of getting married,' I say, accepting the glass of punch, and glancing warily at the marrieds-and-engaged.

'Well I won't say that's not predictable,' says Miss Gibb, quite kindly. 'And is that what Johnny is thinking too?'

'I think so.'

Miss Gibb lifts her eyebrows.

'Well, I haven't gotten it in writing if that's what you mean,' I say, sounding more defensive than I'd intended. Glad comes to join us in the corner. 'I'm tipsy as a jaybird. Either of you want to throw back your heads and wail a bit?'

'You're a good girl, Glad,' says Miss Gibb.

'I won't get married. I'd like to see Los Angeles,' Glad tells us — Los Angeles is where the next Olympic games will be held. 'You won't see Los Angeles if you're married. Don't get married, please, Aggie. You must come too. We'll train together. It will be just like it was!'

'I'm not fast enough,' I say, and I recognize the truth in it. It strikes me that the truth should

215

make me sadder than it does. Instead, I feel unexpectedly freed. No more races. I can do something else instead.

'She is so fast enough, isn't she, Miss Gibb?'

Miss Gibb inclines her head and examines me. 'No,' she says simply. 'I must agree with Aggie. Aggie is not made for the sprint distance.'

I swallow the rest of the punch in one burning gulp. It's one thing to say it for myself, and quite another to have it confirmed. I can feel my breath accelerating as my future contracts. But Miss Gibb isn't done. 'Aggie is not a sprinter. She's something else instead. Aggie will go a long, long way, mark my words.'

Glad throws her head back and laughs. 'I think you're tipsy too, Miss Gibb.'

'You may be right, Miss Wright.'

'She always is, you know,' I say, but the conversation isn't mine anymore. I am drifting elsewhere, into another story that might just be mine to claim. I am imagining myself as Mrs. Johnny Tracy, and the thought of it makes me want to leap in among the girls on the sofa, drowning in punch, crying and laughing with my head thrown back.

But that isn't my way of being. I couldn't really do such a thing, cross over the invisible boundary that keeps me always apart. Maybe the distant gaze I've perfected in photographs is not an invention, but a true telling of myself. My imagination stops here. I've come as far as I can in this game of being Aganetha Smart, Golden Girl runner.

'More punch, Miss Gibb?' says Glad.

'I am a godawful chaperone.'
'And we thank you for it, Miss Gibb.'

★ ★ ★

Not long after falls Black Thursday. October 24, 1929.

Nothing is the same again, although we can't guess that, not immediately, and none of us do. I am preoccupied in any case. I am not thinking about Black Thursday. It does not occur to me that Mr. P.T. Pallister of Rosebud Confectionary will shutter his sponsorship of the Rosebud Ladies' Athletics Club effective immediately and fire Mr. Tristan, nor that most of the track clubs in Toronto will vanish — those for women most suddenly — and that hundreds of factory girls will be laid off and there will be no more girls' softball teams, or hockey teams, or track teams.

I am caught up in another problem altogether, a private problem that seems to belong only to me. I tell no one for the time being.

And Johnny says nothing further of marriage.

14

Two Stories

'Mom, she thinks you're Edith.'

'Isn't that something.' The woman locks the brake. She's got me facing the galley kitchen, where the girl has gone and helped herself to a tall glass of juice. I see the ice cube tray left out on the counter, already melting.

The woman comes around before me. 'Do I remind you of your sister Edith?'

I sit up straighter in my chair. Do you know Edith? The kettle whistles.

It isn't herbal tea I'm wanting, but the girl places a cup of steaming peppermint under my nose.

'You look the same as always, Miss Smart, not that we ever really had the chance to speak up close like this,' the woman says, going to the counter to put away the ice cube tray. My eyes fill with sudden tears. She has called me by my proper title. It would seem she knows me better than her children do, better than anyone I've met in years. It would seem she knows me.

'Honey?' the girl says, and I think, for a flash, that she is addressing me. *Honey.* But she stirs a dollop into my cup before I've had a chance to refuse. She plops into the chair beside me and guzzles from her glass. She doesn't think to spoon me my tea, which I cannot otherwise consume. Distractedly, the woman directs the girl to help.

And so she lifts a spoonful and blows on its liquid surface. I open my mouth.

'I've found something for your movie, Max — I just have to go and . . . ' The woman drifts around the room, plucking at the stacks of papers, exits hazily.

'I think it's going well,' the girl tells her brother. He pours himself a glass of juice identical to hers, and sits at the table in the vacated chair.

I see the tray of ice cubes once again out upon the counter-top, melting.

'I hate this place,' the girl adds in a low voice. 'Mom's got to sell. Mrs. Smart too.'

'Miss Smart.'

'Miss Smart,' the girl repeats automatically, and shivers. 'It's almost like it's haunted.'

What's wrong with that, I'd like to know?

Here is Fannie, as if she's been waiting for her cue, coming in through a crack that runs down the plaster wall on an angle from top to bottom, like someone's carved it there, though I know its cause is nothing more than the shifting of rocks and earth under a rotting foundation. Fannie slips into the room and walks around the perimeter, her face turned from mine. I can't catch her eye.

She's troubled. She circles the room, faster and faster, becoming a whirl, a shadow. She wants me to follow. She's gone, smashing insubstantial through the window that is visible when I turn my head.

Out the window, a ploughed field and a stand of pines, and I see what Fannie's trying to tell me: I'm sitting on the wrong side of things.

I grip the table, but cannot rise.

The woman's footfalls shake the floor on approach. 'Here it is!' She's waving a scrap of glossy paper. 'Look, Miss Smart, it's you! You were in a magazine. I found the clipping on my mother's dresser after she passed. It was in an envelope with your name on it, Miss Smart, but never licked shut. Mama's husband cleared everything out — her second husband, that is, not my father. They were living in Vancouver and I was in Toronto, so I couldn't rescue more than letters and photos to carry home on the plane. Car accident, Miss Smart, tragic. You never really get over a shock like that. But it was years ago now. Kaley wasn't even born.'

She pauses in her story. Already, I know too much about her; I recognize the type, a woman comfortable foisting intimate, unwanted details of her life onto strangers. Next, she'll be telling me about her cervical polyps and divorce settlement.

The woman continues: 'Mama always clipped things to give to people — recipes, news stories, book reviews. I assume she meant this for you, Miss Smart, though we never had any back-and-forth. We always knew you were some kind of famous runner. That's what gave Max the idea for the movie! We remembered you running in our back field.'

I can't see the envelope or the photograph. 'My glasses,' I mutter, but I haven't got any. Lost

220

them years ago. Never found them, though I look from time to time, pawing in jacket pockets, thumping around my bedside table.

'It's you running past the lighthouse,' the girl tells me.

'The lighthouse? Is that still standing?' Surprise grinds the words out of me.

'Of course!' she says. 'We're going to take you there.'

'Kaley!' Max's tone is warning. He's standing on a chair, aiming his camera at the photo flattened on the tabletop.

'Read out the caption,' he directs.

The girl's sleek head leans over the tiny black text: ' "Miss Aganetha Smart, age seventy-six, and a gold medalist in track at the 1928 Amsterdam Olympics, runs on her farm west of Toronto. This summer's Games is the first at which women will contest the marathon distance." '

'What's the date?' he asks.

'Doesn't say, but it had to be 1984,' she tells him. 'Los Angeles. The Canadian women's marathon record was set way back then, and it's never been broken since. Crazy, huh.'

'That's your job, right, Kales? And they'll put you in magazines too.'

She doesn't answer him.

'I meant to give it to you.' The woman smoothes the crumpled magazine page, as if she hasn't followed along with the conversation but is still thinking of her mother. 'I kept it, after all. I did mean to give it to you, Miss Smart, but after I moved back here with the kids, and I brought over a coffee cake — you know, meet

221

your neighbours — and your sister invited me in, and you were so upset by it — well. We never had any back-and-forth.'

I don't remember that. I don't think she's telling that story at all the way it really happened. Does she mean to imply I've cast unfair judgement on her? Who does she think I am? She won't let it go. She repeats herself deliberately, rolling her observation around. She wants me to consider the implications, but it means nothing to me: *We never had any back-and-forth*.

'Do I know you?' I demand.

★ ★ ★

Across the field behind the line of pines is the Granny Room. Behind the pines is my mother. She is not afraid to step forward and show herself, spine straight, her eyes deep with calm like the colours of an ocean shot through with sun.

There are two stories to get straight in my head. They don't belong together, and they do, and I want them straight in my head.

Both stories are about my mother.

My mother is a woman of grave and particular knowledge, and she helps many girls and women, but in the manner of how she helps them, here is the problem. It is the kind of help that draws a stark line between people: for it, or against.

My mother is not like most.

My mother thinks in practicalities. She does

not judge a person's situation in moral terms. She seems incapable of it. She listens, and she responds.

'Is Mrs. Smart in?' 'Is the lady of the house in?' 'I was told there was a lady here could help.' 'Help me, please.' Hushed whispers. Begging. Fear.

The men, the husbands, they come differently, loud and hoarse and excited, to fetch Mrs. Smart to birth their brand-new sons. The fathers always hope for sons, and mostly, so do the mothers. Sons never turn up whispering for the aid of Mrs. Smart.

Fannie is four summers buried when what happens happens. I am fourteen years old, and I've begun my monthlies, which are not yet regular. Mother doses me with a tonic when she thinks I look peaky. I look peaky more often than not this summer, but it isn't my monthlies, which haven't come since April, it's a general restlessness building in me. George's letters, now infrequent, invite me to come and visit.

George writes about seeing a dance marathon, the girls and men whirling the open floor for hours, even through the night and into the next day; he tells of how he won a bet by picking the winning couple, an unlikely pair, both girls, sisters. He writes about Sunnyside Amusement Park, and the rides, and the gigantic swimming pool churning with bathers.

Carefully, I read out George's invitation to my mother. ''If you come, I'll take you to the races.''

'The races?' Mother is distracted, paring and soaking small whole cucumbers for pickling.

'Horses, I think,' I say.

'Do you want to see horses race?'

I am silent.

'Let George come home to visit,' says Mother. 'Toronto is a big city. You would need chaperoning. And what is he thinking of, asking in the middle of summer, our busiest time?'

She exaggerates. Late summer or early fall is our busiest time — harvest, more precisely — but I know *no* when I hear it.

'But I want to see George. He's my brother!'

'Edith is your sister. Go visit her. Cora, you go too.' Cora has come into the kitchen with another basin of freshly picked cukes. 'Bake Edith a cake,' says our mother. 'Take her some beans and tomatoes from the garden.'

We don't want to, Cora and I. Reluctantly we shuffle around the kitchen, gathering ingredients for a sweet loaf with a crumb top.

There is a knock at the summer kitchen door. Olive, who is packing beans into glass jars in preparation for canning them on the hot stove, answers. She comes quickly into the house.

'Mother,' Olive says quietly. 'A girl for you.'

Cora and I look to catch a glimpse of the girl, but we see only that she is not much older than us, and that we do not know her. Someone has brought her here and dropped her at the end of our lane, and she has walked slowly up it, wondering what she will find in this house. We lower our eyes as she follows Mother through the dining room. The sound of Father's hammer comes from upstairs. He is building cedar closets in unlikely corners of the house. The tang of the planed wood perfumes the air and fragrant boards are stacked in the great room, through which Mother and the girl must pass.

Cora measures flour and soda as I read off instructions from a 'receipt' written in our mother's hand. Crumb Cake, it's called. We bake it for every day, not company. Butter, oats, flour, brown sugar. Best eaten hot from the oven with a fresh cup of tea, to wash down the crumbs. A bit dry by the second day.

'Two eggs, well beaten. One cup of sour milk.'

'You sour it.'

We have poured the batter into pans, ready to bring to Olive in the summer kitchen, in hopes that she can watch them for us in the oven out there, when there is another knock. This time it's at the door that opens into the dining room. But we hear the man already backing up into the yard, calling for Mrs. Smart, as if the windows might answer him.

The hammering above stops briefly before resuming again.

I look at Cora and Cora looks at me. Olive comes in from the summer kitchen, drying her hands on her stained apron.

'Busy day,' I say.

Olive opens the door to the man, who won't come in. He's from the neighbouring county, and it's their first baby, and he doesn't know what to do, but he can't leave her, his wife, for long, she's moaning, can Mrs. Smart hurry, please!

Olive fetches Mother. Mother comes calmly, asks a few questions about the type of pains, the frequency, has there been a gush of water, and she determines she must go.

'But the gir — ' Mother stops Cora's question with her hand.

'I'll gather my things and follow you right away,' Mother tells the man, and she shuts the door on him, and turns to us. 'You will look after the girl who has come. Her name is Betty, and she will need much watching, just now. Olive, you know how to apply the cold compresses. Brew some of my Woman's Tea with fresh garlic to fight infection. She is comfortable now, but she could become very ill, and if she takes a turn for the worse, you must find a way to fetch me. And keep your hands washed and very clean.'

'But our cake for Edith?'

'Leave the cake for later. I know you girls will be of help to Betty. One of you must stay with her at all times, do you understand?'

And then, just before she walks out the door, she says to me that I must not run for the doctor. 'The doctor will not be able to help.'

The ordinary summer day is changed, like that.

Our mother gone down the lane, Cora and I follow Olive on hushed, eager feet toward the Granny Room, where a bed is kept for the girls who come. The girls rarely stay longer than a night or two, sometimes a week at most. I do not wonder whether my mother accepts payment, or whether the girls offer it, or their families. I know nothing about the transactions that go on here, or even, it must be said, about the work itself that my mother does on behalf of these girls. I have not, until today, been permitted to enter the Granny Room, not while a girl rests there.

Olive leads Cora and me through the great room, littered and crammed with our father's detritus, and through the front hall, which no one ever uses as an entryway, although there is a door, and into the parlour, which belonged to our grandmother. I remember her not at all, but Olive and Cora claim bits and pieces of memory: horehound candies kept in a glass jar with a cork stopper, handed out to little visitors, and a scrap of black netting she wore pinned to her tightly knotted hair to signify perpetual mourning: she had much to mourn, having lived through the deaths of her husband, four grandchildren, and a daughter-in-law.

Grandmother's furniture remains: a stiff horsehair chair and matching sofa, with carved dark wooden legs and backs, and a china cabinet of dark wood and glass, in which Mother now keeps her tinctures, medicines, and preparations. There is a red rug on the floor, richly patterned with vines and flowers, leaves and birds.

I would like to stop and examine it more closely. Are the birds speaking to one another? Are there wild animals among the vines?

We pause outside the closed door: the bedroom.

'Not all of us at once,' says Olive. 'We'll frighten her.'

'She deserves to be frightened,' says Cora rather breathlessly. 'After what she's done.'

'What has she done?' I'm confused.

'Nothing that concerns us,' says Olive.

'It concerns us now. She's in our charge.'

'And we'll look after her like Mother would,' says Olive, becoming suddenly fierce and turning on Cora: 'And if you won't, then stay away. Do the beans and bake the crumb cake and go off and visit Edith, and leave this girl to me and Aggie.'

Olive turns the handle on the door, gently pushes it open, calling out, 'It's just me — Olive — and my sisters, come to see how you are.'

The girl who lies in our grandmother's bed rolls her face on the pillow to see us. It is a hot day, but she has pulled the sheet to her chin. I occurs to me that she may not be decently dressed underneath it. I spy on one of the wooden chairs her folded dress and hat, and her good shoes are placed neatly underneath. The girl looks as if she does not care about much of anything. She looks quite blank, preoccupied. She pulls her bare arms out from under the sheet and rests them silently on her stomach, her mouth and forehead twisted, as if she is struggling not to make a sound.

Olive quickly pulls over the other wooden chair and sits beside the bed, leaning to touch the girl's hand. 'Are you in some pain?' she asks quietly.

'Something's happening,' says the girl.

'Well, then. My mother's help is doing the trick,' says Olive.

'Will it hurt?' the girl whispers. Her eyes are full of fear.

Olive doesn't answer, not exactly. Instead she promises, 'We will stay with you. We will be with you.'

I am impressed. Olive could be our mother, she is so sure, so confident. Cora makes a noise with her mouth closed, a *hmpf*, a scoffing sound. I give her a poke, make a face at her. *Stop it.* Cora stares at me unblinking, pretending she's done nothing.

The room is too hot, and I go to the window and open it. 'Maybe we'll catch a bit of breeze,' I say, trying to be cheerful. I still do not understand what has made the girl sick, nor what is happening to her. I stand by the window with my arms hanging at my side, wondering how else I might help. Cora stands in the doorway like a statue. When our eyes meet, she crosses her arms over her front, her legs slightly apart, like a sentry. She won't enter the room.

'Cora, Aggie,' says Olive, without turning her attention from the girl, 'could you brew some tea, please, as Mother suggested, with fresh garlic? I will stay with . . . ' she pauses fractionally before saying the girl's name, as if she's afraid she's betraying her privacy by naming her at all — 'Betty.'

'Might as well put the cakes in to bake,' I tell Cora as she fills the kettle and sets it to boil on the big stove in the summer kitchen.

'You don't know what that girl did, do you,' says Cora in a steady tone that I recognize. She is about to tell me something that I don't want to hear, and she's relishing the moment.

Silently, I walk away from her into the kitchen to fetch the filled cake pans.

'That girl has a baby in her stomach that she doesn't want.'

I walk the cake pans right past Cora, who is hovering in the way. I push her aside with my elbow, but she only shrugs and follows me closely. My elbow is a sign of weakness. She knows she's upset me, and she's pleased.

'Our mother is helping that girl kill her baby.'

My hands shake as I set the pans on top of the hot stove, beside the rattling kettle, and open the oven door.

'And now we're supposed to help kill the baby too.'

'You're lying.' I turn on her, oven door hanging open and cake bottoms beginning to cook on the stovetop.

Cora says nothing. She doesn't need to.

'How big is the baby?' I whisper, thinking of the only infant I've ever seen up close, when I was no more than five myself, and Little Robbie was born to Edith and Carson.

Cora doesn't know. She looks suddenly not quite so certain.

'Have you seen the babies? What does Mother do with them? Does she bury them? Why is the girl's stomach so flat? Shouldn't it be very big for a baby to fit inside it?'

Cora cannot answer me. She doesn't know.

'You think you know, but you don't!' I am flustered and hot from the oven, which I suddenly remember is open, and I shove the pans in and slam it shut. The kettle begins to steam. Using a thick flannel pad, I carry the boiling kettle past Cora and into the kitchen, and begin to prepare the tea, as directed, with smashed fresh garlic mixed with the dried herbs, slowly pouring the hot water over top.

When everything is ready, I make up a tray with a pretty embroidered tea towel, and a china cup, and a small bowl of honey, and a little spoon that came from our grandmother. Something in me wants to make the tray look pretty, like I would for any guest.

Cora follows me.

'You're helping her,' she whispers accusingly.

In truth, it would never occur to me not to help the girl, or Olive, or most especially my mother. Mother has told us what we are to do. I cannot imagine choosing to defy her wishes. The alternative is quite impossible to fathom — inconceivable, you might say, though under the circumstances, I should probably not put it that way.

I carry the tray through the parlour and the open door to the bedroom, and set it onto the dresser just inside the door, where my mother keeps sheets and bedding fresh smelling with sprigs of lavender. The girl is rocking her head from side to side on the pillow. She does not look well. Her forehead is wet.

'Make up a basin with cool water and some clean cloths for compresses.' Olive speaks quick and low. Her voice remains calm, but her eyes, as they meet mine, are worried. I can feel my heart beating faster. I understand why my mother has kept me from the Granny Room until now. This is what she's been hiding from me: illness, fear, the suffering of strangers.

I push past Cora, who stands like a stone in the doorway, and run for a basin. I'm back as quickly as I can come, and have to push past Cora again, water sloshing onto both of our dresses. I frown at her, but she doesn't budge, and won't even look at me. I'm not sure who or what she's looking at, exactly. I place the basin on the wood floorboards.

'Shut the door,' says Olive. Cora doesn't move. 'Shut the door!' Olive raises her voice, and Cora challenges her in silent refusal. 'In or out, Cora, make up your mind!' Cora hesitates, and Olive stands, suddenly furious, and pushes her out of the way and leans onto the door to close it, with some difficulty, as Cora appears to be leaning back. As soon as the door is shut, and Olive returned to the girl's side, Cora opens the door. I can see that Olive might strike her, she's that angry, but Cora simply steps inside and pulls the door shut behind her.

Why? I mouth the word.

We soak the cloths, Olive and I, and begin bathing the girl's face and arms. Olive moves the sheet to wash down her legs. I have never touched another person's body before, not like this, and I am surprised by how pliable she seems, how easy it is to lift and position her limbs, and how she responds to our touch — she relaxes against it. I feel for a moment that this is going to turn out just fine, whatever *this* is. But then the girl almost sits up, sharply. Her stomach is hurting her, and it must hurt very much, for her eyes are full of fear. I realize that blood is pooling from under her hips, spreading on the sheet, and I stare at Olive.

Olive's eyes open wide, but her instructions

232

give the impression of calm.

'Lie back down, gently now,' to the girl. And to me: 'Lift just now, just here, and . . . ' Olive opens the drawers for more sheets — I see that Mother is keeping old sheets in these drawers, not new, not nice, these are torn and mended and stained and greying with age. Olive spreads the old sheets under the girl. The smell of lavender rises thickly. I am grateful for the sleepy perfumed scent, which fights against the raw animal smell of fresh blood.

Olive presses on the girl's stomach, kneading it with one hand, the other holding the girl's hand, bringing forth more blood.

'Stop!' I whisper frantically.

'This is how it is done,' says Olive. 'This is how I've seen Mother do it.'

'What is happening?'

'You are killing her baby,' says Cora.

At that, the girl makes a sound, her first, just a quiet helpless cry that comes from her throat as if she can't stop it, though she wants to. Tears stream out of the corners of her eyes, but she forces herself to stay silent inside her fear. I think, *you are being very brave*, but I don't say it out loud. I hope she can hear my thoughts, read my eyes.

'We are not doing harm,' says Olive firmly. 'She is suffering a miscarriage. She needs our help.'

I look across the girl's body, which lies between us, into Olive's eyes, and I believe her. Almost. I believe her enough. I can't decide, just then, whether it matters that I believe Olive's version or Cora's, because what matters is that Mother has told me to help, and so I must help. Besides, I am here and helping, and now I want to, no matter what. I feel that I couldn't leave. It is the girl I'm thinking of, not the girl's baby, that is true, and perhaps it is unfair of me, and unimaginative, but it is the girl who is suffering, and whose suffering I want to soothe. I keep washing her cheeks and brow, and her arms, rinsing out the cloth, washing again. I'm running the wrung-out cloth over her hand when she turns it palm up and wraps her fingers around mine. That is when I understand: she wants something steady and strong to hold on to. It is a want that I can answer. I let her hold my hand. I stop daubing her. My other hand folds on top of hers.

Olive checks under the sheet from time to time. I look away, to give the girl what little privacy I can.

'We need another basin,' Olive tells Cora, but Cora won't go. She is the witness in the corner, the angel of stone, the truth teller. Olive must go herself. In the moments that Olive is gone, Cora and I face each other across the room.

The room is silent and still, except for our breathing. And then I am holding my breath until Olive returns, briskly, prepared for what's next. Into the basin goes some fleshy unformed dark red tissue that looks livery. I stare quite hard, while pretending not to, but I can't find a baby in that basin. I can't find anything that looks human, or shaped, or recognizable. I can't find anything but clotted blood. I see Cora looking too. She seems surprised. I think she expected to see a whole baby come out of the girl.

'We'll just keep pressing and kneading, until it's all clear,' says Olive. 'But you may sit up now. You must have some tea.'

Olive discreetly washes her bloody hands in the basin of cool water, curlicues of colour spin out, and the liquid swirls a pale pink. I try to pull my hand from the girl's, in order to pour the tea, but the girl holds on. She wants to tell me something. I shake my head to warn her that Cora is in the room, and Cora is not someone with whom you want a secret shared.

'He said he'd marry me. I don't want to marry him. I don't want to see him ever again.'

Shhhh, says Olive. Hush.

'Can you help me?'

I don't know what she means. We've helped her, surely. What more can we do?

And then I know. We can do nothing more. This is it. This is all Mother can do too, and the room knows it, and the house around us, and the heat of summer, and the promise of the turning seasons. The distant smell of acrid smoke knows it: a summons from the burnt-up crumb cakes in the oven, which beg watching by the girls who bake them, for it is never boys who bake cakes.

Later, when we are getting supper on and waiting for Mother to come home, Cora points out there is blood on the back of my dress. But it's not the girl's. It's my monthlies, returned.

That is my first story.

★ ★ ★

The second story is mine, all mine. Because I too have been the girl in the Granny Room, lying abed, shivering, in need of my mother's merciful help. I will keep this story short. It is too sad to stand up under the weight of words. I will tell it thin and plain, if I tell it at all. There is no one alive, now, who knows the story, and only a few knew it, ever.

I'll tell only what I've spent my life promising: that I regret nothing. And it will be a lie, of a kind. But it is also the truth.

15

I Think I Know

'You don't know me,' says the woman in Edith's kitchen, 'at least not very well. My name is Nancy. I should have introduced myself earlier.' Nancy, she says. Well, I know this kitchen, don't think I don't, untidy as ever.

'I'm very sorry to disturb you,' I say firmly. 'I will leave now.'

'You're not done with your tea!' The girl is flustered.

'We've still got footage to shoot,' explains the young man.

'Take me home,' I demand, clear as a storm on the horizon.

'Won't you stay?' says the woman. 'I'm sorry I've upset you.'

'It's your story we want to tell,' the girl insists.

Everyone crowding in on me. A crowd of crows. Well, well, well. What makes them think my story is theirs to tell? What makes them think I'll cooperate any further? Don't they know — they are dealing with an expert in the telling of other people's stories.

Edith, I say to the woman who has got me by the hands with her strong, fine-boned fingers, no rings, dry and calloused. Edith, I'm very sorry to have come here, and I will be going now.

'Miss Smart, my name is Nancy.'

237

So you say. In Edith's kitchen. With Edith's mess all around you.

'Miss Smart, I'm sorry to tell you that your sister Edith is no longer alive. She died many years ago. She is buried in the New Arran churchyard if you ever want to visit. We could take you.'

Edith is dead? I do not mean to say this out loud. I do not mean to look old and confused.

'Yes, Edith is dead, Miss Smart.'

Ah. Like everyone else.

'This would be the perfect time to tell her,' says the young man, his camera eager to see me weep.

The woman won't let go of my hands. She insists on burdening a person: 'Miss Smart, my name is Nancy, and I've got something very important to tell you.' Her name is Nancy, so she says. 'Miss Smart, you're not alone in the world. That's what we want to tell you, me and Kaley and Max — we were your neighbours, yes, but we weren't just that. We're family. I moved back to my family's farm after the divorce. The house had stood empty so many years, I thought it might have fallen down, but no such luck. You can see that it stands yet.

'Your sister Edith was my grandmother, Miss Smart. That's why I was so — surprised, I guess. Disappointed. About the coffee cake. When we were kin. I should let it go. It's ancient history now.'

I shake my head. I'm remembering a burnt-up loaf of crumb cake, meant for Edith, could that be what the woman means?

238

But she won't stop her talking.

'My mother moved in with Grandma Edith when I was ten — not that she wanted to. Too much talk in a place like this, she said. But she came back to look after her mother. She was a good daughter. Like my kids. Yes, you are, both of you. I was a teenager when Edith died. And then we got the heck off the farm, me and Mama. We flew like birds across the country till we reached the ocean. I never imagined coming back. To this. Place. But here I am.'

'You're Edith's.' That's what you're saying.

'Yes. Isn't that wonderful?'

'You're Edith's?' Prove it. Can you hear my fury? It pours from me, fear distilled. My hands slam down onto the tabletop.

'I know there was a rift somewhere along the line,' says the woman stiffly. 'Mama didn't know what had happened. And Grandma Edith never said a word wrong about you, Aganetha, though she wasn't fond of your sister — I've forgotten her name — but who would be? I wasn't half-fond of her either, when we'd meet in town. 'How is your poor grandmother keeping these days?' she'd beetle for me, digging around. 'And do you see your father from time to time?' A person who liked to poke a person where it hurt. Still, and all, she took the coffee cake and invited me in, and you weren't a force of welcome, exactly, it must be said.'

'Mom,' says the boy in a tone of warning.

'I'm sorry, I'm sorry. I don't know why I can't let it go. Silly, isn't it?' The woman pauses, but only for the time it takes to sigh. 'I know there was a rift between you and Edith. But it shouldn't matter now, should it, after all these years?'

'Ask Edith.'

'Edith is gone, Miss Smart. I'm sorry. She died many years ago now.'

MILLER, EDITH (née Smart). Of New Arran, Ontario, where she lived on the Miller family farm, known as 'The Flats,' from the time of her marriage to Carson Miller at age seventeen until her death as an old woman, long plagued by ill health. May she rest with her brothers and sisters in peace.

★ ★ ★

The woman isn't done, even with Edith buried. She tells me, as if I don't know: 'You weren't at the funeral. Your sister came to the reception afterward — uncommonly friendly, she was, but my mother didn't trust it. Mama said there was no love lost between Edith and her Smart sisters.'

'Half-sisters.' I gut out the words, but the woman doesn't hear me. She is slowing down, now that she's poured out what she means to say, drifting as she remembers out loud. Nancy's her name, so she says. I mouth it to try to keep it with me. 'For your sister Edith's funeral, my mother and I filled the church hall with flowers from Edith's own garden,' Nancy says. 'Edith was a great gardener in her old age.'

Edith, a great gardener! My mouth opens in steady, pounding revolt. Pshaw. There's my

240

proof. You must be speaking of another Edith, not my sister. Edith was no gardener. Edith never coaxed a living thing from the soil under this house.

★ ★ ★

I think I know at the moment of conception: I feel a pinch, like a sleeve snagging on a branch, the thread pulling loose, the story unravelling. Too late.

Oh! No.

Over me, I can make out the vaguest contours of Johnny's face in the room that's gone dark since we began. Our silence amidst our movements is mutual, choked, giddy. I do not mean to cry out.

'Are you quite fine?' His concern fills me to bursting. I pull his face down into my neck, so he won't see. I don't answer him otherwise. We breathe together and I am glad. I am foolish in my joy.

Already Johnny grunts and presses upright. Already he flips over and jackknifes his body, leaps to his feet, dressing quickly in the dark. He laughs as he stumbles into his pant leg, hopping across the wood boards of the floor, nearly toppling.

'Hush! Johnny! The girls will hear you.'

'I thought they were out.'

'That was hours ago. I'm sure I heard them come in.'

But all of this is beside the point. What am I to do? Already the bedsheets are cooling where his body has been. Already I feel a regret I can't express, even to myself. I know — I do not love him as much as I should. Desire is not love. It cools as soon as it is slaked.

We are the sum of our actions, and of our inactions, yes, that is easy enough to understand. What comes harder is finding ourselves the sum of our emotions, which flicker, altered by experience, by the things we cannot bear to tell ourselves, by the trouble we accrue, the flattening and tamping down as we learn how not to be hurt. As we learn protection and the easiest means of protection.

I am not ready for Johnny to leave the room.

But he goes to the door, and unlocks it. Returns and bends over me for the briefest kiss, as if this will cure me. I roll onto my side, away from him, but he seems not to notice, and away he goes. I hear him thumping down the stairs.

I hear voices in the kitchen, below, rising as lightly as a swirl of fallen leaves caught in an up current. He's staying. He isn't going home yet. He's in the kitchen, where he's found the girls. He's laughing with Glad, who loves to laugh.

I am the furthest thing from laughter, a sour sombreness preventing me from rising and cleaning myself and dressing and jauntily wandering down the stairs to join them. I think, *What is wrong with me?*

I decide: this is a mistake I'll only make once.

What can Johnny say in protest? Nothing to persuade me again.

★ ★ ★

I take myself to visit Tattie, the woman who is not George's wife, the mother of his children, and the secret he's asked me to keep from the rest of our family. I knock on their door during the day, guessing George will not be there, and he is not.

'Tattie,' I say, without much in the way of pleasantries. 'How does it feel to be . . . with child?'

Tattie nurses her littlest. She says, 'Are you worried, then?'

It is not a question that needs reply.

She says, 'Does he love you enough to marry you?'

'I just need to know how it feels,' I say.

Tattie laughs a little, wryly. 'You'll be tired like you'd like to die, and' — she touches her breast with her free hand — 'you'll hurt, and maybe some pains here' — she presses her stomach — 'and it won't be long before you start swelling up. And then you'll know and so will everyone else.'

'Is it the boy from the photos in the newspaper?' she asks me after a pause. 'Handsome. Does he love you?'

'Yes,' I say. 'I think so.'

'Then you'll want him to ask you to marry him.'

I nod. I haven't thought of how to do that, but I see she's right — it won't be up to me to do the asking, my job is to maneuver him into the position to do so.

A tiny crack of fear opens, somewhere in the back of my mind. I can't do this.

Tattie is watching me. I can see her doubt.

'Not every man is like your brother,' she says proudly, and I recognize with surprise that she is complimenting George on his fidelity. George, my brother, who keeps her and the children in this sagging row house, who lives at the racetrack, who drinks steadily when he has the chance, and sleeps steadily when he does not. George, who's never offered her the protection of marriage, who swears up and down that love is all that matters — when it's clear, to me, that he's holding out, hedging his bets, like he always has, like he always will.

'He owned up to what's his,' she says. 'Every night, he comes home to us.'

I try to smile in return, but it is a struggle. The truth is, I am a terrible actress — stiff, unnatural — even after my training, or perhaps my training is to blame. *Enunciate! Smile with your eyes! Be emphatic!* What good are these tools of the trade against Tattie's pretty face, sallow and anemic, her wild gypsy hair? She wears no wedding ring, and my mother and father have never heard of her existence, but she seems to believe she has enough — as much as she deserves, or even more. I see why I've wanted to come here. I see that I cannot be like Tattie.

'Well,' I say, 'it's probably nothing. Just a bit of a flu.'

She nods. The kettle comes to a boil and steam fills the little room. 'Could you get that, please?' She is occupied by the infant at her breast.

I pour boiling water over black leaves, steeped many times over, in a cracked teapot. We drink

244

the weak stew unsweetened, and we do not speak of my trouble again. So I count her among those who do not know.

★ ★ ★

She is my best friend; still, I don't tell Glad.

I haul myself out of the water and sit down, hard, on the slick tiles, my head between my knees at the edge of the pool. Glad swims close, pulls herself up by her elbows, and clambers to my side. She kneels and pets my wet hair. 'Are you all right?'

This is November, late into the month that I've always loved least, nagging and spindled and dull, pressed for light and colour. There is nothing to do in November but wait.

I think: I'm dying. I'm dying or I'm pregnant, one or the other, and I don't even care which.

'Are you okay?'

'Dizzy,' I mumble, although dizzy is the least of it. I am sick, through and through, all the way to my bones.

Glad gets me towelled off and changed. She gets me home to our apartment, and tucked into my bed. She boils water for tea, but brews it too weak. I'm feeling better and do not complain. When Johnny comes hurrying up the stairs, banging open the door to my bedroom, I've heard his approach and I pretend to be asleep under blankets pulled high.

'She's got the flu, she's resting,' I hear Glad tell him. She is just a little bit out of breath. Protective. She leads him out of my dark room.

245

Olive brings me broth. For three days, I lie in my bed. I can't think what else to do, too unwell to escape the apartment and run against the bitter wind and shrinking light. Bone-crushing weariness washes over me in cycles, so that I feel briefly better and allow myself to consider the possibility that I've guessed wrong, only to be swung back toward sickness, made worse by the feeling of certainty. This is what is happening. This is going to be my story.

I gag into my pillow.

'You haven't got a fever, so that's good.' Olive sits on the side of my bed, home from work, and wearing her smeared apron scented of chocolate. The smell makes me gag. She strokes my cheek. I think she is trying to be reassuring. But she is our mother's daughter, too, and when I turn to look at her — directly at her — I tell her with my eyes, and she reads my diagnosis. *No, I haven't got a fever, have I, Olive.*

'Oh, Aggie.'

We hold hands. She does not ask me what I am going to do. She is our mother's daughter. She waits instead for me to tell her what I am going to do.

I push my way out from under the unwashed blankets. 'I haven't talked to him,' I say, standing and wandering about the room, feeling caged, mildly frantic, weakly reaching for the cool plaster wall.

'You need to eat more, drink more. You'll feel better.'

'I'm getting dressed, and I'm coming downstairs,' I say.

Unfortunately it is Glad's night to cook: fried fatty slices of ham served with onions, slightly burnt.

I am surprised to find Johnny at our table too. He is waiting, holding out his plate with an expectant look on his face. Glad stands at the stove wearing a pink polka-dotted apron trimmed with frills. She does not look quite exactly like herself, though I can't say precisely why not. I have the sensation that I've stumbled onto an illicit scene, even though everyone is fully clothed and Olive has come down before me, and sits at the table too, waiting her turn.

Glad serves Johnny first, stabbing a dry hank of ham out of the pan and scooping blackened onions on top.

'Sit,' she orders me, and she pours me a glass of thick milk, which I manage with some effort to work down. But I can't for the life of me swallow even one bite of ham and onions. The mere act of cutting the fraying meat has me sweating and gritting my teeth. The milk is churning a sour froth in my gut, and the smell and sight of the pale pink flesh coming apart under my knife and fork triggers a gag, and another, and I stand abruptly. Without excuse, I run from the room.

I can hear that I've been followed. I flush the toilet, grateful for indoor plumbing. I rinse my mouth. I lean my head against the door. I don't want to go out there. I don't want to talk to him. But he is waiting for me, I know.

I open the door.

'Johnny?' I whisper.

His arms are crossed and he leans with one shoulder against the wall. I can't read his posture, nor his face. I want to see concern, tenderness, but that is not what I see. I see idle interest, vague disgust. He shouldn't have followed me. I'm angry that he has stood outside the door, spying, intruding on the private sounds of my sickness. I stalk past him to the bedroom and sit on the edge of my bed, my hands loose in my lap. They're shaking and I let them lie there on my lap, one wrist on either knee, palms facing up while I stare down with a sense of distance, as if I am removed from my own body.

Johnny takes his time walking down the hallway. *He knows*, I think, when he closes the door and stands with his back against the long mirror. I see no dainty way to wrest open the conversation, and so I plunge directly in, as if into frigid water that arrests my breath.

'I might be . . . I am . . . I think. Having your baby.' I look at my shaking hands, not at him. I can't bear the sight of his reaction, yet I can't bear not knowing. I glance up at him with those words splashed into the air — *having your baby* — feeling shy, hot, humiliated, infuriated, and he does not deny that this might be so. 'It's my fault,' I offer because I feel that I should, that he expects it of me. I hope to catch his eye now that I've found it in me to look at him. I'm braver. The cold is bracing, but it won't kill me. I turn my hands to grip my legs, wrapping the knee bones, unconsciously pulling myself into a protective hunch.

I'm ever so slightly reassured to see that the

news has stirred him up.

But he won't look at me, and can't seem to take it in, moving restlessly around the room. 'Are you sure?'

'I don't know! It's never happened to me before.'

'What are you going to do?'

I have no idea. For once in my life, I want him to tell me. No, I want him to say, with absolute hope and kindness and ardour: *Here is what we are going to do*. Maybe he could shout it. Would that be too much to ask? He could lift me in his arms, swing me in an elated embrace. Why doesn't he? He could win me over and have me for good, if he tried even a little bit. Instead he paces the room, avoiding my eye. He plucks items from off my dressing table and stares at them. He goes and lays his fist against the windowpane, staring out across the street, his shoulders tight, the back of his neck shaved to short bristles. All the hope goes out of me.

The days are short and the deepness of night is already out there, beyond the glass. I can't see another way.

'I'm going home,' I announce suddenly, with what passes for conviction. 'I need to see my mother.' Still, he doesn't turn.

Nor does he prevent me.

And suddenly it becomes too late for whatever might have been, whatever might have come to me, and to us, if only he would kneel before me and put his head in my lap, and say — but, no, I shall stop myself from going on in this way. Because that is not what happens.

249

This is the way it goes, instead.

Johnny turns from the window, says, 'That sounds good. Your mother must miss you.' As if we are now talking only about a visit.

'She does miss me, yes,' I say.

'Let me help. Let me pay for your train ticket.' He comes nearer, his fingertips tucked into the palms of his hands. It's a habit he has. His fingernails and the grooves of his fingerprints are stained black and oily from his work with automobile engines. As if I mind. How will he get to medical school? Oddly — with sadness — I think of this even as we're saying good-bye.

'That is very kind,' I tell him, of his offer to purchase a ticket, 'but no, thank you.'

'I insist.'

'So do I.' My blood rising, my spirit. 'So do I, Johnny!'

He stands in silence. We could turn the ship, yet, couldn't we? There's still time. Silent before me, head dropping to chest. Quietly he says, 'Write me, won't you, Aggie?'

And he goes, like that, quietly, shutting the door behind himself with care and caution. I would like to say that tears are shed, teeth gnashed, passion stirred, but instead I sit frozen, my eyes hooked on the thin line at the bottom of the door where the electric light from the hallway shines under. My room is quite dark. It is lit only by the pale yellow glow that rises up from the streetlights below, fogged and haloed.

I do not protest.

And there is no returning to this room or this moment, nor will there be, ever again.

Olive accompanies me home for Christmas, early. She tells Mother as soon as we catch a private moment together, because I can't bring myself to. It is just the three of us. I stand silent, teeth gritted, staring out the kitchen window at our snowed-in fields, at Cora stalking grimly to the barn in her grey mittens, carrying a basket to collect the morning's eggs.

'I thought there was something peaky about you,' Mother says. She is as level as Johnny's prairie. She does not fall into imagining the worst for me. She brings me to the Granny Room, and lays me on the bed, and palpates my abdomen through the silky fabric of my dress. She tells me I am about three months on, and what would I like to do?

I would like to undo what's happened. Or, I would like Johnny to come for me. Both, I think.

She waits. When I do not reply, my mother says that a young woman in my situation has options, not many, just a few. 'You could birth the baby, and we could find a home for it, or you might miscarry and the baby will come too early.' She does not say that she will help bring on a miscarriage. She does not say that I might keep the baby.

I can't think clearly.

'There is not a great deal of time to wait,' she says. 'When the early months have passed, the baby is quite settled and will grow regardless. Do you understand?'

'I thought Johnny . . . ' I falter.

'Does he know?'

I nod and look at her helplessly. How many versions of this old story has my mother listened to, without judgement, and though never foolish herself? Now here is a question for which I would love the answer, and failed to ask when given the chance: why does my mother choose to help foolish girls?

'I'm sorry, Mother,' I tell her and her face goes soft and her eyes fill with tears, for me, and she strokes my face. 'I know.'

She knows her help can only encompass so much, and after that I'll be on my own, as you are, if you are brave enough to know it — though I could put that differently, I suppose. I could say you're on your own, as you are, if you're stubborn enough to know it.

'Let me help,' my mother says.

Here it is, told plain and thin. I'm become a girl in the Granny Room.

★ ★ ★

I return to Toronto in the spring, coming the same way I'd gone: by train.

Johnny is waiting for me at the station. Glad too. They stand near each other — not too near — but she looks at him and he at her, only a glance, brief as lightning, as the train shudders to a stop. They cannot know that I am watching them. It is like intercepting enemy code. Their seriousness, their silence, their unity as they wait for me is frightening. I know, instantly.

Still, when the three of us meet at the bottom

of the steps, we appear to go on as before, as if nothing has changed. Pretence erects a stiff structure around me, dictating what I can and cannot say or do, lest I crumble — or the world beyond me crumbles. There are rules. I must hold fast.

Glad is quick to throw her arms around me and reach up to kiss me on both cheeks, and I receive her offering warmly, my heart beating wildly. She does not seem a stranger, and I want to weep with relief.

'Are you all better then? Are you quite well?'

I bite my lip and nod yes. I cling to Glad. I've missed her.

I don't dare look at Johnny to guess his thoughts. Did we ever really know each other? It seems unfathomable. It is as if he is that much greater than me, and I am that much smaller. If she notices, Glad doesn't let on. She holds me at arm's length, a whirlwind of information, reporting on our apartment, and on the irritating habits of the roommate who has replaced me, and on how I am not to worry, because I can stay in her room — Glad's — for now.

I don't want to stay in Glad's room.

We are following a script we can't step away from.

I'm a wretched actress, never worse, but Glad and Johnny read their lines naturally, believably, and I can only look on and admire their fluency in dissemblance, quite out of my reach.

Johnny does not kiss me, of course. I am surprised when he squeezes my hand. The hope that leaps in my heart at his touch is dreadful. I think, *Couldn't we continue like this, the three of us? Couldn't we, just?* I think how happy we could be, the three of us. I don't need him all to myself, I think. I could let her have as much of him as she liked. I wouldn't be jealous, if only I could keep them both, like this.

Johnny is squeezing my hand, and my heart soars, but just as abruptly, he lets go my fingers from his. I struggle to find a reason to keep breathing. Jealousy attacks me like a coward, leaping from behind, and I know that I can't share, after all — either of them.

'I'll stay with Olive,' I say. I don't make an excuse for turning down Glad's offer to share her own room.

'Oh!' says Glad, as if I've hurt her, but I don't care.

★　★　★

The roommate with the alleged irritating habits who has taken my former quarters is not a runner. She works days, dawn to dusk, piecing gloves in a factory, and passes her spare hours at the pictures. She seems genuinely excited to meet me — a girl whose picture she's seen in a magazine — but she does not take to me. In real life, in the flesh, I disappoint. All the qualities projected onto a girl photographed in a fur coat pale when the girl herself steps into one's kitchen, wearing gloves and a hat and a blue serge coat with plain black buttons. Especially when the girl is me. Girl of projection: beautiful, self-possessed, elegant, bold. Girl of reality: in

254

need of a hairbrush, distracted, scattered, cool.

The roommate is the sort of girl who takes care of her clothes and hair. She keeps the door to her room closed and spends plenty of leisurely time before the bathroom mirror, or so I assume. When we pass each other in the hallway or the kitchen, the silence is awkward, broken by mistimed statements about the weather that cross each other in the air.

The ginger tom has forgotten me, and hisses whenever I come near. I try not to take offence, but it seems a judgement. My spirits are that low. I am not prepared to be the person I have become.

This is the thick of summer. I practice exercises in Olive's room, between the bed and the wall of windows. I place my hands flat on the floorboards to stretch my aching legs. I jog in place and perform jumping jacks that shake the rafters. The windows are open and the air off the lake is humid. It is far too late in the season to qualify for the Canadian championships, even if I wanted to.

'Come join us at the track,' Glad offers, but I decline.

'I'm still mending,' I say, and cough lightly, touching my chest with my fingers to prove it — Olive and I agreed last winter it would be best if she returned to the city and spread the word that I'd taken ill, and that my mother was caring for me. Even the suggestion of tuberculosis would be better than the whisper of unwanted pregnancy. As I cough, I realize that I almost believe the lie myself. It's so plausible: of course

I cannot run with Glad and Johnny. My cough is to blame. My cough has made me weak.

And it is true that I am weak, or weakened. I've pushed myself down too far inside, sanded off my edges, narrowed my hopes. I've got a secret now. It dare not be spoken, lest it ruin me.

Where to start again, after that?

Staring at myself in Olive's mirror, I think that I look essentially unchanged — slender, tall, pale, my hair long, almost transparent — yet I feel strange within the apartment, my former home, its high white walls and huge open windows somehow confining. This is a place where I've been so free, so certain of love. Thinking of it, reminded, I can hardly breathe. But I cannot bear to leave its safety. I hide in Olive's hushed room, relieved that she works long hours and that I am all alone. Sometimes I lie flat on the wide wood floorboards and bathe in radiant sunshine that streams through the windows, soaking in the warmth, as if it might liven me to wakening.

At night, I share the bed with my sister.

Sometimes I wake and I am holding her by the hand. Sometimes I wake and she is already awake, peering at me with concern. 'You were talking in your sleep again. Shouting, more like it.'

I tell her I can't remember.

'Just a dream,' she says, and I agree. But it is hard to relax. I curl in on myself and draw to the edge of the bed, as far from Olive as I can get, and try not to focus on her breathing, which tells me she's lying there just as awake as I am, both of us miles from sleep.

I do not leave the apartment for an entire week, and then another, and another, and another, long enough to lose the roommate, who gives her month's notice at the end of July, which is bad news, as I can ill afford to pay my share of the rent.

The tomcat switches his tail at me in disdain.

I hear Johnny's voice, occasionally, in the rooms downstairs, and I take care not to go down, and he does not come up. Once I step unguardedly into the kitchen and discover him sitting at the table with a cup of tea, his feet bare and propped up on a chair, his hair slicked down and wet, perhaps with sweat. It is almost as if I've been electrocuted, so violent is my reaction. There is no hiding the way I crash against the doorframe, continue like an automaton to the cupboard over the sink, open it, stare inside blankly, leave it open, and stumble out of the room, smashing my shoulder again against the frame, as if my trajectory, once set, cannot be changed. As if I can't see the opening, only its hard edges.

* * *

I am inside the apartment, alone before Olive's mirror, brushing my hair one hundred strokes, one thousand, when Glad wins the 100-metre dash for the second year in a row, retaining her reign as Canadian women's champion. Johnny takes third place in the hurdles, and promptly announces his retirement. He intends to go to

257

medical school instead.

Olive carries home the afternoon paper and knocks on the door. She knows I'm in here, but she doesn't choose to disturb me, even though it is her room, by rights. I hear the sound of newsprint sliding under the door, paper crinkling and rustling, and of Olive's soft retreating footsteps. She's folded the pages in such a way that I am certain to see the two of them the moment I turn to look. Here they are, pictured in black-and-white, Glad and Johnny, the two of them together. Yet they are no more together than they were when I saw them beside the train. They do not touch, they face the camera, they grin in tandem. But I see it clearly: I've been forgotten — no, it is as if I don't exist. I feel clammy, though it's hot.

I don't say to Olive 'I'm going out.' I overtake her in my rush down the stairs, and I don't stop running until I'm outside. I feel like a bug whose rock has just been overturned, exposed suddenly to the blaring massive world from which it has been hiding.

I stumble along the crowded summer street: electric trolleys and horse carts and automobiles sounding horns and bicycles and dogs and children underfoot or chasing balls and I know that I must look for a job, and soon. No one is going to hire me to pose in a fur coat or a bathing costume. My time has come and gone. So soon. I can hardly believe it. The understanding fills my body from the outside in like cold water is being pumped into my bowels. There is no money anymore, the money has vanished in the crash. This new decade has stumbled before it can get properly started — where will it go?

I begin to run, between people, around them, my feet in their hard-soled black shoes tapping the paved sidewalk. I run even though I know how ridiculous I must look in my long dark skirt and elbow-length sleeves. I run south until everything crowding in on me grows indistinct and loses shape and doesn't matter, until I meet the lake, and then I stop and hold myself still, and watch the water lap the shore.

Is it possible that I am twenty-two and already at the end of the best part of my story?

★   ★   ★

Glad cries.

I hear Olive on the stairs, coming in from outside, and I hear her pause, and retreat and go back down and close the door. I hear the click of Olive's key in the lock, shutting us in. She's guessed, too, what we all know, and she's been waiting, like all of us, for what must finally be done about it.

Glad and Johnny are in love.

That is not what Glad says.

She says, 'We'd like to marry, Johnny and me. Oh, Aggie.' She slumps in one of the hard, velvet-covered chairs I bought with my fur money, and which we arranged in front of the fireplace that has never worked. The sounds that accumulate on a hot city sidewalk rise and spill through our open window and into the long narrow room. We'll never fill the room with enough furniture. It echoes. Glad wipes her eyes and blows her nose exhaustively into a handkerchief.

'This is awful,' she says, looking up at me.

'No, it's not,' I say, leaning my tall frame against the plaster wall beside the fireplace, suddenly as languid and easy as a blade of meadow grass moving with the wind. I'm relieved it is up to her to tell me, and not Johnny, although it seems cowardly on his part, fundamentally unfair. I suppose it speaks to their relationship: Glad is happy to spare Johnny the suffering, and Johnny is happy to be spared. I suppose it speaks to my relationship with each of them too. I see that I trust Glad in a way that I never trusted Johnny. I've always been sure of Glad.

I come close, kneel before her, and lay my head in her lap, and hold her hands.

'I'm a terrible friend,' says Glad solemnly. 'You deserve better.'

'You're not. You're the best friend I ever had.' I mean it too, even as I hear the past tense eliding us into once upon a time. I see Glad in that claustrophobic change room in the bowels of Rosebud Confectionary, marching up to me and telling me what to do. I see her sleek bobbed head cresting inexorably past mine on the track, and I remember looking for her as I cross the line and steal gold. What do I care of Johnny? I've had many months to foreclose on that loss. I can convince myself that I never really knew him, the distance between us like a long railroad line between the East and the Prairies. What we had seems ordinary, I guess, something anyone else might have too, and I can pretend that ordinary comes easy, goes easy.

It's Glad I want to keep.

'Where will you live?' I wonder, and stop myself. 'No, don't tell me. I don't need to know.'

'We won't get married right away,' Glad says all in a rush. 'We'll wait. Until everyone is ready.'

'Ready?' I cry, pulling away from her. 'Everyone?'

I am ashamed, my desolation circling her ankles like a beaten dog.

What went wrong between us? I want to know, as if she's done this to me deliberately, just to hurt me.

She is distracted and rises, pacing around the room like she's marking out a track for a race we've yet to run.

I want to tell her about being a girl in the Granny Room and have to curl into a ball to stop the truth from flowing out.

Please get up, she says to me. I'll always be your friend. Please believe me.

16

Alone

There. I've just denied my own sister. I've said I don't know her. I've said she couldn't be who they say she is. I've told a terrible lie, and the room is rocked by it.

'She's not making sense anymore.'

'No, it's that she doesn't believe us.'

'I'm going to cry!'

'Don't get dramatic, Kaley,' the woman says. 'We'll take her to the lighthouse, like we planned. It's this house. She's not happy here.'

I've told a terrible lie, and my heart is rocked by it.

I'm experiencing an old familiar itch. It isn't good. It's the urge to confess, to tell all, like a bared and humbled person who wants to scrape herself clean, to cut from herself a balled-up truth that's so ingrown it will leave an ugly hole in its absence.

I've hidden this scrap so long, I thought I'd killed it, but here it is, beating like an extra heart.

I want these people to know. I very particularly want the girl — the runner — to know.

Is this why I'm here, in this room where I shouldn't be, looking out this window at a stand of pines, with no one to reassure me that I am who I believe myself to be? Something has rushed us toward one another, some clarity of purpose that I can't recognize. But I will. I will get to the bottom of it. It is my job, after all. It is a job I'm very good at, no matter that I'm a woman: I get to the bottom and bring up every piece of it and hang it out clean and simple, without adornment, plain and true and utterly, intractably mysterious.

★ ★ ★

Our grand apartment over Yonge Street empties out like it's been lifted and turned upside down, its contents pitched into the trash heap of begone and good riddance. Glad escapes home to her family; that is all I know, and I don't want to know more. Olive and I move without leaving a forwarding address, together, into a different apartment, a rooming house with a landlady who cooks the meals. We bring with us the hard, velvet-covered chairs, which we stuff into the single shabby respectable room we share, like we did before I'd gone golden.

'You look familiar.' The landlady scrutinizes me, almost accusingly, when Olive and I come to arrange about the room.

'I'm Olive Smart, and this is my sister Aganetha Smart,' says Olive. 'Aganetha won gold for Canada at the Olympics.'

The woman gazes blankly between us.

'She beat a German girl in a running race.'

No, the woman shakes her head. That isn't it. She frowns at me. Even though the weather is merely mild, I am wearing the fur coat from the advertisement that I made for Canada's most famous department store, and which I kept as part of my payment, and which I have not sold, even though Olive and I could use the money. Olive is the one who tells me not to: 'You're better off keeping something like that, in the long run. Who knows when it will come in handy?'

The fur coat offers courage and disguise. I turn the collar up around my neck and strike a pose. Recognition flickers across the woman's face. She appears to be any age between thirty and fifty, with skin as waxy and smooth and plain as a clean white potato.

'Aganetha also modelled in advertisements.'

'I knew it! I knew I knew you. Come in, see the room. You're boarding together, are you? Sisters?'

'Sisters.'

Olive also finds me a job at Rosebud, even though half the girls have been fired and those who remain have taken a pay cut. The Rosebud Ladies' Athletics Club has vanished as presumptively as it arrived. The track goes unkempt. Mr. P.T. Pallister himself is rumoured to have gone insane or tried to kill himself. It is his wife now in charge of the business, and she is hard as stone, because it is her duty to keep what he couldn't safe for her children. Mothers can be hard when it comes to their children.

Leave it to Olive to get me hired under such circumstances.

Olive is resourceful like that. By spring, having got me settled, she will find herself a husband in similar fashion, applying sheer determination and persistence, even if he will move her to Australia. She will blend in with her new circumstances. She will farm sheep, her fair skin broiling under a foreign sun. She will do battle with herds of wild rabbits. She will raise a handful of hearty Australian children. Her letters to me, arriving several times a year, seem to drop in from another planet, a world only remotely connected to my own. I can't read them without being moved to tears. The thought of Olive — sturdy, practical, indispensable — claiming a brand-new life, stomping her own path in rubber wellies and trousers, her dark hair gone to wild grey. I ask for photographs. She'll travel home for our mother's funeral, but not our father's, and after that we will not see each other again.

But for now, we are together. For now, I take us for granted, and our pairing in times of need, the comfort of sharing a bed and sleeping side by side, her shallow night-time breath warm on my neck.

GUNN, OLIVE. Born June, 1904, in Canada, Olive moved to Australia in 1931 and never looked back. Died June, 1999 in Middle Park, Australia, shortly after celebrating her 95th birthday. Predeceased by husband, Herbert (1985), and survived by two sons and two daughters, and by grandchildren and great-grandchildren too numerous to name here. Her declining years were diffi-cult, but Olive never lost her generous spirit. *'A life lived well!'*

★ ★ ★

I feel hollow. I go about my tasks in a haze, removed from the ordinary sensations of living. 'Keep moving,' the girl beside me has to prompt as the greasy moulds pile up at my elbow, and I stand staring blankly into space, thinking of nothing, it seems.

I can't enter into my body; it is a struggle. I am drifting. I drift toward vanishing.

Except when I am running.

When I am running I inhabit and exit my body in the same moment. I bear witness to the harshest of physical sensations, even while I feel myself flying free and away. I do not want to remember what has happened to me. I do not want to reflect on the past. I can't, in a way. I'm not made for regret.

I run alone, out behind Rosebud Confectionary. I run evenings, after my shift, even after the snow falls, even after it piles deep, I run with extra socks under my black boots, slipping and sliding around and around, knocking a path flat where my feet land.

I suppose I look a sight. I suppose I don't care a hoot.

I run until the lights on the top floor of the factory go dark. That means the floor has been cleaned for the night, and the women are moving their heavy buckets down to one below, wrung mops slung over shoulders. Then I run the four streets over to the narrow row house where Olive and I share a room. Soaked through, I change out of my wet woollen clothes in a hurry, shivering, chilled to the core. There isn't enough hot water to draw a bath, but Olive fetches a boiling kettle from the landlady's kitchen and fills a basin, and I damn near scald myself sluicing my arms and face and neck with a hot cloth, wringing it out and washing until the water has lost its heat. And then I wrap in blankets and huddle in our shared bed until the shivering stops.

The landlady saves me supper.

★ ★ ★

It's March. It must be just March. The light has changed. Evenings are brighter, the snow is a dirty skiff on the track. I am loosening into my warm-up rounds when I see Glad coming around the side of the squat flat-roofed red brick factory building. She must have slipped through the fencing. I am too startled to stop, though I feel like I've been thrown sideways. Yet I hardly pause in my stride.

I haven't glimpsed sight of her since our parting last summer, the memory of which I've shredded and burnt and buried.

She falls in beside me as I pass by her. We don't say a word as we pace each other stride for stride around the track. I'm on the inside, so she has to work a little harder on the turns, like another race we ran together.

I consider saying to her 'I'm sorry. I didn't mean to beat you, I only meant to win.' But I can't say what isn't true — I'm not sorry and never will be, because gold was what I wanted. I would have given anything to win, yes; wouldn't she have too?

We go twice around like this, in silence,

winding ourselves up, until we're giddy from the absurdity, almost, giggling at our own speechless awkwardness. I can't be the first to speak — it's what I feel strongly when I first see her coming around the building, that it is up to Glad to say whatever she's come to say. But as we run stride for stride, step for step, an easiness enters my bones and muscles, a lightness I haven't experienced in all the months of hard solitary work, and it is all I can do to stop myself from lifting her into a whirling hug. That's how much I've missed her.

'Sprints?' she says to me.

I nod.

We run Coach Tristan's favourite drill, jogging the turns, sprinting the straightaways, around and around until I'm quite certain I'll be sick. We're gasping on the turns, slowing to a crawl as we prepare ourselves for the burn of another go.

I don't want to be the first to quit. From her silence, I know Glad doesn't either.

We've stopped looking at each other. We can't speak. We're too far gone. Without a coach to give us the signal, I fight through the fog of depletion to wonder what will happen. Will we go until one of us drops? Or will we go forever? It seems a possibility.

Glad stumbles — how many laps in? It is growing dark. She stumbles and I grab her hand to prevent her falling into the hard gravel and icy chunks on the track. I feel it before I see it — a ring, a band of cold metal. I pull away.

She says nothing, but her smile is sad. Maybe I'm just projecting.

'You're married?' The words slam out of me. I can't stop them, surprised by the anger in my voice.

'Just,' Glad confesses. 'I wanted to tell you before it came out in the papers.'

'I never read the papers,' I say.

'Well,' she says. 'Well. We're married.'

'That's nice.' What else am I to say? Not that, I think furiously — saying nothing would have been better.

'Isn't it?' Glad leaps on my conventional reply. Her sweet face opens to my pinched envy. 'Oh, isn't it?' As if I might be a friend like any other, but I am not, and she is not. We are not just friends, and never have been, right from the very start. From the very start we've been rivals too, opponents, competitors. Perhaps Glad has always known this; perhaps I did not want to.

She's won. She's beat me. I may have bested her in a running race — gently fading victory — but this time, when it really matters, I've lost, and she wants, sweetly and hopefully — do you see what I am saying? — to be certain that I know.

She wants to hurt me, just a little bit; only now do I understand.

I'm not angry anymore.

'It is nice,' I say, of her marriage, but also of all that I can now leave unspoken between us. I need not apologize for what's gone before. I need only give her leave to be who she is, and love her as she goes, which is all that has ever been asked of me — isn't it? — by the ones that I love. 'It's very very nice,' I say again, flushing as I repeat myself.

'I'm glad,' she speaks confidingly.

'Of course you are, you'll always be,' I say, attempting a joke.

After a pause: 'You're working here again?'

I nod. I don't mention that my job is in the scullery, cleaning moulds. The long metal trays with their inverted rosebuds must be scoured and sterilized in a three-step process that cracks and reddens the skin on my hands and arms, and steams open the pores of my face. My hands look like they belong to an old woman, but my face is clear as a child's.

Glad and I cross the dirty slush that is freezing into hard ridges as night approaches. I offer her a drink from the glass jar I keep by the door. The water is sharp with shards.

When we've drunk, I open the back door of the factory with a key, and we walk along the quiet hall, past the darkened windows, over the parquet flooring, dripping wet, aching, flushed and silent, quite as if nothing has ever changed, as if inside these walls we've stepped into our former selves: teammates, friends.

'Miss Smart,' nods the night watchman. He opens the front door for us, and we pass through and out into the darkening night. The doors are locked behind us.

We stand in the street at the bottom of the factory's wide polished concrete steps.

I need to go home to the room I share with Olive. I need the kettle of hot water, and the scalding cloth, and the blankets, and my bed. I need the landlady's plate of mash with carrots and boiled salt pork. I need what I need.

270

Glad needs what she needs.

'I can't retire yet,' Glad is telling me. 'I want to see Los Angeles! I hear the weather's beautiful. What about you, Aggie? Won't you race this summer? You can't keep training all by yourself.'

I've not been thinking of these sessions as preparation for anything at all. This isn't training, it's survival.

'Johnny's studying medicine — and I've been running with the university's team. You'd like the coach. He's just as mean as Mr. Tristan, not that you'd know about that. You were always Tristan's favouri — '

'Please, Glad. I don't need a coach.' Harsher than I mean it to be. I begin to walk, Glad falling in beside me.

'I'm not a student, I'm just training with them — I'm the only girl — it's really fun, you'd love it, Aggie, and you're just as good as any of us. You could keep up.'

I shake my head.

'But I miss you, Aggie.'

My stomach plunges. *You do?*

'I'm sorry,' I hear myself saying. I see that it is my turn to walk away, to step into the corn and vanish.

'It's for the best.' I quicken my pace. I'm shivering in my damp clothes, and she must be chilled too. We need to get out of the cold.

'You're not saying good-bye?' Glad may be entirely sincere but she sounds like a breathless actress in a movie, a Jean Harlow type. I laugh. I actually laugh. It could be taken as cruel, but

271

Glad laughs in return. 'Of course not,' she says, to reassure herself. 'Of course it's not good-bye, it never is, not really.'

I let her think so.

We part ways on the corner of Queen and Spadina. I run all the way home and resist the urge — this time — to glance over my shoulder, to look back.

★ ★ ★

I've looked back before. I've looked back enough.

That photo at the finish line, taken August 10, 1928 — it does not show what it seems to show. It does not show the victorious stride of a golden girl runner. It shows the finish of a girl who couldn't have won if she hadn't stolen victory from a friend.

In the photo, I am looking over my shoulder, but not at the German girl, whom I'm besting at the line, no — I am looking for Glad. *Where are you? Where have you gone?*

The race does not go as planned.

Right at the start, the American jumps out to a strong lead that begins to seem, far too soon, too wide a berth for comfort. I've woken this morning feeling not quite myself, my nightdress damp with sweat. Nerves? Illness? I don't mention it to Miss Gibb, nor to Mr. Tristan. I can't eat my breakfast; instead sip half a cup of strong coffee, and here I am, tight as a bow, progressing around the track. Here we are. As we complete the first 400-metre lap, I feel depleted, washed with doubt. The emotion is unfamiliar and it is utterly crushing. *You won't catch that girl. You can't.*

There is something wrong.

This happens in races. It happens to excellent athletes: it has happened so very recently to Glad. There are those who shine in practice and training, and who cannot turn their minds to belief, against resistance, when under pressure. I am shocked to find myself in this position as we approach the turn where, I know, I must make my move. But I hurt. It isn't a physical hurt, it is an enveloping, almost sweet-tasting interior pain — the pain of acceptance. I am going to accept that this is happening. I am going to let it happen. I am not going to make my move after all.

I am going to give up.

That is when Glad arrives, at my shoulder. We move as one into the turn, with Glad on the outside, boxing out a girl who presses from behind. As we straighten onto the back stretch I hear her say — *Now, Aggie! Let's go!* — though I can't put straight whether she's said the words out loud, or whether her mind has spoken to mine. We are picking up the pace down the stretch, side by side, and at the final curve, again, she boxes out the girl behind us — it's the German girl — and I see the American falter. Minutely. I see her stride express a stagger of doubt.

Glad makes a move to pull ahead and the space between us stretches like an elastic band, widening. *When it matters, you let her win,* I

273

hear Mr. Tristan's prophecy. *You let her win*. It is astonishing the density of thought that can be compressed into a single moment, into one or two strides on a flat grass course.

The space between us widens, our connection stretched to its limit. But the band does not break. Instead, it is as if I am being flung forward, like a pebble inside a slingshot, as if she is pulling on me, launching me to victory. In a few quick steps, I hurtle past Glad. I feel her giving me something — I feel it like a surge of electrical power, and I open my stride and kick down the homestretch, gaining on the American like she's standing still.

I will win this race.

I have no thought of Glad until that final step, when I turn to look for her.

And she isn't there. Not yet, not yet, not yet.

I cross the line alone, the German girl on my heels, the American fading for third, and Glad well back in fourth, out of the record books. Her joy at my victory seems unconditional. I think that scares me more than if she were to slap me.

Because I've seen her bent over in wailing agony as the girls run the 100-metre dash without her. I've seen her rise up and vanish, helped by Mr. Tristan, under the stands. I've seen her composed that very evening at dinnertime, laughing off sympathy, approaching the American girl who won with her hand outstretched.

Because the pictures do not fit together. How can anyone be so jagged, so broken, and so rapidly, smartly healed?

She was ahead of me, and I chased her down

and crashed past her, and I am certain, sick with certainty, that in those final heedless, aggressive strides I stole what should have been hers, ruthlessly. I don't think she gave it to me, for all that it would make the more comforting tale to tell myself. I think I took it, because I'd seen her weak and fallen, and I knew that I could.

And now. And now. What do I owe to Glad? Aren't we even, after all?

It's just a race.

Let me leave her here, forever behind me, forever beyond me. I wonder at my love for her. Sometimes I think I must have loved her more than I ever loved Johnny. Sometimes I think she must have loved me too, more than him, in some strange way. I know that sounds delusional — may be delusional — but I can't think of a better reason to give and take as we gave and took, except for love.

She sends me a Christmas card, two years running, at the newspaper. She's seen my byline. This is a few years on, after the war has begun. She and Johnny have a boy and a girl — the millionaire's family, she writes — and a home in Calgary by the river. They can see the mountains while sitting at their dining room table.

The second card, the following year, is less newsy. She signs her name and Johnny's under the salutation, 'Merry Christmas and a Happy New Year!'

I reply to neither. I'm not the Christmas card type.

★ ★ ★

275

There is more to the story of this summer: 1931.

I owe the trajectory of my life to Mr. P.T. Pallister, owner of Rosebud Confectionary and, briefly, patron of the elite Canadian female athlete. I'd saint him if I believed in sainthood. But Mr. P.T. Pallister would never have found me save for my brother George. I was a long shot. Improbable. I was a bet made by my brother — a gambler whom no one would ever saint. And so it is to George that I owe the greater debt.

Tattie sends her eldest, the boy, to my door with a message to visit, please, and I accompany the child home, not wanting him to walk the streets alone. It is a summer Sunday and my legs ache from a long early run, pain in my shins.

Tattie greets me at the door with kisses on both cheeks, reaching up.

I don't know what I'm expecting. Not this.

George: 'Come in, come in, sit, recline in our parlour, said the spider to the fly. Tattie, a cup of brew for my world-famous sister.'

I perch on a wooden chair that teeters on rickety legs, missing several rungs.

George is in a fine mood. Expansive, desperate, wrapped in a greasy knitted blanket. He wants to talk and talk, and not about this — what is happening right now. He wants the past to cram into the room, to transport us all. He conjures up his own pestering letters written these vanished years ago to Mr. P.T. Pallister, singing my praises from on high. (I can only imagine their grammatical flaws and hyperbolic claims.)

'I just went on writing 'em till he had to agree to have you.'

'But, George! I never knew!'

'Didn't you wonder why the famous P.T. came knocking at your door?' George wheezes between coughs, laughing.

'It wasn't P.T. himself on the doorstep, you know. Not personally.' I'm near tears, seeing George like this. How could he have got so bad? I wouldn't have known — I chide myself for being a negligent sister, a reluctant visitor — if Tattie hadn't sent for me, thinking I might help, and won't I? I will help however I can.

'So it wasn't old P.T. himself banging down your door?' George wants a story from me. He hasn't got breath for his own.

'It was his secretary,' I say, trying not to spy too obviously around the crowded room that is furnished with unrelated objects, some of them not, strictly speaking, furniture. The curtains are drawn, and I see they aren't curtains, but blankets too worn and thin to be otherwise useful. 'A man in a black suit and proper hat, knocking at the door of 445 Bathurst, sending Mrs. Smythe, our landlady, into fits. I wasn't even there. Remember? Olive had found me a job at her factory — that was Packer's Meats, before we went to Rosebud. She'd got me a job as a runner.'

'Good job for you.'

'Wasn't it? But then P.T. offered me a better one.' I'm embroidering the story, a trick I learned from George himself, because it wasn't Mr. P.T. Pallister who offered me a job, not directly, and I only ever met the man but once,

277

when he shook my hand after the team arrived home from Amsterdam, hauling our gold and silver. That's three years ago, now, and Mr. P.T. Pallister locked up and insane, or so the story goes, but what use such details? I purge them from my version.

'You were quite a runner.' George reclines on his side on what looks to be a narrow bed, although the room we are in seems to be one where the family does its living. Tattie and the children hover in the corners like so many fluttering moths.

'Wasn't I?' I say.

'Still are,' George says.

'Nice of you to say so.' But my words are lost under a spell of coughing that brings Tattie running with a cloth, and I see there is blood. Tattie cradles his face in her hands. I sit stiffly and stare at the wall over George's head, unpainted plaster that is coming away in chunks, exposing the greying lathe.

I think, *I need to tell Mother.* It doesn't matter how old I get, nor how far away I live, I will always turn first to that thought: I need to tell Mother. Maybe she could help. Is he dying before my eyes?

I glance quickly, not wishing to disturb this private moment, and my brother's eyes catch mine and I can't look away, his face streaming with tears. He is six years older than me, and I am just twenty-three.

The sound of his thickened lungs lays waste to the room. The spell is coming to an end. He is still alive.

At last it stops. I've forgotten what we've been talking about, but George hasn't. He wants to make a joke. 'I'm dying. I'll say anything.'

I laugh, but it comes out as a sob.

'You'll run for Canada again,' he wheezes, urgently. 'You're that good. I just know it.'

I can't tell him how my luck is up.

'It doesn't matter,' I say. 'What matters is you getting better.'

Now he turns from me, furious, stares at the wall, the crumbling hole. Slowly, it comes to me that the hole is fist-size, the shape of his fist. He is burning, again.

'I'm sorry,' I say. 'I only meant . . . '

'Not getting better.' Low, in his chest. He starts up the coughing.

I don't understand his anger, but then, I've never understood it. We do not come from angry people, we Smarts. We are born whimsical, maybe, impractical, perhaps, a little bit baffled at the machinations of the world around us, a little bit lost. But not angry, not that. Even Cora, who has trained as a nurse and now works alongside our mother, with the goal of applying different principles to the troubles that come seeking their help — even Cora does her best to engage, to connect with the strangeness of the world in a way that will do no harm. George. He seems to want to do harm. Or it seems that he can't help himself. He will rage. He will lose control and fury will spill from him, he is made impatient — or is it terrified? — by the world around him, and what it owes him, and what it will never yield to his demands.

He wasn't always like this. Remember that. Forgive him.

'I'm sorry,' I'm saying to George, but he won't look at me. I've lit his invisible, unquenchable fuse.

Tattie hurries to attendance, gently urging me to standing. 'It's lovely of you to come, Aggie. We thank you.' She doesn't pretend that George will say good-bye. She doesn't pretend that our parting, now, can be anything other than abrupt.

'George,' I'm saying. 'I'm so sorry.'

Tattie pats my shoulder and pushes me toward the door that leads outside, and opens directly into this room. I do not need to retrieve my hat, which I haven't removed.

'I'm sorry, I'm sorry.'

I don't say good-bye, I don't get the chance, or understand that I am leaving, maybe that's what happens. The door is right there in the same room. Tattie and I are outside quite suddenly. Tattie comes with me onto the crumbling stoop, pulls shut the door behind us, tugs the edges of her sweater close at her neck even though it isn't cold out here — it is very nearly hot. Her hair is covered with a dull-coloured kerchief, tied at the back of her neck.

I am shocked to hear birds.

I dig around in my purse for what money I have, next to nothing, really, loose silver coins and a few copper pennies, which she accepts, thanking me.

I am speechless.

Tattie is waiting for me to leave, and when I don't, she nods without looking directly at me, and goes back inside to the crowded room, shutting the door behind her. I hope this garden belongs to their family. It is only a few feet in diameter, but healthy with greens and tomatoes and runner beans, reminding me of our garden on the farm. I push open the gate in a daze and turn into the alleyway and walk the short distance to the busy street, and then, farther, to one even busier.

My eyes are fixed in their inward focus. I turn down another busy street, a good head taller than any other woman walking here, bumping shoulders with the men.

'Watch where you're going!' 'Look alive!' 'Now see here — '

I spot a narrow opening between two storefronts, a passageway for rats. I press between the buildings and slide down the wall until I am sitting on the damp, filthy ground. I can sell the fur coat. I can sell the gold medal. But it won't be enough.

I am as alone as ever I will be. I'm glad to say so. I'm glad there is this moment, because never will I be so very alone again.

In my head I begin composing a letter to Miss Alexandrine Gibb.

August 21, 1931

Dear Miss Gibb,
For your help in the past, I thank you. I write to you now not for myself, but for the sake of a family thrown into desperate means, and whom I must now support, for

that family belongs to me, in one way or another. I am not asking for a handout. I need a job, better suited than the one I have. I would like to work for you.

Sincerely yours, Miss A. Smart

August 27, 1931

Dear Miss Smart,
I've found an opening here at the paper for a copy girl. If you stick it out, I will find you something better.

Sincerely, Miss A. Gibb

SMART, GEORGE. Formerly of Stony Hill Farm, New Arran, Ontario, and lately of Toronto, Ontario. Died suddenly at the age of twenty-nine. Bravely faced a life of illness. Much-loved brother and son. May he rest in peace.

17

The Obits

The inside of the car smells of forgotten sandwich crusts, spilled coffee, mouldering plastic.

Here is Fannie to warn me against folly, coming in through the car door, sliding behind the steering wheel.

Fannie! I'm so glad to see you!

But Fannie doesn't hear me. She switches on the heater, blasting us with stale air. She is humming something to herself, a tune broken by a few scattered, sung words as she steers us along the road and turns into our lane, inching slowly onward.

I turn to the man beside me — so young, I'm amazed that he's managed to grow hair on his face — and I say, Where are we going?

He stares at me through the remove of his camera. Someone squeezes my hand and whispers *There, there* — it's a woman, a stranger, I'm sure of it, sitting on the other side of me, clucking her tongue. I try to hide my worry because I do not want to upset Fannie, who sits so straight in the driver's seat. *I didn't know you knew how to drive*, I say to Fannie — meaning it as a joke, as we have no automobile on the farm, no motorized equipment, not even a tractor. The joke crumbles.

Fannie?

She turns — she turns! — and I gasp.

Not Fannie. A girl. I've forgotten her name.

'What did she just call me?'

'Fannie, I think,' says the young man with the camera. 'Stop turning around. Keep your eyes on the road.'

'It's hardly a road,' the girl says.

'I'm sorry, Miss Smart,' the woman beside me leans in and says, 'but the lane gets very bumpy back here. Hold on tight!' She reminds me of nurses, like Cora, who are forever telling you things you don't want to hear in cheery, hectoring tones. 'You'll find very little has changed since you left, except that the town keeps creeping closer and closer. Nothing stops progress! The barn's still standing, can you believe it? In that state. And the lighthouse. Such a unique addition to the property.'

'Who built it?' the boy asks, disembodied voice behind the camera. 'And why?'

'Are you asking me?' says the woman. 'Because I don't have a clue.'

'Not you, Mom.' He's mildly annoyed, the way that children are with their mothers these days; I've heard them at mealtimes when we're bumping elbows over the pudding, edge creeping into their tone, not even trying to hide it. The expression of any emotion is acceptable these days. Everything aired in the open.

'Miss Smart.' The boy changes his tone to 'cajoling,' and I have to smile. I pride myself on being impossible to cajole. 'Miss Smart, do you know who built the lighthouse?'

I nod slowly, solemnly. Obviously, my father

built it. His hand touched every building on this property. His hand and his mind's eye.

'Why a lighthouse?'

I'm tired of the question. I'm tired, altogether. I don't bother dredging up a reply that will satisfy neither of us.

Through the windscreen, beyond the girl's hair, which is tucked neatly behind her ear, I can see the barn approaching, what's left of it, and the lane leading out behind the barn where the horses pull the hay wagon up the sloped grassy hill and in through the big double doors at the rear, onto the main floor beside the mow where I help Father toss forkfuls of hay into the loft. It must be that I am very young, because I am sitting on my father's shoulders, 'helping,' my hands clutching his hair as he bends his knees to pitch another forkful, and my brother Robbie is tossing hay too, and Edith, and Fannie, Olive, and Cora, and even George, and my mother, all of us. We are all tossing forkfuls of hay and sneezing in the fine rain of dust.

'Bless you, Miss Smart.'

* * *

The editor, not the chief but my superior at the news desk, calls me into his office. He taps his cigarette into the black plastic ashtray and says, 'We're thinking of assigning you something less taxing than what you've been doing for us, Miss Smart.' He calls me Miss Smart around the office, and I call him Mr. Stephens, and only after work when we meet up for the occasional late dinner, do we drop the pretence. 'Something for our woman reader,' he adds.

'What do I know about your woman reader?' I stand right up, shoulders back. It's happening to me, as I've feared. They're moving me off my beloved beat covering crime, the most vicious and tragic our city has to offer, and the trials that aim to make amends and balance the scales, and cannot, because nothing could. I love my job. I earned it out of pluck and guts and diligence, and just listen to me — I've busted my posterior to keep it all these years.

'Well,' he hedges, flushing hot. 'Being as you're a woman.'

'You know me better than this.' I aim to keep my voice steady, that's all.

'Or obits,' he hedges some more. 'There's an opening. Think about it.'

Unspoken, underneath, is the year, 1945, and the end of the war, and all these fine young men come home to find their jobs filled by women like me, and oughtn't I do the right thing and move along to make room for a breadwinner? I'm just lucky, it goes without saying, that I'm not being shown the door. Which is where I'm headed right now, steam firing from my ears. I need to run this out.

'I'm sorry, Aggie,' he says in a low voice, calling me back. 'You know that, right?'

'Yes, Mr. Stephens. I'm sure you are.'

'You'll be brilliant at the obits. You'll dig up all the good stuff.'

'I appreciate you saying so.' I hold myself ramrod straight, face blank, and I exit before he can call me back again, and try to make it up to me with some gesture I'll despise — hopelessly ignorant of what I care about, and why.

From crime to obits. Sometimes I wonder: what's the difference between the ordinary face of evil and the ordinary face of success? Is it a difference of narrative, fundamentally, rather than character? A story gone off the rails versus a story contained and controlled? My job on obits is to collect the vicissitudes of a life and to freeze them into sense. I work to make the facts stand still, stay put. I stop time. I sum a person up, beginning, middle, end.

This is easy to do badly, and easier yet if one has no conscience, but it is painful to do well, nailing someone's feet to the floor. One begins to think about things like honour, like respect, like the shimmering necessity of not quite telling the truth.

Here's something I'll learn: when you're dead, you don't get to choose who's telling your story. The friends and children and wives willing to be interviewed are not necessarily those most intimate with the deceased; sometimes they are those who wished to have been intimate, or who think themselves more intimate than they actually were, or who suffer from regret, or denial. Getting the honest truth about a person from those left behind is a conjuring act. There exist simple questions, the answers to which build a kind of structure, a skeleton, which can be clothed in a few telling or humorous details. How is a life shaped? By parentage, siblings, class and religion, by schooling, vocational choices, by friends, partnerships, children, by place and time, by illness and accident, and sometimes, but most rarely, by surprising choice.

Surprising choice proves hardest to come by. Most choices, even the disastrous ones, are predictable.

★ ★ ★

The accident was no one's fault. Our mother simply slipped getting out of a bath, struck her head, and died instantly. That is not a detail one would choose to place into an obituary, speaking professionally. A reader might find herself confronted, in imagination, by the long naked body of a stranger, prone between toilet and tub, and a reader might not appreciate the vision.

Though Cora is a nurse, she cannot save her. Cora is not to be blamed.

'Will Edith be at the funeral?' I ask, as I've been wanting to ever since stepping through the summer kitchen door late yesterday and seeing Cora in her dark stern blouse and slacks and not reaching for her. We are three of us, sisters, bumping into each other as we move from cupboard to drawer to sink in the kitchen, a room that once was large and seems to have shrunk over the years.

'I couldn't say,' says Cora stiffly. 'It's a free country.'

Olive comes to stand behind me and strokes my hair, which I've kept long despite my years. I could be young again with her fingers waking my scalp. Olive has acquired an accent during her two decades away, in Australia. She no longer sounds precisely like herself. I can't quite quantify what else the years have done to her, what has been added or subtracted, how the burn of the sun at the bottom of the world has altered what she sees when she looks around this room, but if I were urged to, I would make a case for Olive being bolder than she was, less concerned about appearances. This could make me love her more than I already do, and miss her even in this instant, with her standing here behind me. I know how soon she'll be away again, and how far.

'And Edith's daughter?' I go on. I can't help myself, though I do manage not to say her name. I should stop, but I can't.

'I know nothing,' says Cora, and she drops into a chair, as if she's too tired to continue.

I press on. 'You never hear, not a word?'

Cora lifts and drops her shoulders. But she won't look at me. I think, *Even if she knows, she won't say.*

'Why? What's happened? Aren't you and Edith on good terms?' Olive presses Cora. 'Living side by side all these years?'

'Edith doesn't wish to speak to me. She wouldn't accept a pie I'd baked if I carried it over on a gold platter,' says Cora.

'Well this is news,' says Olive, and her fingers pause at the ends of my hair, which she pulls into a clump, then lets fall.

Cora says, 'I washed my hands of it long ago.'

'Aggie?' Olive bunches my hair into a wad, and drops it again.

But I have nothing to add to the conversation.

'Oh, yes, ask Aggie.' Cora pushes herself to

standing, her knuckles folded over on the wooden tabletop, like she's punishing herself for something. 'It's Aggie to blame. Ask her. She'll tell you.'

I won't. I'm forty-three goddam years of age, and I tower over this wrathful sister of mine, who flings the remains of our breakfast into the sink, and comes at the tabletop with a damp rag as if to smite all worldly crumbs and filth.

'Go ahead, talk! Talk behind my back,' Cora says, dragging on her big black rubber boots to march to the barn and look for Father, so that we can make him presentable before the service.

She slams the summer kitchen door so hard that it bounces open again, rather than shut. Olive and I look at each other and being to laugh so wildly that we're weeping, that it hurts, that I am left some while later with aching muscles in my throat and cheeks and abdomen. Contrary to Cora's accusation, we do not talk behind her back, though perhaps this is not due to worthy application of morality, but only because I have nothing to add. I don't know what has happened between Cora and Edith. Cora won't tell me, nor Edith; and our mother was not a gossip.

But I am not to blame.

⋆ ⋆ ⋆

I look for Edith's daughter, wondering whether I would recognize her, but she is not at the funeral — she would be a young woman by now, not a girl anymore. Edith and Carson come together, but arrive late, and must sit near the rear of the

290

church. I glance over my shoulder. *They look like old people*, I think, unfairly, perhaps. He's lost every trace of his hair, his pate shining and freckled, and she's like a stranger to me, her pretty features grown angular rather than soft; but, of course, she has a different mother from mine, I think, as if that explains away everything.

Afterward we stand all in a row to receive the guests, Cora, then Father, then me, then Olive, then Edith and Carson. Cora is pleased with the turnout, but I am surprised there are not more guests — my mother caught half the county. Cora can't stop saying how pleased she is. She repeats it until I stop believing she means it. Afterward we fall to eating the slices of pie that remain — shoofly, choked with raisins, and a glistening mincemeat that no one wants to try.

Edith and I find ourselves standing elbow to elbow holding matching tiny plates, lifting matching triangles of sugar and pastry to our teeth, chewing and swallowing.

'You are well?' I ask, hearing my own flat tone, my eyes darting sideways to meet and somehow avoid hers all in the same moment.

'I am not,' she replies, gazing straight ahead, as if I'm standing there, instead of here. 'I will miss your mother.'

'She can't be gone,' I hear myself saying, and I think, I could only say this to Edith, because Edith is like a stranger now, and it is the kind of thing you would say only to a stranger.

'I will miss her many cures,' says Edith. 'I am not well.'

'No.' I don't disagree. Edith has never, as far

291

back as my memory can stretch, been well.

'Well,' she says, and I repeat it, perhaps with the upswing of a question. 'Well?'

'I'm alone now,' Edith says, 'like you. Children leave, you know. They grow up and leave you.'

My heart knocks against my ribs like a bird in the house, battering the walls. 'You've got Carson,' I say.

She sighs. 'That's so.'

And that is all.

You wouldn't think such a brief exchange would require so much from a person, but I am too tired to speak that night.

I rise stiff and aching in the morning, as if I've run for miles without stopping to stretch or eat or drink, and have collapsed and slept in a heap on the bare ground.

'Won't you come home, now, Aggie?' Cora asks as I'm leaving.

'What?' I make no effort to disguise my surprise.

'I can't manage him all by myself.'

Our father, she means.

It is September, the leaves on the trees green but tinged with rust, crumpling at the edges. Soon will come the winds of fall and the chill of winter, and I can't even imagine it just now — returning home.

I'm bent over, packing my small suitcase. Can she see it on my face? How eager I am to be leaving, how my mood is already lightened to be so nearly gone? She doesn't repeat her request.

SMART, JESSICA EVE (née Liddel). Suddenly, at home, aged seventy-five. Remembered sadly

292

by her husband, Robert Smart, of Stony Hill Farm, New Arran, Ontario, and by her daughters. Predeceased by several stepchildren. Mrs. Smart was unofficial midwife to many babies born in Clyde County. In later years, she remained a friend to those in need. Her death, the result of an accident, leaves many bereft. May she rest in peace.

★ ★ ★

I find myself considering Cora's request. Perhaps I am flattered to think she wants me. I take myself for a long swim on a Saturday morning, and decide that I might agree to return home, to help with Father. It all looks so clear under the water, the pebbled bottom, the roar inside my head. My breath comes cleanly, every third stroke. My turns are crisp. I am weightless in the water, ageless.

Freshly towelled and dressed, hair brushed flat against my skull and drying into flyaway strands, I walk shivering from the pool to The Peacock to meet Miss Alexandrine Gibb, the news of my decision clapping loudly in my head.

Miss Gibb and I meet every third Saturday of the month for coffee and sandwiches at The Peacock, where they haven't changed the decor since we first started coming here, autumn 1931, which was just after I began working for Miss Gibb's newspaper. Twenty years on, 1951, the cracked red booths, thick tabletops covered in plastic, and steamed windows remain the same. We hold fast to our habits too. We both like the club sandwich on white. I add a side of fries. She doesn't like pickles, but gets them because she knows that I do. Neither of us order the pie, but we always say we might, and if we do it will be the lemon meringue. But we never do. And though I try, I cannot call her Alex, as she would prefer. She will always be Miss Gibb to me.

'My sister Cora wants me home again. I'm stuck at obits. I wonder whether I might as well retire,' I say, tucking my damp hair behind my ears. It is still blond, but fading as blond hair does, by discreet degrees, the white threads silvering out the yellow ones.

'Don't go home,' she says. 'There are few enough of us as it is. You'd be giving up.'

'I've been thinking about success, Miss Gibb. What makes a champion?'

'Don't you know, Miss Smart?' She makes a point of calling me Miss Smart when I call her Miss Gibb, to remind me not to. Or perhaps we're both more comfortable calling each other by the names that belonged to us when we first met, when she was so much my superior, manager of Team Canada's girls, a woman of middle age, if thirty-something is to be considered middle-aged, and I was nothing but an untested runner, a girl of twenty, and we were hurtling forward, not knowing the way, but certain we would find it. 'I should think if anyone would know, Miss Smart, it would be you.'

'But I don't, Miss Gibb. I don't.'

She waves to the waitress for more coffee. We watch the waitress pour. Miss Gibb's spoon clinks against the thick rim of the cup. She says again, 'If anyone would know success, Aganetha

Smart, it would be you.'

'I know that a gold medal doesn't make you a champion. Nor does winning. I know that.'

The clink of her spoon. The spoon upon the shiny table-top. My eyes on the spoon.

'Ah, I see,' says Miss Gibb, and I am reminded that once upon a time we were not friends, once upon a time she was my superior who frightened me with her knack for seeing what I thought was hidden. 'But that was never why I thought you were a champion, Aganetha.'

My eyes shine and I blink hard. My fingers fumble with the tiny silver spoon in the sugar bowl, spilling a trail across the table. I am thinking of our first meeting here in the cafe, when she offered me advice I chose not to take: she told me not to show a story I had written to an editor whose attention I hoped to gain; it was not my story to tell, she said. Wasn't it? I remain certain it was the wrong advice. Maybe she agrees. In any case, she does not tell me now what I ought to do. I rather wish she would.

Instead she asks: 'Where do you want to be, Miss Smart?'

'Running,' I say without thinking.

'Ah.'

'I don't know what that means myself, Miss Gibb.'

'Nor do I.' She waves for the bill. 'More coffee?'

'How about pie?'

'Next time.'

And that's when I know that I will refuse Cora's request, because I would like a next time, and a next time, and someday, perhaps a piece of lemon meringue pie.

'Retire when I retire,' she says, 'and we'll travel the world together.'

Won't we?

GIBB, ALEXANDRINE (Alex). Born 1891, died 1958, Toronto, Ontario. Daughter of John and Sarah (Sparks) Gibb. A talented athlete in her youth, Miss Gibb was also the founder of the Women's Amateur Athletic Federation of Canada (1926—1953), the manager of Canada's highly successful women's Olympic team, Amsterdam, 1928, and for thirty years a distinguished editor and columnist for the *Toronto Daily Star*. Her influence on women's sport in Canada shall never be forgotten. Miss Gibb is remembered by her siblings, her colleagues, and her many kind friends.

★ ★ ★

I am sorry to see the barn come down.

Why does my father begin to dismantle it, board by board, beam by beam, and haul the pieces into the back field beside the pond, where he resurrects its bones in the form of a lighthouse? What could set in motion such a strange undoing?

'He's old,' says Cora. 'That's why.'

'He's not that old.'

'He's over eighty, Aggie.'

'Is he? He's still so strong.'

'You don't have to tell me. I can't make him do anything he's put his mind to not doing.'

Once upon a time, my job is to ask: *why?* Why did she smother her babies? Why did he burn down the house with the children inside? Why did he stab his so-called friend on the street outside the bar where they'd been drinking all night? Well, the answer to that one seems obvious, I suppose. And yet, I can assure you, there are no obvious answers that satisfy. Because the simple rule of the inexplicable is that nothing does.

We will never know why. The person himself cannot tell us, and if he tries to — because some will, as if trying to tell themselves — we won't buy it. It won't cover the ground he's razed.

Eventually I learn to stop asking why. I do my job. I crisply record unvarnished facts. I do it now. I note the fact that my father has drawn sketches onto a series of yellow cards, illustrating a building that appears to be structurally sound — in that regard, quite sane. Here the curving staircase will wind inside the sloped walls, leading to one tidy circular room high above the treetops, to be furnished with a simple cot and a table and chairs, and the means for cooking a meal. There will be windows all around the room, and overhead will swing the great light, a beacon in the night to warn the ships from the rocks, from coming too close to shore — in that regard, utterly insane.

'It's a lighthouse, Cora, he's building a lighthouse.'

'Do you think I don't know it? I'm the one who has to make his breakfast every morning.'

297

'Someone should stop him.'

'Go ahead and try.'

Without telling Cora where I'm going I take the path through the woods to town to pay a visit to the doctor — Peter, son of the former doctor. He sits behind his desk, nodding at my story: sister, father, crumbling barn, lighthouse. When I've laid it out before him, Peter, who used to be my schoolmate, says, 'You're looking tired, Aganetha. I'd advise iron pills.'

'This is about my father.'

'Are you afraid he will harm himself? Or somebody else?'

'No.'

'Does he seem happy?'

'He's buried seven children and two wives, so I don't think happy is precisely the word I'd choose.'

The doctor waits. Doctors are like reporters, if they know their business well. They wait, and the underneath bubbles up.

'He's as happy as he's ever been,' I allow. 'But Cora's not happy, not at all. And I'm in the city, and Olive lives on the other side of the planet with her own family, and that's it, that's all of us. Edith's his daughter, but she doesn't count. She scarcely visits, not according to Cora, and she's never been strong, as you know — she's no help. Think of what we were, think of the farm, think of what it was, Peter. You remember it.'

'I do,' he says.

'If my father wanted to build a spaceship to the moon, I wouldn't blame him. I say let him build a lighthouse.'

The doctor nods to indicate he is listening patiently. We are both aged forty-four years, but do not imagine we are judged the same — he is a man and I am a woman, and the year is 1952. I dye my hair to keep the colour bright. If you were feeling uncharitable, you might describe the hue as 'brassy.' I am not past the childbearing age, but my cycles have changed — not that I will mention it to the good doctor — and the blood arrives scanty and uncertain some months, or not at all, or in a terrible aching flood that brings on acne and cramping. A pregnancy this late would elicit pity, even if I were a married woman.

The doctor's wife is younger. He says they are expecting their third child any day now, and he smiles at me, quite relaxed, as if we will now speak as old friends.

'Are you home often?' he asks.

'No,' I say, and leave it at that. In fact, I haven't been home since my mother's funeral, a year gone by.

The doctor scribbles something on a piece of paper and slides it across the desk, taking care to touch my hand, as if he expects me to turn my palm to him, to give him something in return. I do not. I fold the paper without looking at it and put it into my pocketbook and stand. He reminds me of a certain predictable variety of man, with a modicum of power at his disposal, and assumptions about a single woman's status and desires. Or perhaps he only wants a friend. I've friends enough.

'Do you still run?' The doctor wants to keep

299

me here, with him, awhile longer. Late autumn sunlight, so rare, streams through the tall window behind his desk. He stands and is bathed in it. I remember him as a child. I remember running faster than him — faster than all of the boys — with the skirt of my dress hitched up. I remember that there came an age, around fourteen or fifteen, when a few of the boys could beat me in the short sprints, although I doubt any of them could have held on over a long pounding race. I can't remember whether he was one who was briefly quicker. I think not.

'No,' I say again, though it's not the truth. *Do I still run? What could stop me?* But I will keep saying no until he hears me, now that I think he's shown his hand. Pregnant wife, bawling children, country life. He took his degree in the city, and I remind him of who he thinks he was. Perhaps I spark some dread, some doubt, about his choice, made years ago, to come home and take over his father's practice, to live inside the life his father made for him.

He reminds me of Cora.

My presence draws her dissatisfaction like a good ointment draws a splinter — but the splinter never comes out of the wound. I know Cora wouldn't speak to others as she speaks to me.

I know Cora to be helpful at births, and before, with the women whose wombs are unwilling, and afterward, dispensing teas and salves to new mothers, showing them how to latch their babies to their breasts. I know the doctor likes and trusts Cora, and that she works occasional shifts at the town's new hospital, where most women in the area now give birth, painlessly, drugged and in a half-wake, walking sleep.

Cora does not approve of the new methods. She has told me that she believes the pain of childbirth is essential to the experience, ordained.

'Don't go,' says the doctor.

I stop, my hand on the doorknob. I can pull it open in an instant and exit into the small reception area where his secretary, the butcher's wife, Mrs. Guillame, waits at her desk with ears wide open. The reception area and this office are rooms in the doctor's house, and the sound of a child crying can be heard, faintly.

Now it is my turn to wait, if I care to, for whatever is bubbling underneath to boil to the surface.

'I know your mother has been gone for a while, but I haven't had a chance to tell you how sorry I am for your loss.'

I wait.

'Your mother — ' He clears his throat. He wants me to look directly into his eyes, to register the importance of this moment, and I oblige him, for my mother's sake. 'My father respected your mother to the end,' the doctor says, but he can't hold my gaze after all and drops it to the desktop, where his fingers drum nervously. 'My father said she'd spared more lives than anyone knew. I wanted to tell you. Contrary to what Cora says — and Cora's a good woman, don't misunderstand me — I think your mother was very brave. And you too.'

In shocked silence, I stare at him, the breath gone out of me.

'Your father will be fine,' the doctor says. 'Cora is an excellent nurse, excellent. Leave it to her. Don't worry yourself. You have better things to do.'

I wait. I can't move anyway.

'If you are not running, as you say, you should be. You were . . . magnificent.'

'I write about dead people,' I tell him, as if this cancels out my opportunities to run. 'I used to report on people who killed people, but now I write about lives lived.'

I would like to leave now. I'm trembling.

'Aganetha.' His saying of my name, just the fact of it, stops me a little longer. 'Won't you meet me for a drink, later?'

'No. But thank you,' I tell him in a voice not entirely my own, and with that I go, nodding weakly to Mrs. Guillame, whom I can't make out clearly. My eyes have no time to adjust. The reception area is a small but opulently decorated room that receives almost no outside light. I suspect this puts Mrs. Guillame at an advantage with all comers. I suspect she can hear every word spoken inside the doctor's office, and I suspect he has no idea — it hasn't occurred to him. It won't have.

She coos like a mourning dove. 'Say hello to your sister for me, Miss Smart.'

Much later, when I am in the city, I find the piece of paper the doctor's given me. I am digging around in my pocket-book for a different scrap, one on which I've written a phone number for the daughter of a dead man whose life I am to sum up before press time, and which I can't for the moment locate.

I unfold the slip of paper. The words are written in the doctor's scrawl, signed with his name. It is a prescription for iron pills.

I do not fill it.

SMART, ROBERT. Of RR #3, New Arran, Ontario, on September 12, 1957, in his eighty-seventh year. Robert was born on the same farm on which he died, of natural causes. Son of Robert and Mary Smart. Predeceased by his first wife, Tilda, and seven of their eight children, and one grandson, and survived by their daughter Edith Miller and one granddaughter. Also predeceased by his second wife, Jessica, and survived by daughters Olive Gunn (Herbert), Cora, and Aganetha, and four grandchildren, all of Australia. A private burial has taken place.

Now you come home, Aggie? says Cora. Now that there's no one to look after? Now that you've no unpleasant duties waiting? Now that it's only me and the house? Who says I want you now? Who says you're welcome? Your name might be on the deed but this farm doesn't belong to you. You left home. You left like everyone else did. Didn't that make them sad? Didn't that make them weep? What would you know, Aggie, what would you know about giving up everything?

★ ★ ★

What's a week, a month, a year or forty? It vanishes too.

Slowly, steadily, we empty and shutter room after room until our lives shrink to the space we can manage to occupy. We inhabit no more than we can. Even that can seem too much. One day in winter, I shutter the Granny Room. I empty out the drawers and hang the sheets over the window and door.

Lavender. Crumbling in my stiff fingers, mouldy. Dust.

18

Tattie

The girl's eyes meet mine in the rearview mirror. 'Miss Smart, do you know you have a lawyer? Max and Mother have been to see him, and we don't think he's got your best interests at heart.'

A lawyer, yes, well, I'd forgotten. That would be Peter's son, the doctor's boy? His office the same his father kept clinic in, and there are papers to sign, my hand trembling with age not nerves, while Peter's boy looks on. That would explain who's been paying for the home that is not a home, which bothers me when it crosses my mind. I always paid my own way.

'I always paid my own way,' I tell the girl, but she mistakes my meaning.

'It's different now, Miss Smart. You don't know how much it costs — there's coaching, physio, massage. There's vitamin supplements, travel expenses, gear, gym time, you have no idea, or I can't compete. I'm trying to get to Rotterdam, Miss Smart. If I can lower my time there, I'll make the team, and I'm close. I think I can do it.'

I hear the words, but it's like the girl is speaking a different language. The rules have changed from my day, she's saying. It isn't the same. The path is cluttered with obstacles. The obstacles are lit up in dollar signs.

I would like to tell her what matters, but I know better than to attempt it. She may be right, and it all comes down to the money. Who am I to argue? If I paid my own way, as I claim, who, then, was Mr. P.T. Pallister? I was lucky, as much as I was anything.

But still I say to her, It's the running that counts.

We are coming out around the barn, the field opens before us, and I begin to run the old familiar path. No one sees me running. But I do, each step unfolding in my mind, shaking my body, jarring and rattling it, and carrying me along. This is what it feels like: a catalogue of dull pain from ankle to shin to knee to hip to shoulder. The breath comes hard at first, rough, but will smooth into a rhythm. And when I've been running for a while, only then, the thoughts settle into sense.

I am remembering the races, stealthily entered in my middle years, when I ran with a hood shadowing my face, my hair cropped wiry and short, so that I could pass as a man competing at a distance from which women were barred. Look up my times. In my fifties and sixties, as A.F. Smart, I ran Boston, Chicago, New York, Hamilton. Why did I do it? Why race, when I could run from here to the lake and back in a single day, and often did, leaving Cora at home to mutter and fret? I would carry along boiled eggs, walnuts, and homemade sweetened ginger water.

Somehow it never went out of me — the desire to compete, to line up against others, win

306

or lose, part of a rhythm larger than myself. One turning wheel in a crowd of effort.

If the girl is mine, as she claims, she'll get to Rotterdam, if she wants to. But it won't be money that buys her the race she intends to run.

★ ★ ★

When George dies, I do not hear of it immediately. In dying, George leaves behind Tattie, the mother of his four children, my nephew and nieces. Tattie, short for Tatiana. I believe her to be younger, even, than I am. She sends the eldest to tell me about my brother's passing, but I am not at home. I am at the *Toronto Daily Star*, working the job found for me by Miss Gibb's favour. My brother has died and I do not know because I am in a windowless office downtown transcribing copy for a reporter who has been on the scene of a factory fire — suspected arson — and the landlady tells me nothing.

The following day, the boy comes again, this time to ask for money for the burial, and the day after that to say a man has been by their house with a letter that Tattie cannot read, and still the landlady does not say a word of it. Placidly, she serves up her fatty cuts of meat and soft mealy potatoes, inquiring whether I'd like seconds, without a hint that anything might be amiss. I plan to visit George on Sunday, when I'm free, if I can stomach it, and as I'm not sure that I can, it does not occur to me to visit any sooner.

The boy comes a fourth time. On this

307

occasion, he is sent by his mother to tell me that someone in a dark suit is going to take him and his sisters away.

I hear nothing of any of this.

Perhaps the boy does not know he may leave a message with the landlady, and asks for me only to flee when told I'm not in. Perhaps the land-lady thinks the child is a stray. Perhaps — and I consider this the most likely possibility — she believes that the ragged child is beneath me, beneath my interest. She has ideas about glam-our and style, and she seems perpetually to imagine me a fine young lady in a fur coat, no matter the evidence to the contrary.

I almost cannot bear to think of Tattie waiting, waiting, each time, for the boy to return home. I can't bear to think of the silence ascribed to me. The help denied.

On the Sunday, at last, the boy finds me home. This time he is carrying his baby sister in his arms. I hear his story, all in a rush, a cascading urgency of need. There isn't time to question the landlady; I'll state my case against her silently, by leaving before month's end without notice, even if it means abandoning the hard, velvet-covered chairs. What does anything matter? All in a rush, I learn of my brother's death and pauper's burial, and of the letter that Tattie cannot read, and the man in the dark suit who has clearly terrified the boy with his threats. All of this tumbles out of the child in one long exhalation.

We hurry along the dirty streets. The first leaves of the season are falling from the trees, brown and ugly, swirling around our feet as we run, the child just ahead of me. Burdened by the infant, he refuses my help, and keeps a stoical businesslike pace that I admire.

We enter through the garden gate, the late summer fruit hanging heavy and overripe and bug-bored on the weary tomato plants. A patch of lettuce has gone to seed.

The boy climbs the back steps almost wearily, like an old man, and hesitates, after all that rush, at the door. I look at him and try the handle. It isn't locked. Inside, we hear a strange cry, thin as gruel, persistent as life itself. I take heart. I open the door. The strange cry is silenced.

'Tattie, I'm here! I've come! It's Aggie, your sister,' I call as we stand on the threshold, our eyes adjusting to the dark room. I want her to know that I think of her as a sister. I want her to feel centred inside the embrace of family, even a family like ours, that with its instinct for secrecy does not know she exists.

There is no answer and the strange cry is silenced.

It is only one room, as I've said already. The room is dark. Along the wall nearest us is a small kitchen area, a few cupboards, a low shelf for preparing food, a greasy cookstove that warms the space in winter. The infant in the boy's arms has begun to whimper.

I see the children first. They could be asleep, flat on their backs, lying on the wide board floor with a pillow beside them. But they are not asleep. And that is when I see Tattie kneeling in the corner, head bent as if in prayer.

A calm enters my body with the efficiency and

speed of an injected drug. I push the boy behind me, toward the open door, I say, 'Run!'

I move as if I know exactly what to do. I approach Tattie.

'Give me that,' I command, and take from her willing hand the heavy knife with which she's been nicking her wrist, unable to make the first cut.

'I can't live,' she tells me in an urgent, private whisper, but I won't hear it. The calm floods out of me as I turn my back on her. That is when I see the boy. He hasn't gone. He stands in the doorway, a shadow against the light of day.

The boy, he can't be more than seven. The summer I first arrived in Toronto, he was an infant.

I remember meeting him, when George decides I am ready for it. I remember meeting them, I should say: the babe in arms, and the girl in whose arms the babe lay.

'I got something to show you, Aggie. It's a secret. You won't tell?'

I understand secrets. Our house is the location of many kept, and never told.

I agree.

George and I are walking in the street, as there are no sidewalks here. The houses are crammed together — shacks, I think. I push the thought down.

'You won't tell Olive. Promise.' Olive will have nothing to do with George, in any case. She does not like him.

'I won't tell Olive. What is it, George?'

He grins suddenly, ear to ear. 'You'll see.'

Whatever his secret, it makes him happy.

We enter without knocking at a house split into two sections, no porch, no steps, a rough door scraping across the dirt, one window, broken and covered with a nailed board. I hear the baby's cry as my eyes adjust to the dim interior. A chilly room, a bed on the floor. This is where they are. The girl rises quickly, straightens her skirt, sweeps her fingers through her hair.

'This here's Aggie, my little sister,' George says. It surprises me to hear his voice busting with pride. 'Aggie, this is Tattie. Tattie, show Aggie my son, Rob, we call him.'

Tattie cradles the baby expertly, lifting and displaying him against her chest. He is big enough to hold up his head, and he is surprisingly chubby, filled out like a properly fed baby should be, toothless and chortling. Instinctively, I reach for him, and he jumps as if he wants to meet me too.

I hold him squashed against me, under my chin. I breathe in his musty spoiled-milk warmth, his graceless rubbery limbs flailing, his tiny fingers and toes clutching for my hair, my dress. I suppose I get a bit lost in him. Maybe it is kinship — love. My brother's son.

'You're married! Why ever didn't you tell us?' I say at last, looking up to see the two of them watching me, leaning against each other. She has her arms wrapped around his chest in a posture of intimacy to which I have never been witness, certainly not between my mother and father, not even when Fannie walked into the corn with our brother-in-law. I feel my face go hot. I have

311

misunderstood. I have blundered.

It should have been obvious: George is not married to this girl. This girl, the mother of his child, is not his wife.

'I'm sorry,' I say. 'I didn't mean . . .'

'Who needs it?' says George. He kisses Tattie, or she reaches up to kiss him, full on the mouth. I feel like I am glimpsing through a window a scene I am not meant to be witness to — compelling, illicit. I stare down at the lovely lightly curling black hairs on the baby's head. He is beginning to fuss, for which I am thankful. I hop him up and down in my arms and walk the room, away from them, humming his name into his hair.

'She looks broody,' says Tattie.

'Maybe she'll take him home,' says George. 'It'll be just the two of us again.'

'Oh, Georgie.'

I assume they are joking, but I disapprove nevertheless. I bring the baby over to them, and pass him, wriggling, into Tattie's arms. 'He's perfect,' I say.

'Isn't he?'

Isn't he? He remains perfect in my eyes as he stands on the threshold of that other room, seven years on. He is a small child, stunted by diet, rickety, all jutting wrists and ankles. He holds his baby sister like a package he can be trusted never to drop, no matter what comes.

I don't want him to fear the knife I'm holding, but what am I to do? He's waiting for me. I cross the small room in three leaping strides and push the boy in front of me, out into the back garden.

Rows of houses crowd around, intrusive, indifferent.

We are quite stunned, I think. The baby arches her back and howls. I toss the knife — an ordinary kitchen tool with a blunt blade — in among the fruiting plants overgrown with weeds.

'Police! Murder! Help!'

The boy, he hears the word *police* — or is it *murder?* I should not have used that word, nor this tone, entirely hysterical — and he takes off running. Good, I think, forgetting, briefly, that he is only a child and in my charge. 'Police! Police!' There flies the boy, the baby in his arms, disappearing down the alleyway. After a moment's confusion, I tear after him. He knows all of the neighbourhood's hiding places; but he can't outrun me. I follow at a small distance, keeping him within sight.

I want to let him go, to let him lose me. I can feel what he is feeling — or so I imagine. I can feel the world collapsing around us. I can feel the weight of the baby, like an anchor, like an extra heart. I can feel the need to run, to keep just ahead of everything that is falling like an avalanche behind our passage — if only he can keep ahead of it, he can outwit destruction. He can hide out. He can keep what little is his.

But I know it will never do to let the child go, not like this. I track him until finally he is too weary to continue. I catch them in my arms. I hold on for as long as I can, and then I can't anymore. It is my duty to let go.

Isn't it?

It is only later that I wonder why it didn't

occur to me to go along with him, to sweep them up in my care and escape, the three of us. Surely I could have outrun any threat. We could have made our own fugitive family, somewhere else.

Instead the baby, and the boy, both are taken from me. Their only legal relation is their mother, now a murderess. I am prevented from making a claim, as the children are not considered my legal relations. The state will see to it that the children receive care. All I can do is hope the boy forgets everything that came before. I hope he begins life anew, as the infant surely can. To comfort myself, I imagine them adopted into families of wealth and prosperity, I give them tennis lessons, and pressed white shirts, and the smell of roast chicken with rosemary wafting from a clean kitchen streaming with light.

Every day during the trial, which is less than a week in length, I attend in the courtroom. In the evenings, I work the graveyard shift at the newspaper, writing headlines and photo captions for the morning edition. I sleep little but take care each morning to arrive in the courtroom neatly attired with my hair pinned into a bun. When it is my turn to be called as a witness, I reply in plain statements of fact. I identify myself as a friend. Do I believe my friend to have been mad? Surely it was a mad act, I say, with no rational explanation.

I try to catch Tattie's eye, to tell her through mine — but what? What would I tell her, if I could?

I stay. I take notes throughout the week. I

write my notes into a story. The story of the trial.

'You are not a crime reporter, that is clear,' says Miss Gibb. She urges me not to show my story to the local editor at the newspaper where she's gotten me work, but in this instance, only, I refuse her advice.

'Mr. Stephens, have you got a moment? I . . . I've been sitting in on the case of the mother who smothered her children . . . I've been working on a story. Would you be willing to take a look?'

'Interested in crime, are you?'

I give away nothing. I watch his eyes scan my carefully typed-out page of text. He shows no emotion as he returns the piece of paper to me.

'Strong. Colourful. But this isn't balanced reporting. That's what I'd be looking for. Balance.'

'Oh.'

'You make it sound like you knew the woman or something. You can't go around expressing your sympathies so obviously. That's not your job, as a reporter.'

Fact: being a reporter is not my job. Yet.

Fact: it will be by the time this conversation is over.

'Aren't you the girl who won the race? The one Miss Gibb brought in?'

'Yes. I am she.'

'You've got good grammar, nothing to sneeze at. And you're not afraid of a gruesome story — I like that. That's not something that can be said about most women. We're always looking for fresh blood, a new angle. There's a murder case

315

coming up, man bludgeoned his wife to death in front of the kids.' He watches for a reaction. 'It's yours if you want it.'

'Thank you.' My tone is calm, my expression clear. I do not find his test difficult.

'I don't mind a bit of the sentimental if you feel a need to add a feminine touch, but don't pick sides. Maybe the wife was a shrew, or worse, what do we know? Keep it clean. But remember — a touch of shock keeps 'em reading, see what I mean? And readers are what we want. Eyeballs on our paper. It's a bloodbath out there.'

I nod, as if I understand completely. Bloodbath. Readers. Eyeballs. Shock. I have to resist the urge to yank out my notebook and take notes.

'Thank you, Mr. Stephens.'

'Call me Rudy.'

'I prefer Mr. Stephens, if you don't object.'

'Whatever tickles your fancy, miss, tickles mine.'

'I did know her,' I say after a moment of pause. He is shuffling papers on top of his desk and his head snaps up. 'That women in my story. She was someone that I knew.'

'Bit of advice — don't go around telling people things like that. You should know better. Don't make me regret giving you this murder case.'

'No, sir.'

'Call me Rudy.'

'Thank you, Mr. Stephens.'

'Don't foul this up, Miss . . . '

'Miss Smart.'

'And may I call you Miss Smart?'

I open my mouth, close it. Ah, he's joking. He grins.

Fact: it will be another three years before Mr. Stephens can talk me into a drink after work. Whiskey and soda for him. Fruit juice for me. Once an athlete, always an athlete.

Fact: he is married.

Fact: we're never more than friends, whatever anyone else may think. We get along. We enjoy a meal together now and again. If he hopes for more, he hopes in vain, and — mostly — politely.

I am a woman unattached, a single woman of a certain age. I'm spared some complications. No one to nurse in his declining years, for example. Also, no one to check my little eccentricities, developed over years of solitary habit. It may surprise you what a person would forgo in order to keep her small comforts, her calculated balance of order and disorder.

One thing does not change, no matter how much practice I get. I do not know how to say good-bye. I never learned that trick.

★ ★ ★

Tatiana Lukivny sits beside her lawyer and weeps. Her face does not alter in its expression, and yet the tears flow steadily down her cheeks.

She is asked to stand, to accept judgement, and she obeys. She is asked to confess that she, an unmarried mother of four, took the lives of two of her own children. The children, Margaret, aged four, and Cecily, aged three, are named, and Miss Lukivny groans in apparent agreement: these are the children she smothered to death.

'Did you love them?' the judge asks.

The accused stares unseeingly and does not respond.

'Did you love them perhaps less than the other children, the two you did not kill?'

The accused cannot reply. Her throat is stopped with tears.

'Why did you do this, miss? Why?'

The accused has become a statue. She utters nothing in her own defence.

★ ★ ★

'Tattie, it's me, your sister, Aggie.'

'Come in.' She is sitting in a straight-backed hard wooden chair set before a window in a room that is whitewashed and very small. She is fortunate to have her own room, she has told me. I agree. I sit on her bed.

'And how are you?' I ask, as I always do.

'Just fine,' she replies.

I wonder why she doesn't face the window. She is always facing the door, instead, when I knock and enter, sitting in the chair, her back to the glass. Does she not wish to see the sky, the grass, the trees? Does she fear being overcome with an irresistible urge to throw herself out? But the window is locked, as she must know. Or have I got it wrong, and it is not that she is facing away from the window, but toward the door, waiting for someone to come in?

I don't ask.

'I'm glad you're well,' I say. I have brought her a book, a slight novel of melodrama and romance such as she prefers. They have taught her to read, in here.

'Thank you.' She opens the cover and thumbs through the pages. I think I see her lift the book toward her nose to inhale its scent. She is distracted and already bored with me. I would have to call her unwell, although she does not seem mad, nor has she on any visit I've made since first coming, a year or so after her trial.

We were both of us uncomfortable during that first encounter. When I think of it now, we were both so young. And yet we knew of things that other people, most people, did not. And we were kin, I always felt that, no matter the letter of the law.

She asked me on that visit: could I find her children for her?

No, I said, no more than I could find them for myself.

She drifted after that, and she has drifted during every visit since, and yet I come and sit on her bed, and ask her how she is. It seems to me that someone must. Tattie has told me things, here and there, and I've collected them. I have in mind that I will write for her an obituary, as I've done for so many others. I know that her mother died when she was just a girl, that she did not get along with her father, that she scorned the care of her younger siblings, that she would not 'work like a horse,' like her father demanded, and that she would not do her duty for duty's sake alone.

319

That is not how she puts it, exactly, but it is how I take it.

'I loved horses,' she has said on more than one occasion. Her father was a smithy, and she lived around the animals from a young age.

'Why?' I ask, of the horses.

She looks at me with contempt, for not already knowing. 'Because they were wild things tamed and trapped, as I was.'

As you are, I think, but refrain from saying out loud.

Today she withdraws into silence and I see that she is already drifting from me. I let myself drift from her too. I look out the window at the sky, grass, and trees. It is 1951, and my own mother has recently died. I am permitting myself, in this room, to think of my mother, to let myself go, just a little bit. My eyes sting and I dig around in my purse for a handkerchief to blow my nose.

Tattie sighs deeply. Her eyes gaze vacantly at the door, which is ajar.

'Tattie,' I say, leaning forward. Always a small woman, she has become almost insubstantial, while I've grown to be something of a scarecrow, bony, stretched thin and long. I touch her hands with mine, and she startles and stares at me, disturbed into this moment, this room.

I say, 'My mother has passed on, George's stepmother. A good woman.'

She squeezes my hands in response and I am moved by her sympathy.

'You'll wonder why I did it, as a mother,' she says, 'but I did it as a mother. You wouldn't know, not being one yourself, but your own mother would understand.'

'Yes,' I say, to encourage her. She has never spoken of that day, nor have I tried to shake memories from her, let alone explanations.

I can't decide whether she seems entirely rational, as we stare at each other, or entirely mad.

'I knew they would be taken from me. A woman like me, unmarried, alone, how could I keep my children? They would be taken from me. I did try to think of another way to keep them. I did my best. But there was no other way and so I made a plan. I was going to take them with me, that's all. It's all I wanted.'

'The boy came and fetched me, with his baby sister,' I say.

'He fought me,' she says simply. 'He got away.'
Oh.

'He was to be the first.'

'Please, you don't have to tell me anything more.'

' "Don't move, Mama, don't do anything, I'll come back with help." '

And I wonder, sitting across from her, holding her hands in my own, if I will be able to come back to visit her again, or whether she will sit and stare at the door and wait for me in vain. I don't know.

I let her hold my hands, but I say, 'Let's be quiet, now, there's a good girl,' like she's a child. If I treat her like a child it is easier to be gentle when what I feel is rough, harsh. Stupid woman! I think. It is not that hard to give up a child. You just make up your mind and you let that child go. You just do it.

LUKIVNY, TATIANA. On February 13, 1963, after a long decline. 'Tattie' was born in Russia, in 1909, location and precise date unknown, and shortly thereafter came to Montreal, Canada, with her family, then to Toronto where she wed George Smart and became mother to four. Mr. Smart succumbed to illness (1931), a loss from which Tattie never recovered. She was predeceased by two daughters, Margaret (age four), and Cecily (age three). If you have information regarding Tattie's two other children, Rob (born 1924) and Judy (born 1931), it is requested that you contact A. F. Smart at the following P.O. Box. All confidences kept.

Replies: none.
Confidences kept: all.

19

What Remains

I don't recall the lane going this far. We rise and fall as if plunging through waves. I am fortunate that I've never suffered seasickness. I've always had a sturdy constitution.

I see the field gone fallow, gone to weed.

We're slowing at the top of the hill overlooking the pond. You should step on the gas, I lean forward to tell the girl. But where is the water — is it gone? I had a brother who drowned in that pond. His name was, his name was — James. There is a shallow indentation in the dirt. A person wouldn't know a pond had ever been there, but for the lighthouse towering beside it. But this makes no sense. Why build a tall lighthouse beside a puddle of a farm pond? I am surprised to recall that it was mostly completed when Father stopped his work. The boards went unpainted and are grey with weather, but the shape of the structure is unmistakable, and I see its purpose.

It has taken me all these years, but I see now as the tires spin, and the young man beside me observes, 'We're stuck,' as the woman on the other side says, 'Never say never!' as the girl jams her foot into the gas pedal with increasing futility, that the lighthouse was meant to guide us home safely. All comers. All goers.

My father was calling us back home.

Well. Here I am, safe in this sinking ship as ever I'll be.

The boy has not stopped filming.

'It won't go,' the girl says in disbelief, lifting her foot off the gas pedal, silencing the whirring tires, giving up. 'I can't make it go.' She bends her head briefly, then turns to address me, carrying upon her shoulders some small shame. 'Miss Smart, this is going to sound really bad, but I have to tell you. We're broke — I'm broke. I can't afford to keep training. That's why we brought you here, that's why we're making this movie, that's why we need you to sell your land. We need you to sell your land, Miss Smart. I'm sorry, Mom, but I'm just going to tell her. What do I have to lose? Our farm is only worth something if you sell it.'

The woman beside me shifts uncomfortably. I wonder — does she want to sell what's hers? 'There's your dad,' the woman says mildly.

'Dad.' The girl is scornful but does not elaborate.

'I only meant,' says the woman, 'that we must not put this all on Miss Smart. It is a big decision to make. To sell land. Family land.'

We are quiet for a bit.

Then the girl turns again and says, 'Miss Smart, there's a developer who wants this land, ours too. He's got a plan. Lighthouse Commons, it's going to be called. But he won't buy Mom's land unless you're selling too. Max and I — me and Max — and Mom — we . . . we looked really hard for you. Mom called I don't know

324

how many nursing homes in, like, a hundred-kilometre radius. Maybe you didn't want to be found. Maybe we're not who you want, but — '

'Kaley,' her mother interrupts gently.

'You know what. What does it matter? — I might not even make these Games.' The girl grips the wheel, turns away from us, muttering to herself.

'You'll make these Games,' the boy tells her. 'Why else are we making this movie?'

'You think it's that easy? Decide to, and I will? Find the money, and I will?' She whacks the steering wheel with her hands. She roars. I like that. She opens the car door and leaves it swinging wide as she leaps into the mud and she runs.

'Oh, Kales.' The young man, who must be Max, sighs.

'Too much pressure on her,' says the woman. 'I think we're all pushing her too hard.' She climbs out of the car and closes her door gently, and the other one, before setting off after the girl, but heavily, not hurrying.

The boy waits to disagree till she's gone. Then he says, perhaps to me, 'It isn't us, it's Kaley. None of this is us. It's all her.'

I lean for the handle of the door nearest me, and tug on it. I hook my imprisoned fingers around the polished metal. I've never been more sure of anything. I push with thickened hands and the door gives way. I won't fall out. I'm swinging my frozen legs and kicking, and creaking bone by bone to standing. Sinking in the muddy spring field, clutching at the roof of the car to stop myself from toppling, I clear my head in the late afternoon light that angles down over the ancient row of sugar maples, and I clear my throat to call, 'What was her name?'

The words are coming through, ringing like a bell, straight from my brain to my mouth.

The boy is at my side, the girl's brother — Max. 'They can't hear you,' he says.

'She's a good runner? Very good?'

'She's amazing! She's run the fastest Canadian women's time this season, and she'll only get better if she gets the chance. She needs time, but honestly, Miss Smart, Kaley's, like, the best. Just not everyone sees it.'

He stops. It seems he can only look at me through the lens of his camera.

'What was her name?' I ask again.

'Kaley, you mean?'

'No. No.'

'Nancy's my mom. I'm Max, remember?'

No! The final piece of proof. Her name, her name, her name! *Edith's girl*.

'You mean, my grandmother? She died a long time ago, like Mom said. I don't remember her at all. She was called Fannie, I think. But it was short for something else.'

She was called Fannie. I don't need to know anything else.

'Look — Kaley's coming back, I knew she would,' he says. 'Sometimes she just needs to run. It's like her answer for everything.' He trains his camera across the field and we watch the girl stride effortlessly up and down the rises, stray weeds batted down as she makes her path. Her mother stands between us, as mothers do, watching, in a posture of adoration. She glances at us as if to say, Isn't my daughter wonderful? Isn't she remarkable? Do you see what I see?

I, sinking into mud, feel my bones trembling, a shaking up my spine. I haven't stood on my own for this long for years and I'm mildly exhilarated. No — make that wildly exhilarated.

The girl is coming back to me. I can't wait.

I let go of the car and take a step, and another.

★ ★ ★

'There is not a great deal of time to wait,' Mother says, leaning over me, whispering. 'When the early months have passed, the baby is quite settled and will grow regardless. Do you understand?'

I understand.

'I'm sorry, Mother.'

'I know. Let me help.'

It is then that Cora comes into the room. She does not exactly burst in, just enters briskly without knocking, and takes over. 'Mother, you've agreed not to do this anymore.'

My mother moves out of Cora's way, silently.

Cora comes directly to me, where I lie, and begins pressing her fingers and palm into my lower abdomen, like my mother has done, only harder, harsher. I wince. 'Three months, I'd guess,' she tells me. 'As Mother's likely already said. You can stay here. We've had girls stay regularly since you and Olive left for Toronto. We can always find a place for the baby, so don't

327

worry about that. Mother?'

'Yes, Cora.' Her tone is flat, neither question nor reply.

'You'll find things much changed around here,' says Cora, addressing me. 'If you stay, that is. You'll find this place is not what you remember it to be.'

But when Cora goes, my mother leans down and whispers, 'What do you want, child? I will help you.'

And I find I do not want to fight Cora. I want to wait for Johnny to follow me. I want to wait.

As you wish, Aganetha.

Cora is wrong. Home is as I remember it, changed, yes, but only by the thinnest layer of strangeness. The plaster walls are poked full of holes, Father's wires tunnelling deep, tying the house together, but the windmill turns atop the barn, and the woods are quiet, and I may walk where I wish, despite my ungainly body, though I take care to stay out of sight. If I hear footsteps on the path, I hurry the other way, or hide, crashing deeper into the woods, trying to lose myself in brush and bramble.

I drape myself in a heavy plaid shawl. I pin my thickening hair to my skull in braided coils and brush it out at night in the stillness of the back room so that it floats around me like a cloud.

My sister Fannie visits. I can hardly be surprised, and find myself grateful, comforted, anticipating her surprise arrivals like I would those of a friend. She comes through the holes Father has bored in the walls and I wake to find her nearby in the room, gazing out the window into the unlit night.

I tell her that I will name the baby for her, should it be a girl. This is wrong of me. I have agreed not to keep the baby. But I wait in hope that Johnny might change his mind and come for me, although I do not write to him and ask. The Johnny I wait for is not the Johnny I left, you will understand. He is an attractively vague character in a story I'm telling myself, a figure both much embellished and entirely emptied out. I imagine myself too like Tattie, nursing this infant in a cramped room hidden away from the world and I begin to understand how Tattie might be happy, or at least agree to the situation, and not be miserable in it, because she has her baby in her arms, her little ones around her, gathered near.

My mother has a plan. Cora does not like it, because she thinks it will cause talk and trouble. My mother disagrees, and to quell Cora's arguments, I promise to accede all claim: the baby will never know of me.

'It is a great gift you're giving,' my mother tells me.

But when I make my promise, I've given nothing at all. It is possible that I agree to the plan only because I keep on believing, against all logic and evidence, that Johnny will come.

★ ★ ★

I am walking the woods, a fat and aching vessel, the baby's weight stirring my insides, when I hear a distinct pop, like a bottle of champagne

329

uncorking — a sound that reminds me of the luxury of victory — and warm water rushes down my legs in a splash that quickly eases to a trickle. At almost the very same instant, my belly is seized with a tightening, and pain radiates from a tiny central point that I can almost see, somewhere deep inside. The exit point.

I find that I am not afraid.

I find that what I want is to stop right here in the woods, on hands and knees, to crawl just off the path, into the trilliums, and do this all by myself. It seems a challenge that should be managed alone, a private roaring urge that only I can understand well enough to answer. I feel as if I were made for this. And perhaps I would birth my baby all by myself, and perhaps the ending of this story would be quite different, but instead I hear footsteps hurrying along on the path, and my instinct is to waddle away from their approach as quickly as I can manage. Someone is coming, as happens only rarely, from the town to the farm, and I must not be seen. I hurry, pausing only during the most intense crescendos of pain, and soon I am out of the shelter of the trees, and running past the barn and to the house. If this can be called running.

Strangely, it is Edith, I learn, who has come along the path behind me.

I have not seen Edith during all this time. I tell myself I haven't been avoiding her, but it isn't true. I've been avoiding her. I've been avoiding everyone, of course, but most especially I've been avoiding Edith. And here is Edith, tracking me, just out of sight, stopping by the house on

330

her way from town to home, coming the long way 'round.

And so this story goes as it has been planned by others, not by me.

I crouch on hands and knees beside the bed on the hard floor, wishing I were in the woods, on soft earth. 'Edith's here.' Cora raps on the door to the Granny Room but does not enter. The noises I am making are unmistakable.

My mother leaves my side for a moment, returns. It is just the two of us. 'You are doing so well,' she tells me. Palm on forehead. Palm on the bones of my lower back.

I've lost myself inside the familiarity of pain. The discipline of birth is similar to training and racing. Both are explorations of extremity, the sensation of leaving the physical self by means of pain. How can I explain? You give what you have in you to give. You may have more than you know, and you can only know how much, exactly, by slamming head-on against the limits of toleration. This is easier done once you've accepted what needs to happen. Once you cease worrying about how you look, or who you might be, and you simply are.

I am muscles, strength, opening. I am rest, utterly at ease, waiting. I am efficient, powerful. The pressure will split me, but I bear down against it. I always run fastest when I'm pushing against a wind. I am pushing. Anyone might be in the room and I do not care. But I think it is just my mother. Just her. Her finger hooking under the caught shoulder, her voice suddenly risen to urgent command. She shifts me — *push,*

331

no matter what you're feeling, push, push, push
— and we shake the baby loose.

What do I know? I flood with joy. I collapse. I laugh and I cry.

Cora is in the room. She pulls me onto the bed, flat on my back, and she is taking care of something unpleasant. Apparently my work is not yet done. 'Push,' she instructs, kneading my belly, which is slack and barren like a flaccid sack. She is tugging something from me and it releases all at once, in a gush, a rush. I'm suddenly overcome with nausea, and I gag and retch into a basin that Cora provides for me.

I haven't even heard the kitten cry of the baby. She is rushed from the room in my mother's arms immediately, the cord between us cut. I do not see her.

'It is easier to let go that which you never had,' my mother tells me.

Is it?

How can I know? All I know is that there is nothing easy about what I am doing. I will have to keep doing it my whole life. I'm doing it yet.

Mother brings me broth, and toast with butter and jam. Mother brings me cabbage leaves to tuck around my breasts, to relieve them of their useless fevered milk. She kneads my lower abdomen and tells me that all is well, that my uterus is contracting as it should, back into its walnut self, hidden inside.

I cower at the pain, the cramping that flickers at her touch.

'Your body is doing its job.'

I sip her red raspberry leaf tea, poured from a

china teapot into a delicate cup, sweetened with honey. My head bends over the steam, breathing it in, bathed in it.

'You will be fit to begin running again, soon,' my mother says.

My whole body shudders, turns in on itself. 'I don't want to,' I say, weeping helplessly. The weeping seems connected to the general leakiness of my state, the discharge, the rich brown droplets of early milk, the tears, even a strange perspiration that soaks the sheets at night. Seepage. Cleansing.

I do not recognize myself: where is my trusted toughness, my innate daring, my willingness to suffer? Have I birthed a new self, vulnerable, tremulous, fickle?

'You'll want to, in time. It's too soon,' says my mother.

'What if I don't? What if I never want to, ever again?' It seems possible, just then. Possible that I have turned into someone unrecognizable, that I've crossed into an unknown mirror landscape where nothing makes sense, and from which I cannot return. Weak body, collapsing mind, empty arms, leaking breasts, loose skin, muscles as sore as if I've run a long race; but I haven't. I have nothing to show for this. Nothing.

'Aggie. You will have another child, someday, other children.'

I fall back against the pillows with tears leaking wildly, tea sloshing over the quilt. I do not know until she says it that this is what I need to hear. My mother lifts the cup from my hands, sits beside me on the bed, strokes my face. She blesses me with her promise, even if her prophecy will prove untrue. She trusts in the possibility. She trusts in me.

What has my father to say?

He is silent, and I do not see him. He does not come to my room, nor do I expect him to, nor want him to. It is almost as if he refuses to know what is happening, what has happened, in his own house. His dead wires tunnel the walls, binding the rooms together, but they don't come this far.

What has Cora to say?

She interrupts without knocking.

'Aggie should rest,' she says with a frown, as if my mother is a naughty child caught misbehaving. Cora does not ask permission, or explain, just comes at me and digs into the same place, between the hip bones, where my mother has kneaded. Cora's touch is dark, piercing. I can feel her judgement.

'Stop.' Mother pulls Cora's hands away, roughly. A cry hangs in the air. Mine.

'It's going down nicely,' says Cora, looking down on me, her hands loose at her sides, as if she has not just hurt me unnecessarily. Sisters. The things we take. The things we give. The ways in which we are nothing like each other.

Her disgust, hiding in plain view, decides me. I will tell Johnny that the baby died. It doesn't occur to me that I'll never get the chance to tell him anything — I'm still comforting myself with the impossible, imagining now that this is over, we can start at the beginning, as if nothing has happened. He needs to know nothing of this

— for him, it can be as if nothing has happened. That is the gift of the Granny Room. I feel my heart empty out, clear of bitterness.

I say, 'I'm thirsty,' and Mother brings me a fresh cup of cooling tea.

'Thank you.' I lift the cup and drink steadily, a tonic, a comfort. If I turn my head just so, away from them both, into the light, blinding myself, if I do not glance over at the mirror, I can make myself believe that I too can go on as if nothing has happened.

And so I have done until now. Now, will I try to tell them — my granddaughter, my great-grandchildren? What am I to do?

★ ★ ★

I go to see her once, the girl.

I walk across the fields on a visit home, the next summer.

I slip away from the house. It is easy not to tell anyone where I am going — perhaps I don't even tell myself. The corn is taller than I am and I follow the rows like a child, pretending that I'm exploring, until I come to Edith's yard and there is the girl sitting fat and content, as far as I can tell, on a quilted blanket in the sunshine. She hears me cry out the name I would have given her: *Fannie*. She hears me and sees me. She pushes herself upright and toddles toward me on her rounded baby feet — has she recognized me? Does she trust me, know me for who I am? I feel sure I am doing some terrible wrong — or might do something even worse — and in my fear I

335

back away, whispering 'No. Don't come near.' As if I am composed of something toxic.

And then Edith comes from around the side of her house with a clothes basket pinned on her hip, her expression pinched and clouded, and I cry, 'Edith, am I never to see her, then, never?'

I regret the outburst. I try to apologize, but Edith snatches up the child and covers her with the quilt, as if she too believes the sight of me might harm the girl, and she runs with her into the house.

I can't leave, not knowing what to do, tearing my hair, turning in circles, until Carson comes and finds me and walks me home. We walk along the road, not through the corn. He guides me with his hands on my upper arms, a kind touch, a warmth that I imagine drew my sister Fannie. I'm weak enough to be grateful.

Carson doesn't accompany me up the lane. He says that the baby girl — Frances, they've named her — is a good baby and happy, and Edith too. Edith is happy too. He and Edith, they are both happy, together. He thanks me.

I am glad of that. It means something. Not enough, maybe, but something.

And then he says, 'Leave us be, won't you?'

He sees my expression, gutted and raw.

'It will be easier for all of us. There've been rumours — I'm not accusing you, I'm just saying. It only upsets Edith.'

I draw myself up, straighten my spine. 'I understand,' I say with difficulty. I see, in a way, that Cora has been right — that talk and trouble comes from a gift like this, so close to home, so

336

close to the bone — and I want to prove her wrong.

I take Edith's daughter's name, and shout it away across a chasm I'll never cross — Frances, Frances, Frances — and I hear only now, from the boy's lips, its echoing refrain. *Fannie*. Is it a gift for me, from Edith, in return for mine? I receive it as if it were.

20

The Land

They want the land.

I suppose it is mine to give, lawyers be damned, as much as the land is anyone's to give.

My great-grandfather Robert Smart bought this section from a Mr. MacDoughall, a Scots entrepreneur who purchased plots from the Indians, who had been titled the land by the British government for help in the War of 1812, and therefore I suppose it is mine, now, as the closest surviving direct descendent of my great-grandfather, but I suppose, also, that it is no more mine than it has ever been any of ours, who claimed ownership all the way along.

The young ones want to sell it so that strangers can haul in earthmovers and tear and raze and plot and erect. The idea does not upset me.

I see that houses and barns and gardens and fences, even the trees, are as transient as we. The pavement, the concrete, the very foundations, even the most massive of inventions and corruptions cannot last, nor hold. I see the contours of the land slowly shifting, rising, falling, turning up new stones each spring. I see the wildflowers that belong returning.

I could give this all to you. I would like nothing more, for what it's worth.

The girl is breathless with relief, and her hands are cold. 'Mom, did you hear?'

'It is yours, by rights,' I tell them, but do not add, *because you are mine*. Do with it as you wish, children of the line of Edith.

Look at the girl leap and whoop and grab me and rock me and almost pull me down, staggering. I can't understand how she's so small when I was so tall.

'She was always like this — bigger than she looked,' says the girl's mother, proudly. 'Threw herself out of her crib before she could land on her feet. Walked before she could crawl. Never afraid to fall.'

The glass lens of the camera catches the sun and throws its light into my eyes. I say, as clearly as I can, that I wish to give my property to this family, my only known living relatives, directly descended from my sister Edith. The glare from the lens is all I can see, and then it moves off, and I see again the woods, and the mud, and the lowering sky. I'm glad to be here, and a bit surprised, it must be said.

'Is that it? Have we got it?'

I say, more quietly: a promise is a promise. Maybe what the woman claims is true — that Edith was a great gardener, while I — I must have been born to run. I gave what I had.

I take a step away, and another. Drawing apart.

It makes sense to see Fannie here, beckoning me. It makes sense that she would be walking the field and quietly making for the woods. It makes sense that I am to follow. There is a crack in everything. I don't know that I can run that far. I don't know that I can run at all, but it seems that I am. I am running. Fannie calls me, ever ahead. She knows me as I was, as the girl I will always be.

She's kept her watch. She knows.

Fannie has reached the woods. I am catching up to her. The trees loom up before me and cut off the fast-slipping sun with their cool stand, their long shadows, their pale flowering under-growth. Fannie pauses, just ahead, her hair thrown out around her head as she turns.

She turns. Her face is full and kind.

She waits.

I'm coming.

Author's Note

Aganetha Smart is a fictional character whom I've imagined into the 1928 Amsterdam Olympic Games, the first at which women were allowed to compete in select track and field events. I was inspired by real athletes who participated in the Games, specifically 'The Matchless Six,' as Canada's female track and field team came to be known. The six women performed above expectation and returned home to great celebratory fanfare, having earned medals in a number of events, including gold in the 4 × 100-metre relay and the high jump.

Contrary to my storyline, it was not a Canadian woman who won the inaugural 800-metre event: that honour went to Karoline Radke-Batschauer, of Germany, with silver to Kinue Hitomi, of Japan, and bronze to Inga Gentzel of Sweden. Canadian runners Jean (or Jenny) Thompson and Bobbie Rosenfeld placed fourth and fifth, respectively, in the final, a race that instantly became subject to controversy. This was the slice of history I chose to explore in the book.

It was reported in some contemporary news sources that at least half of the 800-metre finalists collapsed or failed to finish the race, a story whose accuracy was only recently called into question. There is no doubt that the pace of the race was gruelling — the winner broke the world record by several seconds — and it is possible that the athletes showed fatigue, as athletes do, at the finish line of a hard-fought race. But as noted in an article published in 2012 in the magazine *Runner's World*, film evidence exists that shows the entire field finishing the race, and only one woman stumbles and falls at the line before recovering her footing within seconds. (That woman appears to have been Bobbie Rosenfeld, one of Canada's greatest all-around athletes, in whose name an award is given annually to Canada's top female athlete; hardly a weak specimen.) In my own research, I came across at least three differing and contradictory versions of the race, and find it impossible to declare with any degree of certainty how it unfolded. What is not in question was the fallout: a committee was immediately struck and women were banned from racing distances farther than 200 metres in future Olympic Games.

It wasn't until the 1960 Games in Rome that women were again allowed to compete at the 800-metre distance.

Lest one imagine discrimination is gone from distance running today, in 2011, the IAAF (track and field's world governing body) ruled that official records could only be set, by women, in women-only races. This is to prevent women from being paced by faster male athletes. How men are to be prevented from being paced by faster male athletes is left unaddressed by the IAAF. The ruling would nullify records formerly set in mixed-gender races. Presumably the women who set records in those races ran on their own legs, not riding on the men's backs, but perhaps I lack a nuanced understanding of the issue. And perhaps one can see from that last sentence why I chose to write about the subject in fictional form; when I consider these issues in any other way, steam comes out of my ears. And steam coming out of one's ears makes for an argument undercut by its own stridency.

Hence, Aganetha, girl runner, for all girl runners, now and then.

There is one character in the book who is based on a real person. Miss Alexandrine Gibb was as I portray her to be: a former athlete who became a driving force for Canadian women in sport, and served as team manager to the Canadian women's team in 1928, while also writing about women in sport for the *Toronto Daily Star*. When researching this book, I began quite by accident with her columns covering that summer's Games. Alex Gibb's independence, vision, wit, and force of personality seemed integral to the story of the 1928 Games, and I chose to write her into Aganetha's story in what I hope is a tribute to the women and men who work supportively behind the scenes, in administrative capacities, to spark changes so that others may shine.

As I was finishing revisions on the manuscript, history was made. On October 20, 2013, the Canadian women's record for the marathon, which stood for twenty-eight years, was finally surpassed by Lanni Marchant of London, Ontario, and, in the same race, thirty-two seconds later, by Krista DuChene of Brantford, Ontario. I think Aggie would be pleased.

Carrie Snyder
October 2013

Acknowledgements

This book was a pure pleasure to write. I think Aganetha must have been there waiting to be found, because she seems as real to me as if I'd transcribed her voice rather than invented it.

As always, there are many people to thank for the existence of this book. I thank my agent, Hilary McMahon, for her dedication and energy. I thank my editors: Janice Zawerbny of Anansi for her thoughtful initial reading and Claire Wachtel of HarperCollins for respectfully pushing me to dig for clarity. I thank everyone (publishers, editors, designers) involved in turning the manuscript into a finished book, a magical art that I will never tire of witnessing. I thank Lisa Highton at Two Roads, and all of the publishers who've signed on to bring this Canadian story to a wider audience.

Thank you, friends and family, for your unflagging support, and for spontaneous celebrations when the moment calls for it. Thank you, Angus, Annabella, Flora, and Calvin for giving me the time and space to write, and also for invading that time and space — you keep my head in the game and my feet on the ground. And, thank you, Kevin, for a partnership that includes but is not limited to meals prepped and schedules juggled and optimism shared; but most of all, thank you for changing as I've changed.

When I started this book, I knew only that I wanted to put into words the deep joy of becoming and being a runner. My final thanks goes out to all runners everywhere, whether you run in body or in spirit. May your path be your path.

SMART FAMILY TREE

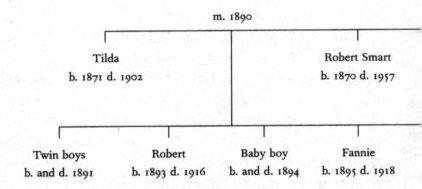

m. 1890

Tilda
b. 1871 d. 1902

Robert Smart
b. 1870 d. 1957

Twin boys
b. and d. 1891

Robert
b. 1893 d. 1916

Baby boy
b. and d. 1894

Fannie
b. 1895 d. 1918

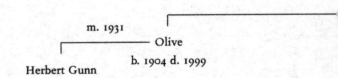

m. 1931

Olive
b. 1904 d. 1999

Herbert Gunn

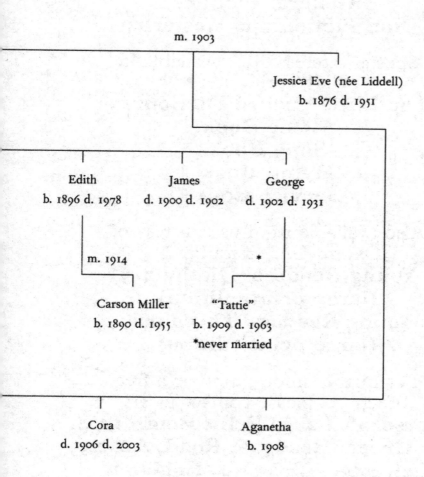

m. 1903

Jessica Eve (née Liddell)
b. 1876 d. 1951

Edith
b. 1896 d. 1978

James
d. 1900 d. 1902

George
d. 1902 d. 1931

m. 1914

*

Carson Miller
b. 1890 d. 1955

"Tattie"
b. 1909 d. 1963
*never married

Cora
d. 1906 d. 2003

Aganetha
b. 1908

We do hope that you have enjoyed reading
this large print book.

Did you know that all of our titles
are available for purchase?

We publish a wide range of high quality
large print books including:
Romances, Mysteries, Classics
General Fiction
Non Fiction and Westerns

Special interest titles available in
large print are:
The Little Oxford Dictionary
Music Book
Song Book
Hymn Book
Service Book

Also available from us courtesy of
Oxford University Press:
Young Readers' Dictionary
(large print edition)
Young Readers' Thesaurus
(large print edition)

For further information or a free
brochure, please contact us at:
Ulverscroft Large Print Books Ltd.,
The Green, Bradgate Road, Anstey,
Leicester, LE7 7FU, England.
Tel: (00 44) **0116 236 4325**
Fax: (00 44) **0116 234 0205**

THE CURIOUS CHARMS OF ARTHUR PEPPER

Phaedra Patrick

Arthur Pepper gets up every day at 7:30 a.m. He eats his breakfast, waters his plant, Frederica, and does not speak to anyone unless it is absolutely necessary. Until something disrupts his routine. On the first anniversary of his beloved wife Miriam's death, he finally sorts through her wardrobe and finds a glistening charm bracelet that he has never seen before. Upon examination, Arthur finds a telephone number on the underside of a gold elephant. Uncharacteristically, he picks up the phone. And so begins Arthur's quest — charm by charm, from York to Paris to India — as he seeks to uncover Miriam's secret life before they were married. Along the way, he will find hope, healing, and self-discovery in the most unexpected places.

HAG-SEED

Margaret Atwood

Felix is at the top of his game as Artistic Director of the Makeshiweg Theatre Festival. His productions have amazed and confounded. Now he's staging a *Tempest* like no other: not only will it boost his reputation, but it will heal emotional wounds as well. Or that was the plan. Instead, after an act of unforeseen treachery, Felix is living in exile in a backwoods hovel, haunted by memories of his beloved lost daughter, Miranda — and also brewing revenge. After twelve years, his chance finally arrives in the shape of a theatre course at a nearby prison. Here, Felix and his inmate actors will put on his *Tempest* and snare the traitors who destroyed him. It's magic! But will it remake Felix as his enemies fall?

BLUEPRINTS

Barbara Delinsky

Jamie MacAfee's life is almost perfect. She loves her fiance, and adores her job as an architect on her family's home renovation TV show. Her beloved mother Caroline has built up her own confidence after a painful divorce, working as the very successful host of the show. Everything is going to plan . . . and then the lives of both women are changed overnight. When the TV network decides to replace her with Jamie as the show's host, Caroline is left feeling horribly betrayed. Then tragedy strikes, leaving Jamie guardian to her small orphaned half-brother, and fiancee to a man who doesn't want the child. *Who am I?* both women ask, as the blueprints they've built their lives around break down. It's time to find out what they really want, and where their future lies . . .

THE DAY I LOST YOU

Fionnuala Kearney

Contentedly sipping a cup of tea at home after a fun-filled afternoon at a Christmas fair, Jess receives the most terrible news a mother can get: her daughter Anna has been reported missing after an avalanche while on a ski trip. Though she's heartbroken, Jess knows she must be strong for Anna's five-year-old daughter Rose, who is now her responsibility. As she waits for more news, Jess starts to uncover details about Anna's other life — unearthing a secret that alters their whole world irrevocably . . .

THE OUTSIDE LANDS

Hannah Kohler

Jeannie is nineteen when the world changes. The sudden accident that robs her and her brother Kip of their mother leaves them adrift, with only their father to guide them. Jeannie seeks escape in work and later marriage to a man whose social connections propel her into an unfamiliar world of wealth and politics. Ill-equipped and unprepared, she finds comfort where she can. Meanwhile, Kip's descent into a life of petty crime is halted only when he volunteers for the Marines. By 1968, the conflict in Vietnam is at its height; and with the anti-war movement raging at home, Jeannie and Kip are swept along by events larger than themselves, driven by disillusionment to commit unforgiveable acts of betrayal that will leave permanent scars.

DEVASTATION ROAD

Jason Hewitt

Spring, 1945: A man wakes in a field in a country he does not know. His name is Owen. Injured and confused, he gets to his feet and starts to walk. A war he has only a vague memory of joining is in its dying days, and as he tries to get back to England he becomes caught up in the flood of refugees pouring through Europe. Among them is a teenage boy, Janek, and together they form an unlikely alliance on their way across battle-worn Germany. When they meet a troubled young woman, tempers flare and scars are revealed as Owen gathers up the shattered pieces of his life. Nothing is as he remembers, not even himself — and how can he truly return home when he hardly recalls what home is?